Chili
con
Corpses

ALSO BY J. B. STANLEY

Carbs and Cadavers
Fit to Die

FORTHCOMING BY J. B. STANLEY

Stiffs & Swine

Chili
con
Corpses

J. B. STANLEY

MIDNIGHT INK
WOODBURY, MINNESOTA

FIRST EDITION
First Printing, 2008

Book design by Donna Burch
Cover design by Ellen Dahl
Cover image © 2007 Linda Holt Ayriss / Susan and Co.

Midnight Ink, an imprint of Llewellyn Publications

Library of Congress Cataloging-in-Publication Data
Stanley, J. B.
  Chili con corpses / J.B. Stanley.—1st ed.
    p. cm.—(A supper club mystery series ; bk. 3)
  ISBN 978-0-7387-1259-8
  1. Henry, James (Fictitious character)—Fiction. 2. Librarians--Fiction. 3. Overweight men—Fiction. 4. Shenandoah River Valley (Va. and W. Va.)—Fiction. 5. Virginia—Fiction. 6. Dieters—Fiction. 7. Clubs—Fiction. I. Title.
PS3619.T3655C48 2008
813'.6—dc22

                                                                    2007033875

Midnight Ink
Llewellyn Publications
2143 Woodsdale Drive, Dept. 978-0-7387-1259-8
Woodbury, MN 55125-2989, U.S.A.
www.midnightinkbooks.com

Printed in the United States of America

For Dad

Because of you
I saw a bullfight in Mexico
a view of Paris from the Eiffel Tower
a carnival in Finland
Roman Baths
Lenin's Tomb
the Lion of Lucerne
the Panama Canal
and so much more

Thanks for broadening my perspective
and for believing in taking kids
on long airplane rides

My doctor told me to stop having intimate dinners for four. Unless there are three other people.

—ORSON WELLES

ONE

TURKEY BACON
RANCH WRAP

Sodium per Serving: 2024 mg

"I'm SICK TO DEATH of being on a diet," Bennett complained as he curled two free weights up and down from his waist to his collarbone.

James heartily agreed. The lunch he had eaten composed of a turkey bacon wrap with lettuce, tomato, and fat-free ranch dressing served on a whole-wheat tortilla seemed like a faint, unsatisfying memory.

"I know what you mean." James pushed himself backward on the leg press machine, his thighs and buttocks burning as he moved the grudging stack of weights into the air. "Thinking about the nutritional content of every item I put in my Food Lion shopping cart is killing me. And I used to really enjoy going to the grocery store."

As James got up from the leg press and selected a pair of twenty-five-pound free weights, Murphy Alistair, the editor and foremost reporter of *The Shenandoah Star Ledger*, entered the cardio/weight-training room. Even though this was the only YMCA within a hundred-mile radius, and was therefore always busy, Murphy was hard to miss. She was wearing black nylon sweats, a form-fitting yellow tank top, and a yellow headband. Waving hello to James in the mirror, she stepped onto a treadmill and began to jog. Murphy's chin-length brown hair, streaked with golden highlights, flapped up and down on the sides of her head like bird wings as she moved. She looked completely at ease as she ran, her hazel eyes glued to the early news program playing on the wall-mounted TV, a towel draped casually round her neck.

"Spot me while I bench, will you?" Bennett asked James a few minutes later while preparing to lift a heavy dumbbell above his torso.

James examined the size of the circular weights attached to each end of the bar over his friend's chest. "Two hundred pounds, huh?"

Bennett scowled. "Hey, man. I'm gonna do more than one set."

"No, I'm impressed. That's quite a load you're lifting," James quickly soothed his friend, noting how muscular Bennett's arms and legs had become over the past several months. "You meant it when you said you'd be spending the summer getting buff. Well, now you're buff."

"Thanks, but I'm still the short mailman with the big gut." Bennett took a deep breath and removed the weights from the stand. "*You're* the guy who needed all new belts and pants."

James stole a glance at himself in the wall-length mirror. It was true. After pursuing a low-carb diet with his supper club friends and then counting points and pursuing a regular exercise routine, James had lost over thirty pounds of unwanted flab and several inches from his doughy waist. Even his second chin, which had once given him a rather bullfrogish profile, was nearly gone. He still had slightly floppy jowls and was a long way from resembling the fit and toned specimens that paraded around the cardio room in tight biker shorts and T-shirts advertising the previous marathon they had run.

"Okay, James." Bennett lifted the barbell so that James could settle them gently back onto the stand straddling the padded bench. "Let me just catch my breath before the next set." Bennett closed his eyes and focused on his breathing. While he waited, James watched Murphy's trim figure as she ran with a seemingly effortless stride and the black rubber of the treadmill moved beneath her feet like a fast-flowing stream. As he stared, Murphy's attention was drawn to the reflection of two blonde-haired women entering the cardio room. Her face broke into a smile and she waved at the pair vigorously.

James did his best not to drool, nudge Bennett in the side, or blatantly ogle every square inch of the newcomers. He believed the women must be visitors because he would have certainly noticed the gorgeous blondes if they lived within the county, which was located in a rather isolated area of Virginia's Blue Ridge Mountains. His town, Quincy's Gap, did not have a shopping mall, trendy restaurants, or boutiques selling the latest in haute couture, but today, apparently, two movie stars were present in the middle of Shenandoah County. After all, James reasoned to himself, no one else but a starlet could have such shiny blonde hair, flawless skin, enormous blue eyes, and a body with more curves than a road on Skyline Drive. And what's more, there were two of them. Twins, it looked like!

The young women moved with languid grace as they crossed the room, seemingly unaware that all of the men had ceased their activities and stood like mute statues in front of weight machines, ellipticals, or stair climbers.

A squeaking noise below James's chest distracted him from the sight of the beautiful women. Bennett, who was slowly suffocating beneath the weight of the barbell resting on his chest, was desperately trying to get his friend's attention.

"Oh, sorry!" James grabbed the barbell and struggled to return it to its metal holder.

Bennett took in a great breath and then, his lungs recovered, hollered, "What kind of spotting is that? You almost killed me, man!" Bennett sat up, rubbing his sore pectorals. "Do I have to send you to Gillian for some of her hocus-pocus herbal remedies to improve your attention span? Jeez!"

"Hey, you can't blame me," James mumbled, poking Bennett and pointing in the mirror so that he'd see the two blondes who were standing next to Murphy's treadmill, beaming at her with two sets of blinding white teeth.

"Damn." Bennett stopped rubbing his chest. "Those girls are *not* from around here. You think Murphy's doing some kind of Miss America story or something?"

"Twins in the same pageant? Doubtful."

"They could be from two different states," Bennett argued. "The one on the left could be Miss Virginia and her sister could be Miss West Virginia."

"That's pretty unlikely, Bennett." James observed the women more closely for clues as to who they were. "Look, the one on the right is wearing shorts with the Blue Ridge High Red-Tailed Hawks logo."

Bennett cleared his throat as he gawked. "Those shorts never fit any high school girl like that! They're tight as a wetsuit. That sweet thang must have dug that pair out of the lost and found at the elementary school."

James laughed. "They're a bit snug, that's for sure."

"And those two are almost as dark as me," Bennett continued his appraisal. "Where'd they get color like that?"

"Probably from tanning."

"In the dead of fall?" Bennett asked in disbelief.

"Yep. There are salons where you can go just to get a tan." James smiled at his friend. "Some people spend their hard-earned money to look like they've been to the beach when really they've been sitting inside a claustrophobic capsule, frying beneath light bulbs supposedly free from ultraviolet rays, while they wear purple goggles and listen to relaxing music."

"Sounds like sitting in a coffin while your own cremation's going on." Bennett gave James a strange look. "And exactly *why* do you know so much about this tanning nonsense?"

"I'm a librarian, remember?" James said as they headed over to the water fountain. "I read lots of magazines. In this month's issue of *Time*, there was an article about 'tanorexia.' Fascinating stuff."

"Tan-a-what?"

"It's a new addiction, like alcoholism or being addicted to drugs, shopping, coffee..."

"Now, now. There's nothing wrong with coffee," Bennett interrupted defensively. "The caffeine in regular coffee speeds up the metabolism, reduces the risk of heart disease and certain types of cancer, and can even stop an asthma attack."

"Bennett, I've never met someone who knew as much trivia as you. You have *got* to try out for *Jeopardy!* some day."

"They're comin' to D.C. again this year," his friend said quietly. "You know, for a contestant search."

James took a long drink of cold water and then patted his dripping mouth with his sweat-soaked gym towel. "When?"

Bennett shrugged. "This winter."

"You've got to go! You always said it was your big dream to appear on *Jeopardy!*"

His friend looked forlorn. "I don't think I'm ready."

"Just go to the tryouts. What have you got to lose?"

Bennett brightened. "You're right! Besides," he opened the gym door, casting one last look over his shoulder at the three attractive women clustered by the Y's single treadmill, "I could use a bit of a shake-up. My life has gotten kind of dull these days. Same old routine, day in and day out."

"I know what you mean," James said, eyeing the beige parka he had worn for the last six winters with distaste. He looked at his watch. He didn't want to go home, as his father was repainting the dining room and would demand help, and he didn't feel like making a last-minute date with Lucy because their previous one had ended awkwardly. Still, he felt strangely restless and wanted to do something other than drop by Food Lion or rent another lackluster movie from the video store. Suddenly, he got an idea. "Feel like spoiling your dinner?" James asked Bennett once they were in the parking lot. "We could stop by Custard Cottage."

Bennett zipped his navy blue uniform coat provided by the United States Postal Service and shivered. "Frozen custard in November?"

"Willy's got a coffee-and-custard deal going on right now. We'll get Sweet Lucy Light custard and skim milk in our coffees. A no-guilt snack."

"Twist my arm, why don't you?" Bennett sniggered. "You're on."

"Well, well!" Willy beamed as James opened the canary-yellow door of the purple and pink Victorian abode known as the Custard Cottage. "It's good to see you, my friends!"

"What happened to your garbage cans?" James asked, pointing out the window where the trash cans shaped like giant ice cream cones were normally placed.

"Graffiti." The jolly proprietor issued a deep belly laugh. "Apparently, Billy loves Jamie and in ways I don't think Jamie's parents would appreciate."

"Ah," James and Bennett replied in unison.

"I've got the stuff to clean 'em up with, but I figure they can stay inside for the winter anyhow. No one's eatin' outside these days—not even the teenagers who like to act like they're too cool to feel cold." He tugged on his starched, pinstriped apron. "Now what can I get for the most eligible bachelors in Quincy's Gap? I've got the most delicious Pumpkin Nutmeg custard you'll ever get on your tongue. Wanna try some?"

"Better not, thanks." James gestured toward a nearby chalkboard. "We'll each take your Cup & Cone special. Decaf and Sweet Lucy for me, please."

"I'll have full octane and a Chocolate Mousse cone." Bennett shot a glance at James. "I burned enough calories today—I gotta give myself a reward sometimes."

7

"Nothin' wrong with that." Willy completed their orders and then came out from behind the counter to sit with them while they ate. He stirred a packet of sugar into his own coffee mug and then took a sip. All of a sudden, he looked out the front picture window and began spluttering and fighting for air. Bennett thumped him on the back while Willy gasped. During the commotion, the front door opened to the tinkle of merry bells.

"What a *darling* place!" stated an appealing but unfamiliar female voice. James turned to see what the speaker looked like and was surprised to see Murphy and the gorgeous blondes hustling through the doorway, rubbing their bare hands together against the chilly November evening air.

"Don't worry, I'm not stalking you guys," Murphy teased, winking at James. "I'd like you all to meet my friends, Parker and Kinsley Willis."

The twins said, "Hi, y'all," and smiled. James could feel his heart flutter.

"Aren't Parker and Kinsley names of towns in Kansas?" Bennett asked once he found his tongue.

"Wow! You're the only person who's ever known that without us saying something!" The twin named Parker exclaimed. "You must be a master of geography."

"Well..." Embarrassed, Bennett looked to Willy for help, but the proprietor seemed to have forgotten all about the notion of providing customer service.

"Can we interrupt you for some hot tea, Willy?" Murphy prompted kindly.

Willy leapt out of his chair while issuing apologies. "Forgive a man for staring, ladies, but are you two famous or something?"

Kinsley laughed. "Nope. Just tall, blonde American girls with big white teeth. And these teeth would like to sink into a double scoop of Chocolate Cookie Dough Chunk, if you please."

Her sister examined the ice cream flavors carefully. "They all look delicious, but I'll just have a Diet Coke."

"And for you, Ms. Alistair?" Willy handed the twins their orders. "The usual Peanut Butter Cup Perfection?"

"You got it, Willy." Murphy linked her arm with the blonde sipping Diet Coke through a straw. "Parker and I were roommates at Virginia Tech," she explained to the three men. "Can you imagine what it was like to share a room with someone who looked like a supermodel and had the brains of a neurosurgeon?" Murphy smiled fondly at her friend. "But Parker was so nice that I liked her despite the fact that boys only hung around me to get inside info on Parker. What was her favorite flower? Was she dating anyone, yada yada. Now she's a vet with her own practice in Luray and between our two crazy jobs, we don't get together nearly enough."

"But we're working on it," Parker chimed in. "I've got a wonderful partner at my office, so I can leave the animals in good hands and we can hang out some more."

"Don't leave me out! I'm hoping you give Mr. Perfect Partner Dwight lots of furry clients so that you can show me all the sights," Kinsley said to her sister.

Turning back to the men, Kinsley offered them a winsome smile. "See, I'm brand new to town—a transplant from the North." She then paused in order to devour her frozen custard with gusto. James was amazed at how fast she could eat. After she licked a stream of custard from the back of her hand, Kinsley added, "but don't hold being a former fast-paced New Yorker against me."

"I don't think I could hold much against you, sugar," Willy said in appreciation while watching the beautiful young woman polish off her frozen treat.

After downing a cup of water, Kinsley wiggled the fingers on her left hand in farewell and headed back outside with Murphy and Parker.

———

"Did you get a load of those blonde bimbos?" Lindy squawked as she entered Custard Cottage a few seconds later.

"They're kind of hard to miss," James said with admiration. "And I don't think they're bimbos."

Lindy chose to ignore James. "I saw your mail truck outside, Bennett, and thought I'd join you. I need some sugar to perk me up after finding out that Barbie Number One is going to be joining the staff at Blue Ridge High."

Bennett gave Lindy an odd look. "What's the problem with that?"

Lindy thumped her fist on the counter. "What's the problem? I finally decided that I'm going to ask Principal Chavez out ... well, by the first of the year anyway. And now how am I supposed to do that? I'd be competing with a Heidi Klum lookalike. Every man in this town is going to be licking his chops over that girl."

"Ask him out anyway, Lindy," James advised.

"It's about damn time you did," Bennett commented. "You've been dreaming about that man for over a year, so why wait until January?"

Lindy ordered a hot chocolate with extra whipped cream and caramel drizzles. "Because I want to lose just a few more pounds.

Especially now, with that young Christie Brinkley on staff. I need a boost of confidence."

"You don't need to lose any more weight," James offered. "You look terrific." It was the truth. Lindy had had her long black hair cut just above her shoulders. Layers snipped at sharp angles softened Lindy's round face, and she wore subdued makeup that enhanced her latte-hued skin and enormous dark eyes. Though Lindy was still quite curvaceous, especially around the bosom and hips, she had lost enough weight that her new and improved hourglass figure was strikingly voluptuous. Lindy had gone from being pudgy all over to being soft in all the right places.

"I wouldn't kick you out of bed for eatin' pork rinds," Willy teased as Lindy blushed.

"That's two resolutions for the new year then." Bennett raised his coffee cup in the air. "Here's to you bagging your man, Lindy. Me? I'm trying out for *Jeopardy!*"

Willy looked at James. "And what about you, Professor? You five always do stuff together, so you must be planning something big, too."

James shook his head and stared fixedly at the light brown drips swimming around in the bottom of his mug. "Not me. I'm fine with the status quo."

But he was lying. There was something he would very much like to change, and for once it had nothing to do with his appearance. Suddenly, James felt the beginnings of a major headache coming on. He never used to get headaches, but lately they had been plaguing him more and more frequently. Rubbing his temples, he said goodbye to his friends and climbed into his old white Bronco.

For a moment, he gazed at his own reflection in the rearview mirror and then answered Willy's question truthfully. "I'd certainly like to change something. Yes, indeed. I'd like to know what a guy's gotta do to score with his girlfriend."

TWO

FRIED WON TONS IN SOY SAUCE

Sodium per Serving: 1260 mg

"I HAVE AN ANNOUNCEMENT to make," Lucy Hanover declared after she tapped a pair of wooden chopsticks against her glass of Chardonnay.

"It must be big news, too," Lindy interrupted, "since you're springing for the tab for this extravagant feast."

The members of the supper club group, who had adopted the self-effacing moniker "the Flab Five," had been pleasantly surprised to accept Lucy's invitation to change the location of their meeting from her house to the Dim Sum Kitchen.

The Dim Sum Kitchen was famous throughout the Valley for its authentic and delicious Chinese cuisine, but because it was so small, reservations were required for any party larger than two. Located in a tiny brick house, which had formerly been home to an interesting group of businesses including a dentist's office, a psychic, a barbershop, and, in the 1800s, a ladies' hat shop, the building's Colonial architecture seemed unsuited for an ethnic restaurant.

Luckily for the area inhabitants, Mr. and Mrs. Woo disagreed. They gutted the space, installed bright red carpet, painted the walls gold, and hung paper lanterns and several magnificent dragon kites from the ceiling. After hanging a simple plaque outside the front door in jade-green lettering, the Dim Sum Kitchen opened in the middle of a three-day blizzard. Folks slowly became aware of the restaurant's debut and, bored by the storm, piled into their four-wheel drives and filled the place to capacity from eleven in the morning until ten at night. The Dim Sum Kitchen became an instant success.

"This sure beats cooking," Lucy said, her face breaking into a grin as she stared up at one of the dragon kites. "Besides, I'm not going to have as much time to cook as I used to." James thought he had never seen her so happy. She was glowing like a new bride or an expectant mother. "You see," Lucy continued, "I passed both the written and psychological exams and am now only one step away from becoming a deputy for the Shenandoah County Sheriff's Department!"

Bennett, Gillian, and Lindy clapped heartily, while James followed suit in a mechanical manner. He was torn between sharing Lucy's joy and feeling hurt that she hadn't told him about her triumph first. Ever since Lucy had been employed as an administrative assistant for the sheriff's department, she had longed to exchange her computer keyboard and telephone headset for a pair of handcuffs and a firearm. All summer and into the early fall, Lucy had studied and exercised, preparing herself for a challenge she hadn't felt ready to face until now. James was proud of her, but he was upset, too. Wasn't he her boyfriend? Wasn't he supposed to be privy to all of Lucy's life-changing events before everyone else?

Lucy accepted the praise of her friends and pointedly avoided meeting James's eyes. Biting into a crispy won ton, James thought back to their last date. As usual, they had gone out to dinner at a restaurant where they could select a healthy meal that wouldn't require them to spend the entire next day on the treadmill. Afterwards, they had seen the latest movie that had generated the biggest buzz in Lucy's beloved *People*. The film was a dud, in James's opinion, as it had a weak plot and stilted dialogue unsuccessfully disguised by expensive special effects and a group of staggeringly beautiful actors. Of course, Lucy had completely loved it and called James a snob in what he hoped was a teasing manner.

Back at Lucy's house, after she had barricaded her three enormous German shepherds called Bono, Benatar, and Bon Jovi in the kitchen, she and James settled down on her fluffy sofa. Pretending that they were going to watch *Seinfeld* reruns on Lucy's ancient TV, they barely made it through Jerry's opening monologue before they were fervently kissing. Trouble arose as it would always invariably arise at this juncture, for this was the point during each date when James would attempt to unhook Lucy's bra. As predicted, Lucy twisted her back away from his determined fingers and whispered, "Not yet."

As he had done several times before, James repositioned himself on the couch and Lucy got up to collect two glasses of water from the kitchen. They both downed their glasses of water as their overexcited hormones calmed down and then watched an episode of *Dukes of Hazzard*, which Lucy loved and James fell asleep to. After this date, James climbed into his old white Bronco and wondered, for the umpteenth time, what he had done wrong. He hadn't gotten up the courage to ask her why she refused to allow him to touch her in a way that would take their physical relationship beyond a PG rating, but he knew he had to soon. His physical and mental health depended on her giving in, as their current state of limbo was slowly driving him mad.

Watching Lucy now as she speared a snow pea with her chopsticks and chattered with their friends, he took note of her wide blue eyes, her caramel-colored hair, and her creamy skin. His eyes traveled down her neck to her alluring cleavage and then to her shrinking waistline. From there, his examination was blocked by the wooden table, but he had no difficulty picturing the round curve of her hips and the soft cushion of her thighs. Like Lindy, Lucy's body had diminished by a dress size or two, but she was not skinny. To James, she had a perfect feminine physique, and he longed to claim her like some kind of primitive caveman, but he lacked the guts.

"So tell us what some of the psychological test questions were like, Lucy," Gillian said as she shoveled spoonfuls of vegetable fried rice onto a porcelain plate decorated with cherry blossoms. James noted that the orange hue of Gillian's hair almost matched the koi swimming around the outside of the rice bowl.

"Yeah, did they ask you if you wanted to kill your mama and sleep with your daddy?" Bennett teased.

"No." Lucy scowled. "They weren't easy questions, though. You had to answer true or false to almost five hundred questions and some of them … well, let's just say there wasn't a simple true or false answer each time."

Her friends were intrigued. "Give us an example," Gillian pleaded.

Lucy hesitated. "I don't know if I should."

"It's not like any of us will be taking the test any time soon," James argued, trying to sound playful even though he felt genuinely combative.

Lucy finally fixed her gaze on him, and James felt as though she were really looking at him for the first time since he had picked her up from her house. Her blue eyes sent out mixed messages of tenderness and irritation in an infinitesimal amount of time before she sighed and said, "Okay. One of the easy ones was *Do you often have nightmares?* I don't, so the answer was *false.*"

Gillian helped herself to an egg roll and, after taking a bite of the crispy dough, swallowed and said, "I'm *sure* there must have been some questions that probed into the *deepest* corners of your psyche. Those difficult ethical and moral dilemmas we must *all* face. After all, to uphold the law, to be placed in a position of judgment upon your fellow human creatures, you must be *resolved* of your own internal struggles."

Bennett raised an eyebrow at Gillian. "I never know what you're talking about, woman, but there must have been some juicier questions on that test than whether you've got nightmares or not. Come on now, tell us a tough one."

Lucy took a gulp of wine. "Oh, fine. I admit that I had a really hard time answering two questions. The first was *Did you ever steal anything when you were younger?* And the second was *Do you always tell the truth?*"

"*Did* you steal something when you were a kid?" Lindy raised her black eyebrows inquisitively.

Lucy colored. "Yeah. When I was in the eighth grade, a bunch of the cool girls were swiping little things from the drug store. That was back when those glitter pens, the ones that had sparkly ink, first came out. We all wanted to write with those."

"Your poor teachers," Lindy clucked her tongue. "The ink is so pale you can barely see it."

"Exactly! That was part of the fun." Lucy drank another sip of wine. "Anyway, this new girl had joined our class. Her name was Claudia and she was from England. It took all of five minutes for her to become the 'alpha' girl. I wanted to hang out in her set so bad that when she dared *me* to steal something just for her, I did it."

Gillian's eyes rounded. "What was it?"

Lucy mumbled, "A unicorn air freshener."

"Your first taste of crime was pocketing an air freshener?" Bennett cackled gleefully.

"Yep." Lucy grinned sheepishly. "It had a rainbow on it and Claudia loved rainbows. I got caught, too. The store manager saw me tuck it in my pants. I got *such* a licking when I got home. Lord, I don't think I sat down for two days."

"So, did you put down *true* as your answer to that question?" James wondered.

Lucy shifted in her chair. "Yeah, sure." She added, "But that was hard. It's not like I could say I was a kid or that it was an item worth less than a dollar. All they'd see is that I stole something."

"That second question is totally unfair," Lindy said, twirling lo mein noodles around with her fork. "There isn't a person on this earth who tells the truth all the time."

"You got that right," Bennett agreed. "Sometimes you gotta tell a little white lie to keep things peaceful. Just the other day, my boss showed me a picture of his new grandson and asked if I didn't think that that child was the most beautiful baby ever born. Well, all I saw was a red face with wrinkly skin and a bunch of black hair wrapped in the middle of about a thousand blankets. Shoot, looked more like one of those little Mexican dogs than a kid, but of course I said he was the cutest thing I'd ever seen."

James laughed. "You're right. There are some questions you could never answer truthfully, especially if you're a man. Like, *Do I look fat in this?* or *Don't you wish my mother lived closer?*"

Lindy poked James with her chopsticks. "Or when men ask us women questions about our ex-boyfriends. We have to lie and tell you that they were all unattractive, acne-covered wimps or you'll obsess about them."

Gillian took a sip of green tea. "That test question almost feels like a trick. Who can be truthful all of the time, unless you're Buddha? Lucy, you poor thing, what did you put down in the end?"

"I stared at that question until time started running out," Lucy answered quietly. "Unfortunately, they asked that same question using different wording about ten times throughout the test. In the end, I just kind of circled an answer without really looking and handed in the test." She shrugged nonchalantly, but James saw the tension in her shoulders by the way she slumped slightly forward in her chair. "Guess whatever the answer was, it didn't keep me from passing."

The table fell silent. No one fully bought Lucy's tale of blindly answering her test questions, but none of them felt as though they could have answered a similar question with more ease.

"I think the worst lies are those of omission," James spoke into the silence. "The ones you don't even admit to yourself. I didn't see those kinds of lies until I met all of you and starting thinking about all of the things I was burying inside my layers of fat."

Everyone nodded in empathetic agreement.

He continued. "And I discovered one truth about myself when I was at the Y with Bennett. I want to take a break from being obsessed with dieting. I'm having so much fun tonight eating what I want and focusing more on the company than on counting calories."

Gillian sighed theatrically. "Oh, James! I am *so* glad you shared that with us! I too feel bogged down in the predictable, the *routine* food that we eat now. I love my exercise walks and my closet filled with new clothes," she indicated her kelly green shirt covered with a design of yellow and brown spirals, "but I *long* for more spice in my life! I want *exotic*. I want my tongue to be reawakened, my nose to be invigorated, my senses to be *transported* to other places!" Gillian's armful of silver bangles clinked noisily as she gesticulated wildly during this speech. "I want to *savor* the experience of eating! My friends," she said more quietly, her energy spent, "I spend my days with animals. I love them, don't misread me, but I need something *more*. Like the dying autumn," she gazed out the window and sighed, "I feel as though my days have become more and more colorless."

At this poignant moment, the waiter appeared like a puff of silent wind and placed the bill on the corner of their table, quietly slipping away again without removing any of the dishes. He must have sensed the change in tone that had fallen upon the dinner party.

Lindy began rummaging through her purse.

"This is my treat, remember," Lucy scolded her. "Because we're *supposed* to be celebrating," she added a bit ruefully.

Lindy withdrew a strip of newspaper from her bag. "We know, Lucy, and we're so proud of you. You're the only one who is looking forward to a major change, a new chapter in your life. The rest of us are feeling kind of like sticks in the mud." She beamed her hundred-watt smile at the rest of her friends. "I can't fix everything, but at least I can bring some zest back into our dinner meetings."

"Oh, wonderful!" Gillian squealed. "How, my dear, how?"

"Once a week, on Saturday nights, we're going to take a break from all of this dieting," Lindy announced. "We're going to stick to our light and healthy routines during the rest of the week, but on Saturdays, we're bustin' loose!" Her brown eyes twinkled with anticipation. "Pack your bags, my friends, 'cause we are about to embark on a culinary trip around the world!" Her eyes flickered over the piece of newspaper. "Well, the Spanish-speaking world, in any case, but get your aprons cleaned and gas up your cars. Next Saturday, we're heading out on a new adventure!"

Even though he didn't have the faintest notion what Lindy was talking about, James found himself spontaneously clapping in response. Here was the change he had been looking for. He had no idea what it was exactly, but he was ready for it. At least it would allow him to delay doing what he dreaded most: giving Lucy an ultimatum.

THREE
VIRGINIA HAM

Sodium per Serving:

1275 mg for 3 oz.

JAMES OPENED HIS EYES in the dark. He rolled over on his side and tried to read the clock, but the neon green digits blurred into the black background. As he fumbled for his glasses, a familiar throb assaulted his temples. Another headache was coming on. James peered at the clock through the water-stained lenses of his glasses. 2:14. He let his body fall flat against the bed and closed his eyes. He didn't feel tired at all.

Sighing, James threw back the covers and slid his cold feet into a pair of ragged slippers. He then put on his robe and tiptoed out of his room and into the hall, though he could have marched through the house banging on a bongo and his father wouldn't so much as blink in his sleep. *The old man can't hear anything beyond the cacophony of his own snores*, James thought as he turned on the bathroom light. He helped himself to four ibuprofen liquid-gel capsules and stood in the weak light studying the box.

"Someone should just invent an ibuprofen shot," he muttered at the rubber duck sitting on the tub ledge. "They could sell it at all the coffee bars, beer joints, pool halls, libraries." He filled a glass from the tap and drank it down.

Back in his room he checked the clock again. 2:21. It was going to be one of those nights. James had had three of them over the past week. He woke abruptly after a few hours of sleep, restless and yet drowsy at the same time. His mind would review the day's events, make lists of tasks that needed to be accomplished at the library, ponder over what to eat for breakfast, and fantasize about Lucy appearing at her front door wearing a filmy robe made of white silk, her mouth curved in a seductive smile as she beckoned him inside. This vision was immediately followed by a headache. Tonight, to James's disappointment, the headache had arrived before the Lucy fantasy sequence.

By 3:35, James gave up, switched on the reading lamp clamped to his headboard, and delved into *The Alchemist* by Paulo Coelho. There was something about the simple purity of the writing that soothed James and distracted him from making scores of mental lists that he would forget by morning. Just before dawn, James fell asleep to the image of a large caravan at rest in the midst of crossing the interminable Sahara. He absorbed the sense of the vast, star-pocked sky stretching over the quiet desert. As his room seemed as cold as the desert night, James half believed he was lying down beside the shepherd boy of Coelho's tale.

He had only been asleep for about two hours when he was awoken by the clanging of pots and pans downstairs in the kitchen.

Feeling totally out of sorts, James pivoted the clock and was horrified to see that it was almost eight. He was going to be late to work if he didn't get a move on.

"Pop!" he exclaimed as he entered the kitchen.

His father, Jackson Henry, had taken all of the frying pans, saucepans, and large pots out of the cupboard and strewn them across the floor. A carton of eggs and a jug of milk sat open on the counter while a package wrapped in white paper from Food Lion's deli had been tossed onto the kitchen table. Puddles of milk, several broken eggs, a chunk of butter, and cheddar cheese shavings created a dairy minefield on the floor.

Their beautiful kitchen, which Jackson had completely renovated using the profits collected from the sale of his oil paintings, was in shambles. Surveying the mess, James couldn't understand how a man with such a sour disposition could paint birds and their natural settings in such a moving and realistic manner. How could such serenity and grace spring forth from such a gruff and temperamental person?

"Where's the goddamn *good* fryin' pan?" Jackson demanded as he noted the presence of his only child. "How am I supposed to make breakfast with no pan? And you're just sleepin' away like you're at some kind of fancy hotel with no work to go to and nothin' to do but sit at the pool and sip fancy little drinks with fancy little umbrellas."

Despite his fatigue, James tried not to smile. At times, his father's childish fits could be rather amusing. "Are you hungry, Pop?"

Jackson's furry eyebrows drew together to form a single fuzzy line. "I've been up for two hours workin' in the shed." James noticed that his father never mentioned the word "painting." When he was locked outside in the shed, he was merely "working," just as

24

though he were still tying on his green apron and heading out for the family hardware store, which had been bought out by one of the mammoth home improvement chains several years ago.

"'Course I'm hungry." Jackson sulked.

James examined the littered floor. "Let me tidy up and I'll cook you something, but it's got to be quick." He eyed his father. "If you helped, I could get to the cooking part faster, you know."

"Ha! You won't be able to fry anything worth swallowin' without that pan." Jackson continued to sulk, making no move to assist in the cleanup.

The pan his father was referring to was one of the few remaining from the original set his parents had received as a wedding gift. Jackson firmly believed that all food tasted better when cooked in one of these old pans. James agreed, though he couldn't understand why this was the case. The cooking surface of every pan looked like it had been scratched by a bear claw and the orange coating on the outside had flecked off in so many places that the pans looked like they were wrapped in tiger pelts. Still, anything precious to James's beloved mother, who had died suddenly over a year ago from heart failure, was precious to both her husband and son.

"It's okay, Pop. That pan's in the dishwasher. See?" He dropped the dishwasher door and pointed at the clean dishes inside.

Jackson shook his head. "I just can't get used to these newfangled contraptions."

James glanced at the eggs and milk on the counter. "Would you like scrambled eggs with cheese?"

"And fried ham." Jackson indicated the deli-wrapped package on the counter next to the eggs and settled himself at the kitchen table with the cartoon section of the newspaper.

As James began to cook the eggs, the sight of his father reading the newspaper reminded him of the advertisement Lindy had showed them last night. James had been so distracted by Lucy's announcement that he hadn't fully understood the gist of the ad. He finished with the eggs and divided them equally onto two plates. He then began to fry several slices of Virginia ham in the same pan.

The two men ate their breakfast in silence. Jackson read through the classifieds, occasionally snorting at what he considered absurd prices for "those little yappy dogs that can't even fetch their own tails." He then moved on to the *Goings-On* section while James scanned disinterestedly through the sports pages. He wanted to read the ad Lindy had clipped, but he knew better than to ask for any section of the paper until his father was finished with it.

"What are you up to today, Pop?"

"I'm gettin' goin' on my bathroom. Gonna rip up them old tiles and clean the gunk off the floorboards underneath. I got a pile of new tile comin' on today's UPS truck."

James thought about the wallpaper in his parents' bathroom: a silver, iridescent style fashionable in the seventies. It had always reminded James of tin foil. "Are you going to repaper it, too?"

Jackson frowned. "I'd sure like to, but I'll likely just paint it. I can't pick out that kind of decoratin' stuff like your mama could."

"I could enlist some female help," James offered. "Lucy or Lindy."

"Boy, I can't keep track of all of your female friends. Which one's your girl again?" his father asked, though he knew the answer. He then pushed back his chair, placed his dishes in the sink—still skittish of the new dishwasher—and hitched up his splattered painter's pants. No matter what Jackson ate, he stayed thin as a plank. *I must have inherited my mother's metabolism*, James thought and reached for the *Goings-On* section. He found the ad almost immediately.

ARE YOU BORED BY FOOD?

Sick of Cooking? Join *Fix 'n Freeze* and cook 10 meals big enough for a family of 4. Our first session features exciting cuisine from Spain and Mexico. We provide the <u>food</u>, you provide the <u>friends</u>! Hurry, classes are filling up. E-mail: fixnfreeze@shenmail.net to reserve your space. Classes begin Saturday, Nov. 3rd, in the former Cottage Gift Shoppe, Main Street, New Market. Grand Opening tuition: $199^{00}.

James reread the ad several times and shook his head in confusion. "We cook ten meals in one day? No way am I doing that. I'd be exhausted!" Taking a large drink of coffee, he reorganized the paper and began to make his lunch. As he cut his turkey and mozzarella sandwich in half and packed an apple, a yogurt, and a Diet Dr. Pepper into his thermal lunch sack, he had a vision of a glass dish in the oven, stuffed with plump, oblong chicken enchiladas submerged under layers of golden, bubbling cheese.

"Shoot, I can cook all day if necessary," he relented, eyeing his sandwich as it sat nestled in crinkled layers of plastic wrap. "I'd do just about anything if I didn't have to see another slimy, tasteless piece of low-fat turkey breast for a few weeks." Tossing his lunch into the Bronco, he backed rapidly out of the driveway and right into the garbage can, which was parked alongside the road.

James jumped out to discover a new dent on his beloved truck, just below the rear window. Cursing his own stupidity, he kicked the garbage can, stumping his toe so hard as he did so that he had to sit down for a few minutes until the pain passed.

When he finally reached the library, the Fitzgerald twins were waiting to be let inside.

"You should give one of us a key, Professor," Scott suggested, running a hand through his tousled hair, which seemed to grow wilder and more unkempt each day.

"Everything okay, Professor?" Francis asked when he saw the stormy look on his boss's face.

"Just a headache," James grumbled as he unlocked the front door.

Francis rushed off to empty the book bin of returned books as Scott placed everyone's lunches in the fridge.

"Hey!" Francis announced as he returned with a carton filled with books. "Look what someone left in the book bin!"

"More trash, I suppose," Scott guessed, displaying a rare frown. "What is *wrong* with people? I already put up a sign that says, *This is NOT a trash can!* What is it going to take?"

"What is it this time?" James inquired, fully prepared to allow himself to become even more cross than before. "The remnants of another Happy Meal?"

"Nope. It's a lottery ticket," Francis answered, flourishing the small, colorful rectangle. "For the upcoming Cash 5 drawing." His eyes glimmered behind his thick, old-fashioned, horn-rimmed spectacles. "I don't gamble, but I know that if you get all five numbers right, you win a huge jackpot. A hundred thousand bucks or something."

Scott whistled. "I would buy *such* a cool computer with that kind of dough."

"I'd go to that astronaut camp NASA's got," Francis said dreamily.

"That camp's for kids, bro," Scott pointed out kindly.

"Hey, if twenty-five-year-olds can play high school kids on TV, then I can fake my way into Space Camp. We're only twenty-three, after all." He shoved his glasses farther up the bridge of his nose. "What would you do with the money, Professor?" Francis asked his boss.

James took the ticket and placed it in the cardboard box labeled *Lost But Not Yet Found* behind the circulation desk and sighed. "I'd buy a suitcase full of books and go on a trip around the world. Alone!" He saw the perplexed looks on the brothers' faces and softened his tone. "Better write down the titles of the books that were in that bin, Francis. See who checked them out. In the highly unlikely case that ticket's worth something, we might be able to track down the patron."

"Good idea, Professor," Francis replied in his customary upbeat manner.

James headed into his office and booted up his computer. Along with the other supper club members, he had received an e-mail from Lindy reminding them all to reserve their space for the Saturday evening Fix 'n Freeze class. James sent his reservation by e-mail and immediately felt his bad mood start to dissipate. A few moments later, the owner of the new business wrote him back.

Dear Mr. Henry,

Welcome to Fix 'n Freeze! Please bring an apron with you on Saturday and prepare to have a great time. We will be cooking chicken enchiladas as we snack on black bean dip, fresh salsa, and homemade tortilla chips. (Miss Perez told me that your group of friends is using my class as a "night off" from dieting. I'm honored to be able to tempt you all with sumptuous, homemade food!) See you at 5:00 p.m.

Sincerely, Camilla Fields,
Head Chef, Fix 'n Freeze

James smiled as he read the e-mail. Chicken enchiladas! That was precisely the meal he had been fantasizing about earlier. *Guess I'm lucky,* he thought. *I don't need a lotto ticket. I'm going to taste Mexico and Spain for only $199. And I won't have to cook for Pop for ten whole nights. That in itself might be worth a hundred thousand dollars.*

"Come in from the cold, my friends," Mrs. Fields said, opening wide the front door of the Fix 'n Freeze cooking classroom. "Since I've got even colder bottles of *cerveza* inside." She patted James on the back. "Take off your jacket, handsome. There's a coat tree over there in the corner."

James smiled at the tiny woman wearing a yellow apron that said *Some things are better rich: coffee, chocolate, and men.* Camilla Fields looked to be in her mid sixties. An abundance of curly and rather colorless blonde hair poked from beneath the edges of a white baseball cap that said *CHEF* in bold letters. Her eyes were a silvery blue and her smile felt so warm that James felt immediately at home in her presence.

"The first rule is that we're all here to enjoy food and each other! No debating over politics, religion, or anything serious," Mrs. Fields announced cheerfully. "There are name tags on the side table near the coatrack. I'll only need them this one time and then I'll have you all stored in my mental files," she said and tapped the side of her head. "You can call me Milla. After you've hung up your coats and put on a tag, gather around the butcher block and let's have a toast to the commencement of our gastronomic voyage to Mexico and Spain!"

As James hung up Lucy's coat, the front door opened again and in walked Murphy and the Willis twins. All three wore dark jeans and tight sweaters. The blondes looked stunning in black turtlenecks and Murphy wore a white V-neck with a choker made of rough-cut turquoise. James smiled at her and waved at the two sisters.

One of the twins then turned back to the door and cast a dazzling smile in the direction of a tall, attractive man in a leather coat and faded blue jeans. After he removed his coat and kissed the waiting sister lightly on the lips, he shook hands with Murphy and Kinsley, as though it were the first time he was meeting both of them.

"Ah, here are the other members of our class!" Camilla drew the foursome into the room. "Now, we can have our toast."

James was too busy helping himself to a Corona with lime to notice Lucy glaring at the newcomers. He filled a warm tortilla chip with a load of black bean dip topped with sour cream and a sprinkling of fresh chives and popped it into his mouth. As he chewed, he took in his surroundings. Fix 'n Freeze had taken over a small historic building that had once housed a gift shop. Milla explained that she had simply emptied the downstairs and separated the space into an open cooking area and a section devoted to a pantry, fridge, and two chest freezers.

"I can't tell you how surprised I was to find out what a walk-in fridge costs! Lord, you could've blown me over with a feather! Good thing my husband left me a big enough nest egg that I could take a risk and start my own business, 'cause I'm not *quite* ready to sit in a rocking chair and knit ugly socks." She laughed and the members of her first class joined in. Her joie de vivre was contagious. She reminded James of Willy. He wondered if there was some secret to happiness in owning a small business related to food.

"I'll wrap up before I bore you to death or you demand a refund by telling you that I live upstairs with the love of my life," Milla continued. "He's a corgi called Charles, after the Prince of Wales—that was back before I knew about him cheating on Diana, you see. So if you have any food emergencies—like the time Charles climbed up on a dining room chair and ate our Thanksgiving turkey—you know where to find me."

"I like the colors in here," Lindy said when Milla was done, gesturing at the mango-colored walls and the celery-green countertops. Piñatas in the form of sombreros, donkeys, and bulls dangled from ropes of yarn in equally vibrant hues. Lindy scooped up some fresh salsa from the wooden bowl on the butcher block and groaned happily. "Fresh cilantro?" she asked when her mouth was empty.

"Very good, my dear. A star pupil already!" Milla winked.

Lindy beamed as Gillian introduced herself to Parker, Kinsley, and the good-looking young man who identified himself as Colin Crabtree, a large-animal vet and Parker's boyfriend. Gillian, Parker, and Colin immediately began to talk about animals. Their subjects ranged from grooming practices to which dog breeds were the worst clients, while Colin told humorous tales about having to sedate enormous bulls and about how he first learned to shear sheep. In the meantime, Bennett flirted shyly with Kinsley while James concentrated on the black bean dip. He offered Lucy the bowl of tortilla chips but she shook her head no.

"Has everyone lined their bellies with something?" Milla asked. "Good! Let's don our aprons and prepare to make some mouthwatering enchiladas. Go on and pick a cooking station, and we'll get down to business."

Camilla described the contents of the small metal bins in front of each cooking station. "These are your ingredients for this dish. I'll lead you step by step through the assembly process. Then we'll pop our entrées in the oven and socialize for a bit."

As James ripped pieces of chicken from the breast set before him, he felt completely content. His friends chattered amiably and Milla circulated the room, patting backs and complimenting chopping or sautéing techniques until every person felt like a budding Emeril Lagasse.

"You okay?" James asked Lucy, who had been unusually quiet.

"Sure," she replied hastily. "I'm just thinking about how I'm not going to be able to eat a bite of this dish. It's too fattening, and I'm on a pretty strict routine right now."

James slowed in the middle of stirring the onion and garlic sautéing in the pan on the stovetop he shared with Murphy, who was at the counter space across from him. They each had two burners and seemed to be in perfect sync as they added green chilies to their pans, their movements mirroring one another. Tantalizing aromas from the onions and garlic filled the air. Kinsley's eyes watered and she dabbed at them with a napkin while Parker teased her for being "such a sensitive girl."

"What are you going to do with these enchiladas then?" James asked Lucy.

She shrugged. "Bring them to work. Those boys'll eat anything that's not nailed down." Lucy concentrated on the pan in front of her and added, "But I'm not sure if this class is the best idea for me right now."

At first, James didn't reply, as he didn't know what to say. Finally, he said, rather lamely, "But we're only indulging once a week. It can't be *that* bad for us." Listening to himself, James felt as though his answer was a bit argumentative, so he hastily added, "Besides, we'd all miss you, Lucy." Then he turned his attention back to his enchiladas.

The class flew by. Before he knew it, their dishes were cooking away in the wall ovens while people cleaned their spaces and talked. Once their individual cooking areas were tidied, Milla gathered them all by the butcher's block and they gave themselves a round of applause while she passed around a plate of crescent-shaped Mexican wedding cookies.

"I know these are delicious, my friends." Milla bit into a cookie. "Don't worry, we'll make them in a future class. I'm a big believer in finishing a meal with dessert."

After the oven timers went off and the aluminum pans had cooled enough to be loaded into cardboard boxes, the group untied their aprons and thanked Milla heartily. It was apparent that everyone had enjoyed their first Fix 'n Freeze experience.

As James handed Lindy her leather jacket, he noticed a dark look on her face.

"What's up, Lindy? Didn't you have fun?" he asked as they stepped outside.

Lindy shrugged her coat on. "Oh, I *loved* the class, James. I just don't know if I can come again."

James was shocked. "Not you, too! Lucy doesn't think she can do this because of her fitness training, but why you? Is it the food?"

"No. The menus are totally wonderful." She lowered her voice. "It's the company I have a problem with."

"The company?" James asked dumbly. "It must be Murphy, Colin, or one of the twins then. Unless you've suddenly developed a distaste for one of us."

"It's the bimbo twin named Kinsley," Lindy hissed. "She thinks *my* Principal Chavez is cute! She even asked Murphy if he was single! And, she's going to be taking over for Mrs. Harding, who just started her maternity leave! That means she'll be roaming the high school halls every day starting this Monday!" Her voice shook with agitation. Though Lindy wasn't aware of it, the rest of the class members had also retrieved their belongings and were now passing by her as she practically yelled, "Mark my words, James—and this is *not* just my Brazilian temper talking—that if she goes anywhere near Luis Chavez, I will *kill* her!"

Milla's Mexican Chicken Enchiladas

3 tablespoons canola oil
1½ pounds skinless boneless
   chicken breast
salt and pepper
2 teaspoons cumin
2 teaspoons garlic powder
⅛ teaspoon allspice
¼ teaspoon coriander
1 onion, chopped fine
2 cloves garlic, minced
1 cup corn
5 whole green chilies, canned
4 chipotle chilies, canned
1 small can (4¼ ounces) diced
   black olives

1 can (28 ounces) stewed
   tomatoes
3 tablespoons flour
12 (8-inch) flour or corn
   tortillas
1½ cups premade enchilada
   sauce (Milla likes Las Palmas,
   but use what you can find)
1 cup shredded cheddar cheese
   (Milla prefers "Taco" cheese
   blend, but it's up to you)
chopped cilantro, chopped
   scallions, dollops of sour
   cream, according to your
   taste

Preheat the oven to 350 degrees. Coat a large frying pan with oil. Season the chicken with salt and pepper. Brown the chicken over medium heat, approximately 7 minutes for each side or until it is no longer pink. Blend the cumin, garlic powder, allspice and coriander, and dust the chicken with the spices before turning. Remove it from the pan and allow it to cool. Sauté the onion and garlic in the chicken drippings until tender. Add the corn and chilies. Stir well. Add the olives and canned tomatoes. Sauté for 1 minute. Pull the cooked chicken into shredded strips. Add the shredded chicken to the sauté pan, and combine it with the vegetables. Dust the mixture with flour to help it set.

Microwave the tortillas for 30 seconds. Coat the bottom of 2 (13 × 9-inch) pans with about 4 tablespoons of enchilada sauce. Using a shallow bowl, dip each tortilla in enchilada sauce to lightly coat it. Spoon ¼ cup chicken mixture into each tortilla. Fold over the filling, and place 6 enchiladas in each pan with the seam side down. Top with the remaining enchilada sauce and cheese. Bake for 15 minutes at 350 degrees until the cheese melts. Garnish with dollops of sour cream, chopped scallions, and, if you like, some chopped cilantro as well. Enjoy and don't plan on being hungry for a few hours after eating these!

FOUR
APPLE FRITTERS

Sodium
per
Serving:

360 mg
per fritter

By Monday, James and Jackson had polished off the enchiladas and were both eagerly awaiting Milla's next class. According to the menu, they were going to be cooking Spanish pork chops and vegetable paella.

"Y'all are finally doin' somethin' worth a lick in that food club of yours," Jackson commented after he had polished off his first helping of enchiladas. "This here is a real meal. It sits in your belly and makes itself known. If you made us another salad I was gonna have to go out and buy me a goat to feed it to. Still, you could try and git that teacher of yours to cook some good ole Southern food."

"You don't seem to be suffering too much over this particular south-of-the-border dish, Pop," James retorted, grinning. "Hey, I've got an idea. Maybe I'll hire her to come teach *you* how to cook a few meals. It's never too late to learn your way around the kitchen, and now that you've fixed it up so nicely, it seems a shame that only one of us is using it."

Jackson raised his hairy eyebrows. "At my age? Why should I start cookin'?" He pushed his empty plate away. "You goin' somewhere or somethin'?"

"No." James shrugged. "But I might not always be living here. Besides, I think you would really like Milla. Everybody does."

"What do you mean 'might' not always live here?" Jackson looked concerned. James was surprised that his offhand comment disturbed his father. He had momentarily forgotten that Jackson's reclusive nature made him completely dependent on his son. "You thinkin' of marrying that girl of yours?" Jackson wondered.

The fork dripping melted cheese that was headed for James's open mouth paused in mid-air. "Um ... no."

Jackson leaned forward and stared hard at his son. "In my day, men courted a gal and then married her. Mostly they did it so they could finally git under her skirt, but still, that's how things were done. You've been courtin' for a long time now, boy, so either you don't love the girl or you've already got under her skirt."

"Pop!" James was flabbergasted. "I'm trying to eat!"

"Hrmph!" his father snorted. "You've never had a problem with that. So, about what I was saying," he pursued relentlessly. "Which is it? You don't love her or it's the ole why-buy-the-cow-when-you're-gettin'-the-milk-for-free type of thinkin'?"

James snapped, "I'm not getting any milk!" He then colored and mumbled, "And I'm not too sure about the love thing, either."

Before his father could embark upon a full-blown lecture on his son's lack of masculine prowess, the phone rang. James practically toppled the kitchen table in his haste to answer it.

"I need a *huge* favor, James!" Lindy's exuberant voice rang out from the earpiece.

"Anything," James said hurriedly and turned his back on the quizzical look on Jackson's face.

"I need you to chaperone my field trip to Luray Caverns this week," she pleaded and then rushed on. "None of my class parents volunteered, and we've been given special permission to stay inside the caves after regular visiting hours. My art students are working on a unit called 'Texture and Shadow,' and the Caverns are the perfect place to go. Please say yes, James. I'm really desperate! If I don't get enough adults, then I'll have to cancel the whole trip, and I set it up almost a year ago."

James groaned. He couldn't think of a more miserable pairing than a pack of high school students and a cold, damp cave. Eyeing his father once more, who still sat expectantly at the table with his scrawny arms folded across his chest, James said a silent prayer of thanks that he had replaced their ancient rotary phone with a portable type and headed up to his room.

"Everyone else in the supper club has agreed to help, even though they'll all have to cut out of work a bit early," Lindy added for good measure. "See? You've forced me to try and guilt you into this, even though I know that doesn't affect you Methodists as well as us Catholics." She giggled.

"Why so many chaperones?" James tried to stall. "How many kids do you have in your art class?" He shut his bedroom door and settled onto his bed.

"Because *all* of my art students are going—from every grade." Lindy paused, sensing that she had yet to hook her fish. "What if I told you that you didn't have to ride with us on the bus and that dinner is free? We're having an early meal at Johnny Appleseed before we head underground. *No* one can resist Johnny Appleseed."

James was torn between the thought of Johnny Appleseed's famous homemade fritters rolling in a shallow bowl of powdered sugar and his unwillingness to view the caverns again. Though they were truly an amazing sight, James had grown up near enough to the famous attraction that he had already visited it a half-dozen times. What he remembered most from his student field trips to Luray Caverns were the endless nooks where hormone-crazed teenagers strived to have educational experiences beyond learning the difference between a stalactite and a stalagmite.

He doubted much had changed in the behavior of high school kids left to their own devices in the dark, and he hated the notion of being in charge of sneaking up on a pair of them as they groped each another in the lightless shelter of some rock formation. Even worse was the thought of a verbal confrontation with two teenagers. He might be forced to pry them apart, and he imagined that would be akin to separating a bulldog from its grip on a rabbit's neck. James grimaced with distaste at the thought.

"Think of the apple fritters, James," Lindy taunted. "Still warm from the oven."

James *was* thinking of the fritters. He hadn't tasted one in years. "Okay. I'll do it for you, Lindy."

"Bless you! Now I just need Principal Chavez and maybe one or two more people. I'll ask the school librarian and maybe one of my parents will come through. If not, I can always see if Willy's free. Meet us at the restaurant at five on Thursday. I'll have a whole basket of fritters just waiting for you."

———

Lindy was true to her word. James pulled into the parking lot a few minutes past five and parked the Bronco alongside three black and red Blue Ridge High buses. He took a deep breath and walked into the restaurant, expecting to hear the rowdy cacophony of a large group of teenagers enclosed in a small space. Instead, he saw that the students were seated by tables of four or six and were talking quietly as they sipped sodas or munched on fritters. The adults were all gathered at the largest table and James was surprised to see the shiny blonde halo belonging to one of the Willis twins among the chaperones. He also didn't see Lucy among the adults.

The only empty chair was between Lindy and an elderly gentleman, so James took his seat and immediately helped himself to a fritter. Pressing the crusty pastry, which was ripe with the fragrance of baked apples, into a pool of powdered sugar, he waved to Gillian and Bennett and then popped the fritter into his mouth. "Delicious," he said to Lindy, who looked uncommonly cross. "Where's Lucy?"

"She blew us off at the last minute," Lindy frowned. "Said she couldn't miss her body-shaping class at the Y."

"I'm sorry, Lindy." James didn't know why he was apologizing for Lucy, but he felt irrationally responsible for her behavior. "She cancelled our last dinner date as well," he confessed ruefully. "For Pilates, I think."

As he sipped his ice water, James noticed that the Willis sister—whether it was Parker or Kinsley he couldn't tell—sat next to Principal Chavez. They were sharing a dish of fritters and talking animatedly. "Which sister is that?" James whispered to Lindy.

"I'm assuming she's Kinsley," Lindy muttered unhappily. "She only starting teaching four days ago, but I guess she didn't want to waste any time making a move on Luis."

"But didn't you arrange for the chaperones?" James was confused. A waitress stopped by and he ordered sweet tea and the turkey platter with mashed sweet potatoes and black-eyed peas. "Why include her if you're worried about her charming your principal?"

Lindy ordered a cheeseburger and a garden salad and then turned and answered James's question. "Yes, I recruited all of these folks, but the librarian came down with a nasty cold so she couldn't come. She must have asked Kinsley to fill in for her, and then Adam Sneed's grandfather just showed up out of the blue and volunteered to help out. Said he was visiting from St. Louis and would love to see our famous caves."

"That's the guy on my right?" James asked, and when Lindy nodded he said, "What's his name?"

"Mr. Sneed. He kind of mumbles when he talks, which isn't much. I wish you'd break the ice with him so I can thank him properly. Every time I go near him, he kind of shies away." Lindy popped a fritter in her mouth and chewed mechanically, looking miserable.

As dinner was served, James said hello to his neighbor on the right. The older man was wearing a pair of enormous square sunglasses that James believed were used by people with cataracts, a ratty tweed blazer, and a turtleneck. His face was especially wrinkled around the eyes, and deep lines were etched into his prominent forehead. He had a dramatically hooked nose and his skin seemed to have a slightly orange hue. Most of his hair was hidden beneath a tan fishing hat in which a single black and red fly was hooked.

After reaching in front of James to help himself to the saltshaker, the man cleared his throat and, in a gravelly voice, said, "I'm Mr. Sneed. Pleased to meet you." He then sunk a pair of yellowed teeth into a piece of roast beef coated in brown gravy. Drips of gravy speckled the man's short graying beard and James turned away to concentrate on his own plate.

Shortly before six, Lindy shepherded her students into the buses, and they made the brief trek to Luray Caverns. The parking lot was nearly empty, as tours had ended for the day. Only a skeleton crew of Cavern employees remained—cleaning up the grounds and preparing the site for the following day. The antique car museum, general store, and restaurant had all closed their doors for the night. To James, it felt odd to approach the entrance beneath the dull glow of lampposts and to walk past the one-acre garden maze as shadows stretched out like black tree limbs over the hedges.

The students immediately sensed the uniqueness of their situation and either fell silent or began to exchange excited whispers.

"I hear a girl was killed inside that maze last year," one of the boys said loudly, pointing to the wall of dense foliage off to the right.

Lindy rounded on him. "Knock it off, Charlie. No one's been killed anywhere on these premises. Stop trying to spook your classmates."

At the entrance, she handed their tickets to the gate attendant and then made a brief speech to her students about staying with their given partners. Each pair was free to move about the caverns for thirty minutes in order to scout out the area in which they would like to spend the rest of the time rendering drawings in pencil or charcoal.

"You won't be getting the traditional tour," Lindy informed her pupils, "but the guides will turn out the lights at exactly seven p.m. for an entire minute. By then, you should be set up and working on your sketches. I wanted you to see how important light is in creating shadow. With absolutely no light, you cannot have any contrast." She looked around at the young faces in front of her. "We can't really get a sense of what total darkness is like. Our world is filled with light—both natural and artificial. But early man lived in caves and battled darkness all the time. Yet, he eventually managed to paint in caves just like these. I wanted you to think about how challenging that must have been and to be thankful, for art's sake, that fire was discovered. So remember seven o'clock and have fun!"

"And please do not touch any of the formations," a guide added pleasantly. "The oil from your skin can be damaging to the rocks." Gillian looked down at her hands and then fluttered them in front of her face as if shaking off any impurities. The guide shot her a quizzical look and then continued. "There will be four guides stationed throughout the caves in case you have any questions or get turned around down there. You must remain on the main pathways at all times. And watch where you step. The paths get pretty slick in places." She smiled and continued the speech she may have delivered thousands of times. "I see you've all got your coats with you. That's good. It's in the fifties down there—about the same as outside. Before we get started, I'd advise you to use the restroom now, because there's a lot of stairs to climb if you need to come back up here."

Several girls darted off to the restroom while the rest of the students organized their art supplies. When everyone was ready,

Lindy read the buddy list aloud. To some of the students' dismay, she had paired them by like gender, so that the chances of subterranean hook-up sessions were diminished. James sighed in relief.

"Oh, I cannot wait to view nature's *sublime* architecture," Gillian gushed. She pushed herself to the front of the line, zipping up a bulbous, electric-yellow parka.

As they descended the staircase, Lindy handed James and Bennett a map and informed them that their patrol area extended from a place called Hades to another named Giant's Hall and included a tall chamber dubbed the Cathedral, where the "Stalacpipe" organ played its surreal melodies.

"*I'll* be floating around the Ballroom with Principal Chavez," she grinned sheepishly.

"And where will Kinsley be?" James couldn't resist ribbing Lindy a bit.

Lindy pointed at the map. "She and Gillian will be hanging out near the Leaning Tower and Twin Lakes. Twin Lakes, get it? It seemed fitting. And since Adam's grandfather is the oldest of the chaperones, he's going to remain by the entrance/exit." She pulled a compact out of her purse and reapplied a berry-colored shade of lip-gloss. "Plus, we've got the four guides."

She scrutinized herself in the small mirror and seemed satisfied. "Tonight, my goal is to find out what Luis likes to eat," she confessed in a hushed tone. "I'm going to throw a New Year's party and dazzle him with my culinary skills."

"You gonna test that 'way to a man's heart' theory?" Bennett inquired.

"You betcha," Lindy replied and hustled off, her buoyant spirits restored.

Bennett stared after her, a small smile playing around the corners of his mouth. "Go get him, girl."

James studied his map and began to move deeper into the caves toward his patrol area. Even though he had been there before, the first glimpse of the initial chamber was still breathtaking. As he continued to roam on the walkways, he stared at the immense columns, illuminated by white-yellow light, and observed how some of the formations looked almost fuzzy. The pale, clumpy masses resembled the type of mold that grows on the surface of spoiled yogurt. Other rocks seemed like oversized weapons—covered with sharp edges and growing from the floor or ceiling into deadly points. Those were the ones that were so tempting to touch.

James saw the familiar curiosity dubbed the "fried eggs," which were always carefully guarded by the guides. Even when James was a student, people had lunged over the guardrail in order to brush the "eggs," with their fingertips. Several tourists had even been escorted from the caves and told never to return for disregarding the rules. There was something about those two liquid-looking ovals that screamed, "Touch me!" and over and over again, people tried. There was always a wary guide stationed near the attraction, and tonight was no exception.

Walking by structures that could have passed as the skeletal ribs of a great whale or the splintered hull belonging to a wrecked schooner, James arrived at one of the larger subterranean lakes and gasped. The staff, as a surprise for the students, had lit hundreds of white candles and placed them in nooks all around the lake. The twinkling flames reflected all around the room, and shadows danced wildly off the water. Ribbed rocks, slick with moisture, truly seemed alive in the shifting light. The chamber was completely silent even though half a dozen students had gathered and were standing against the pathway rail, gazing out at the lake in respectful wonder.

James suddenly thought of Lucy. He would have liked to have her beside him at this moment. Even with others present, it would have been romantic to see her face bathed in the soft, flickering light and to stand together without feeling the need to speak. Experiencing a pang of sadness, as though Lucy were drifting away beyond his reach, James turned to look for Bennett.

"Hey, come on!" one of the boys shouted, breaking the magical spell created by the candlelight. He waved a map and gestured at his buddy and a pair of cute girls. "The place where they found that dead girl is this way!"

Bennett appeared around a corner and gestured at James to follow the foursome.

"Is this where the skeleton was found?" the boy asked a young guide while pointing at a dark ledge across the pathway.

"Yes," the guide acknowledged flatly. "She was most likely a Native American girl who lived in this area about two hundred years ago. Her burial ground probably fell through a sinkhole and she ended up down here."

"That's *not* what my daddy says," one of the girls stated emphatically.

"What does he say, Dana?" the boy who had led them there asked with acute interest.

"Well, Jacob," she began, tossing her hair over her shoulder as she basked in her moment of self-importance. "My daddy's a history professor at JMU, and he's studied all about these caves." She paused to make certain she had the full attention of her small audience. "It *was* a woman's body, but no one could tell if she was Native American. Her bones were almost destroyed *after* this place was discovered in, like, the 1800s sometime. So, anyway, the guys who came in here, the first, like, tourists, *stole* parts of her skeleton!" Two of the other students gasped. "One guy took, like, a whole leg bone!"

Even the guide was transfixed.

"That's so totally gross!" Dana's drawing partner exclaimed.

"My mama says that ever since she was little, this part of the caves has been haunted. See, that girl wants her bones back!" She finished theatrically.

The guide gaped at this revelation and searched for a rebuttal. Before he had the chance, Jacob grabbed Dana's shoulders and shouted, "Maybe she's here right now!"

Dana shrieked and then giggled.

"Yeah, yeah," Bennett stated, unimpressed with the ghost story. "And maybe a UFO will land down here, too. Go on and find your spots and get settled down to work." He checked his watch. "Lights are going off in ten minutes. Go on now."

"I don't want to be standing *here* in the dark," Dana's partner breathed. Bennett made a shooing motion with his hand and, reluctantly, the students moved off.

James followed the students to the Cathedral chamber where all four decided to set up their drawing materials and, leaning against the rail, began to study the crevices and crags on the rock faces before them. Not wanting to hover, James meandered around his patrol area, nodding at students intent upon their work, and wondered how Lindy was getting on with Principal Chavez.

Suddenly, an image of Murphy Alistair in her workout attire popped unbidden into his head. James found his pulse quickening, and he began to ruminate on how friendly she had always been to him. Beyond friendly, in fact. There were times when Murphy had been downright flirtatious.

Trying to banish Murphy's cute face and trim figure from his mind, James headed back toward the Cathedral. He noticed that two of the four students who had been working near each other were no longer standing against the guardrail.

"Where are your partners?" he asked the remaining boy and girl. "They were Dana and ... Jacob, right?"

The boy shrugged and wiggled his eyebrows suggestively. "I think they're studying a different kind of artistic contrast."

The girl sniggered as James attempted to translate the meaning of the boy's words. He felt his stomach lurch. Now he would have to find the wayward duo, who were certainly up to no good, and get them back on task. If he didn't, there was no telling what Lindy would do to them—and him—when she found out.

"Which way did they go?" he demanded of the girl, looming over her and implementing the authoritative tone he had perfected years ago as a professor at William & Mary.

The girl pointed to a passage leading back toward the exit and James hustled off. His feet had just encountered a slippery downward slope when the cave was plunged into utter darkness. Unable to halt his forward momentum, James reeled and, unable to see the guide rails, lost his balance. He landed hard on his rump on a patch of uncarpeted and wet concrete. The seat and legs of his pants immediately became saturated and James felt chilled. Fumbling about for the rail, he pulled himself upright and rubbed at the goose bumps that had sprouted all over his arms. Cursing in the blackness, he jabbed at the buttons on his watch until the face lit up with a pale light and showed the time of 7:01.

Within seconds, all of the interior lights came back on in a burst of white and yellow color. James rubbed at his shocked eyes and pulled at his soaked pant legs, which were sticking to his skin, and resumed his search for the two students.

Off to the right, he heard the echo of running footsteps, and Dana suddenly appeared, running in his direction from one of the prohibited pathways. In the near-darkness, her face looked like a moon bobbing in a black sea. James opened his mouth to yell at her but never had the opportunity. As soon as Dana reached him, she threw her arms around his waist and burst into noisy tears.

Removing her sharp nails from the flesh of his upper arms, James told her to calm down. "It's okay," he said gently. He repeated this phrase over and over until he began to lose patience with the girl's blubbering.

"Dana!" he shouted roughly. "Stop it! I can't help you until you get a hold of yourself!"

"I … I …" were the only intelligible sounds James was able to comprehend.

"What is WRONG with you?" he growled. "Are you hurt?"

"N-not, m-me," she stammered, her face blotched and streaked with tears. She wiped at her runny nose with the back of her jacket and tried to breathe. "It-it's Ms. W-Willis!" she wailed. "I th-think sh-sh-she's dead!"

FIVE

SPEARMINT GUM

Sodium per Serving:

0 mg

JAMES TOOK A LONG look at Dana's stricken face and knew that she was sincere.

"Can you show me where she is?" he asked, sounding more courageous than he felt.

"B-back where the sk-skeleton used to be." She pointed toward the path veering off to the right.

James pried three of Dana's talons from the flesh of his forearm and gripped her shaking hand tightly. "Can you show me the exact spot?"

"NO WAY!" she bellowed and ran off in the opposite direction, yelling out Jacob's name.

Once her youthful form had disappeared around a shadowy bend, James became aware of the intense silence around him. Even the water dripped noiselessly from the rock points as he moved cautiously down the path, looking left and right for any sign of Kinsley. His mind raced as he wondered how Kinsley could have come to harm. Had she fallen? Did something fall *on* her? He flicked his eyes at the ceiling where the dagger-shaped rocks jutted downward like dozens and dozens of menacingly outstretched arms.

After several minutes of walking, James saw a spot of blue on the forbidden side of the railing. Kinsley's short, sky-blue trench coat was gently illuminated by the row of lights embedded in the rock walls above. The pale light pooled around her form, radiating a fragile corona in the darkness. She was lying on her side, her face turned toward the back wall, but her legs were clearly splayed at an odd, uncomfortable angle. James had a peculiar thought that her pointy-toed, high-heeled ankle boots, though undoubtedly chic, were very unpractical for a walk through the caves.

Edging under the railing, James timidly whispered Kinsley's name. He hadn't expected her to reply, but it was the only action he could think of repeating as he inched closer to her inert body. He noticed that the belt she had worn on top of her long, black tunic and which had accentuated her small waist had somehow come unbuckled. It lay like an uncoiled snake next to her upraised palm. Kinsley's hair, which had been bound neatly into a low ponytail when they entered the caves, was now tangled and messy. Several moist blonde strands were plastered across her cheek and forehead. Another stuck to her lips, and James instinctively reached out to lift it off when he stopped himself.

It had only taken a few seconds to absorb the details of the scene, but the overall meaning of it took a little longer to sink in. James sat back on his heels, his eyes transfixed on Kinsley's light blue eyes, which were unnaturally glassy beneath the dim lights. He felt as though he were gazing into a shallow pool and, finding his own reflection there, kept staring like some kind of deranged

Narcissus. There was his image, which Kinsley was unable to shatter by simply blinking her eyes. The feathery curtains of her lashes were angled back toward her own skin, which seemed to become less and less pink in tone the more James stared.

"Kinsley?" he whispered once more, now watching her mouth. The full lips were parted, and he could see the gleam of her white teeth. It was only then that he became aware of two shocking details. The first was the presence of a vicious red and purple welt encircling the beautiful skin of Kinsley's neck, and the second was that someone was sitting nearby in the dark, weeping.

Fear filled his stomach, his chest, and finally worked its way up into his throat. Taking in a desperate breath, James slowly backed away from Kinsley's body, his eyes never leaving the figure crouched only feet away in the shadows.

"Is that you, James?" the figure whimpered.

James recognized the voice. He relaxed a fraction and allowed himself to breathe.

"Lindy? How long have you been sitting over there?" James backed away from Kinsley and moved closer to his friend.

Lindy shook her head as if trying to make sense of what she was experiencing. "Jacob found me and told me to come here. He said someone was hurt." She exhaled and continued, her voice trembling along with her hands. "He didn't say who—just mumbled something about a skeleton and ran for the exit. I yelled at him but he wouldn't stop." Lindy laced her fingers together to prevent them from shaking. "I've never seen Jacob rattled—even when his term project blew up in the kiln, so I knew something was up. When I got here..."

"Yes?" James prompted.

Lindy gestured at Kinsley's body without actually looking at it. "She was just like this. I climbed up here and saw...and saw her eyes. Then I realized she was dead and felt like I wanted to hide." Her brown eyes were glistening with unshed tears. "I thought that if I put my head down on my arms and waited, I would look up in a few minutes and find that this whole thing was a prank or some...subterranean hallucination. But then you came and, by watching your face, I knew that this wasn't just a bad dream."

James took his friend's hand and pressed it between both of his own in an attempt to warm it. "It's real, Lindy, and we have to get help."

Lindy nodded numbly. "I'll find a guide."

When she failed to move, James stood and pulled her gently to her feet. As he did, he became aware of footsteps approaching behind them.

"What's happened?" boomed the voice of Principal Chavez.

The young guide who had discussed the details of the ancient skeleton with Lindy's students earlier stood alongside Chavez. Leaning to the side, the guide observed the immobile form lying precisely where the skeleton had once lain. Issuing an involuntary grunt, he fumbled with his walkie-talkie. Talking rapid-fire into the receiver, he grew ashen as he tried to cloak his emotions by adapting a posture of bravado. Squaring his shoulders and drawing himself upright, he directed Lindy and James to return to the pathway.

"Ms. Perez!" Chavez ignored the guide and repeated his question. "What's going on here?"

Lindy refused to meet his eyes. "It's Kinsley," she said timidly, waving away James's proffered arm as she heaved herself over the guide rail. "It looks like ... we think she's dead."

"Good God!" Chavez spluttered. He pushed James aside and grabbed onto Lindy to steady her as she made a wobbly landing from the top rung of the railing. She clung to him for support and seemed to instantly forget that anyone else was present.

"Are you hurt?" he asked Lindy, clutching her to him.

"No," she dropped her eyes. "But poor Kinsley! Someone . . ." She pressed her cheek against his chest, as if to separate herself from the words she was about to utter. "Luis, I think she's been murdered!"

James stared at the twosome. The way they stood, holding one another as the striped shadows from the illuminated stalagmites behind them fell across their faces, they looked as though they were posing for the cover of a romance novel.

Finally, Chavez released Lindy and raked a hand through his black hair. He turned his attention to the body on the ledge. "That's not Kinsley. She couldn't come today." He lowered his voice as a group of curious students headed their way. "It's her sister. That's Parker." And with that, he strode away with a shout, determined to intercept his charges before they could come close enough to see the dead woman.

———————

A half-hour later, the police had finished questioning the shaken and agitated students. They were reluctantly loaded into buses and driven back to Quincy's Gap. Believing they had no more pertinent information to share with the authorities, Bennett and Gillian volunteered to continue their roles as chaperones. They joined the students on the buses, leaving James, Lindy, and Principal Chavez available to assist the police.

Not all of the students were free to leave, however. Jacob and Dana, who stood huddled together sipping root beer in the staff conference room, were not allowed to join their friends. The police made them repeat the story of how they had come across Parker's body while searching for a suitable place to make out.

Dana cried the whole time, begging the officer not to tell her father about her lack of discretion.

"My daddy hates Jacob's daddy," she informed the bemused officer in weepy tones. "They had some fight over some dumb girl in, like, the fifth grade and have been mortal enemies ever since."

"Hey! That *dumb* girl's my mama now," Jacob added in an injured tone. He seemed to have recovered a fraction of his calm in light of Dana's distress. He edged away from her a bit. "Calm down, Dana. It's not like you knew her or anything," he scoffed, referring to Parker.

"Shut up!" she snarled. "It's all your fault I'm sitting here instead of headin' home with my friends. If you hadn't pulled me from the main path, someone *else* could have ... found her."

"Oh, you wanted to break some rules," he said, smirking. "When I got behind that one pillar you were hot as a—"

"That'll do, young man," one of the policemen broke in before Jacob could complete his analogy. "So let me ask you this one more time," the cop stared down the edgy teenagers. "Did *anyone* pass by you as you looked for a place"—he paused and covered a blossoming smile with his hand before he completed his question—"to hang out?"

The students shook their heads.

"And you didn't see a single person until you found Ms. Perez?" the officer asked Jacob.

"That's right," Jacob replied. "Ms. Perez was standing by that lake with all the candles. I told her someone was hurt and then kept on goin'." He cast a sidelong glance at Dana. She glared at him and made a face illustrating her disgust. "Well, damn, *I* didn't want to end up like that poor lady."

"Oh, so it was okay for Ms. Perez to face the axe murderer alone?" Dana inquired acerbically. "I thought you were, like, a big, tough wrestler. Ha!"

Jacob's mouth contorted in anger. "At least *I* ran in the right direction."

The officer cleared his throat and fixed his attention on Dana. "And the first person you came across was Mr. Henry?"

Dana shrugged. "Everyone calls him Professor, but yeah. I was *so* scared. It was, like, five minutes before I could even tell him what I'd seen. Then I ran smack into that mailman guy, and he helped me find the exit." She shuddered. "I am *never* going into another cave for the rest of my life!" Suddenly, a thought occurred to her and her eyes lit up. "You know, my parents could probably, like, sue this place. I'm gonna have nightmares *forever*! That should be worth something."

The officer rose and held on to the back of Dana's chair, indicating that she should also stand. "We're going to take you both home now." He gestured at Lindy, Principal Chavez, James, and the remaining guides. "The rest of you folks may as well get comfortable. Sergeant McClellan from the State Police is on his way to take your statements."

James watched with longing as Dana and Jacob were escorted outside by a kind-faced policewoman. He felt drained—both emotionally and physically. A cup of brown sludge posing as coffee sat on the table before him. He had taken one sip of the brew, which was thick with old grounds and lightened with the type of powdered creamer that fell from its aluminum can in tight, hard clumps. The result was a gray-looking and completely unpalatable liquid that James wished would be magically transformed into a glass of brandy or, at the very least, a belly-warming ale.

"James?" Lindy nudged him in the side and held out a package of peppermint whitening gum.

"Hmm?" He blinked.

Thanking her, James peeled back the foil and pondered the ability of a stick of gum to whiten his teeth. Suddenly, an image of the yellowed choppers belonging to Mr. Sneed popped into his mind.

"Ah, Lindy?" he whispered. "Where is Mr. Sneed?"

She gave him a perplexed look. "Who?"

"Adam's grandfather!" James twisted his neck in order to gain a view of the hallway outside the conference room. "Where is he?"

A flush sprouted on Lindy's latte-hued cheeks and neck. "Good Lord! I forgot all about him!" She leaned in and whispered something to Chavez, whose black eyes sprang open in alarm.

Before anyone could discuss the matter any further, a policeman entered the room, removed his cap, and began to shake hands with the other officers. James found himself staring at the fortysomething officer. The man James assumed was Sergeant McClellan was easily the tallest man he had ever seen. As he greeted his law enforcement fellows, McClellan peered breezily over their shorter heads with a pair of wide blue eyes tinged with green and observed the civilians seated around the table. After clapping the officer nearest to James on the back with an enormous hand bearing inhumanly long fingers, the sergeant settled himself down at the head of the table and accepted a cup of coffee.

As he sipped, the room fell silent.

"Sweet mercy on me!" McClellan exclaimed in a deep but surprisingly soft voice. "This stuff is even worse than what we've got at the station. I did *not* think that was possible." He pushed the cup away. "We'll make this quick so y'all can get on back home. No doubt we'll be speaking to each other again tomorrow," he added. "For now, I'd like to speak to you one at a time." He looked at James. "I believe you were the first adult on the scene, sir?"

James hesitated. The truth was that Lindy was there before him. "Um ..." he stammered.

"Sergeant?" Lindy jumped in, raising her hand eagerly as if she were a student.

McClellan's mouth twitched in what might have been a grin. "You don't have to put your hand up. Ms. Perez, is it?" When Lindy nodded, he gestured at her to continue. "Did you want to say something?"

"I'm sorry to interrupt, but I ... we ... just realized that one of the chaperones is missing."

McClellan's eyebrows rose as he shot a curious glance at the closest officer.

The local cop shrugged. "First we've heard of it, Sergeant."

"I see," McClellan responded emotionlessly. "And who is the missing person?"

"A Mr. Sneed," Chavez answered. "He was the grandfather of one of the students on our field trip."

"My men have done a full sweep of the caves, Sergeant," one of the cops added quickly. "There's no one down there. Just the body, sir."

"Thank you, Ray." McClellan opened a notebook and exposed the point of a black pen with a firm click. He studied James, Lindy, and Chavez and inquired, "When was Mr. Sneed last seen?"

Again Chavez took the lead. "Ms. Perez gave us all different sections of the cave to monitor. Mr. Sneed was asked to remain near the main staircase. We all moved deeper into the caves to take up our assigned areas around six thirty."

"So none of you saw him after six thirty?"

James, Lindy, and Chavez all shook their heads.

McClellan looked at the guides. "Any of you see the older gentleman down in the caves during the course of the field trip?"

"He walked past my post a couple of times," one of the female guides answered. "I was stationed kind of near the stairway, too, but I don't think I saw him after the first fifteen minutes. It was my job to turn the lights on and off at seven, though, and I didn't see him after that."

"That means that six thirty is the last time that any of those present here saw Mr. Sneed." McClellan made a note. He then sat thinking and as he did so, he tapped his pen against the side of his high forehead, leaving a peppering of black dashes on his skin. Finally, the pen ceased and he said, "We'll have to check with the students and other chaperones as well."

"I have a list of emergency numbers for all of the students who were with us," Lindy said, pulling a file folder covered with rainbow stickers from her tote bag. "The number for Adam's parents is the third one down. Maybe we should call them."

"May I?" McClellan indicated the folder. Lindy slid it across the table and McClellan took it in his hands, eyeing the rainbow stickers with apparent amusement. Flipping the folder open, he found

Adam Sneed's name and contact information and quickly dialed the Sneed residence.

"Is this Terrance Sneed?" He waited for an affirmative reply. "This is Sergeant McClellan from the Virginia State Police." He paused. "No, sir. Your son's fine. He's on his way back from Luray as we speak. Didn't mean to alarm you, sir." McClellan hesitated, as if trying to choose his words carefully. "Point of fact, I understand that Adam's grandfather volunteered to be a chaperone for this excursion," he began, but then a questioning voice on the other end of the phone caused McClellan to stop before he ever had a chance to ask his question. "I see," he responded in a sober tone after a few seconds. "I'm sure there's some misunderstanding. I hope I didn't give you a scare, sir . . . Will do. Good night."

McClellan snapped his cell phone closed and gazed, unseeing, at Lindy's folder. He traced the arc of one of the rainbow stickers with an index finger that resembled a flesh-colored stick—long, skinny, and a bit gangly—and then cast his eyes around the room.

"Men, we've got a challenge set before us." He pointed at Adam's name on the list of students. "The man who claimed to be this boy's grandfather is an imposter."

Lindy gasped. McClellan swiveled his blue-green gaze in her direction. "Did he ever show you any ID, Ms. Perez?"

Flustered, Lindy bit down on her lip. "No. He met us at the restaurant, and I'd *never* think anyone would . . ."

"No, of course not," McClellan reassured her hastily. "But did the man ever speak to Adam or did the boy acknowledge this older man as being his grandfather at all?"

Lindy hesitated. Avoiding the penetrating stare of Principal Chavez, she sighed and said, "Mr. Sneed, or at least the man I *thought* was Mr. Sneed, told me that Adam wanted to keep space between them, as he didn't think having his grandpa on a school outing was too hip." She looked helplessly at McClellan. "It sounded just like Adam to say something so insensitive." She shrugged. "So I let it go. And we needed an extra adult, so to be totally honest with you, Sergeant, I was glad to have him along, even if it meant letting his grandson get away with being rude."

"Understood," McClellan replied kindly. He then jabbed at Lindy's folder with his finger and his brow drew together. His face clouded over with a combination of anger and determination. "Folks, the problem now is this: Adam Sneed's grandparents are all dead, so none of them were here today. Somehow, someone found out this young man's name and used it to be invited into these caverns with a group of young men and women. I don't like that." He shook his head. "No, I don't like that at all."

Without any warning, he suddenly slammed the flat of his palm against the table. James jumped in his chair and Lindy let loose a surprised whimper. McClellan stood, slowly, purposefully, and put his hands on his hips. He locked eyes with the other officers, and they straightened their shoulders and lifted their chins as they waited for him to give a command. "What I also don't like is the notion that the man *pretending* to be Mr. Sneed—while he may not be anyone's grandparent—may damned well be a murderer. Let's get going, men. We've got a lot of work to do."

Lindy darted a quick glance and then whispered to McClellan. "There's something else you should know."

"Yes?" The sergeant seemed impatient to get on with his investigation.

Throwing an anxious look at Chavez, Lindy was barely audible when she asked, "Can I confess something to you in private?"

McClellan nodded and indicated that his men should clear the room, along with the remaining citizens.

James was the last to leave and as the door closed behind him, he heard Lindy sigh. "I just wanted you to know that I threatened Parker's sister the other night. I ... I actually said that I'd kill her."

The door shut on the rest of Lindy's confession.

SIX

WOODROW WILSON PALE ALE

Sodium per Serving: 34 mg

ONCE MCCLELLAN HAD DISMISSED James, Lindy, and Principal Chavez, the weary three-some piled into James's Bronco and rode back to Quincy's Gap in a dazed silence. The mountains that swelled above them on both sides of the highway were a dark battleship gray beneath an opal moon. As the road wound over their shoulders, they seemed to emanate a sense of strength and endurance, causing James to think about how quickly a person's life could suddenly end.

After mumbling a good-night to the others, James did not turn his truck toward home. Though he was tired, his unsettled mind replayed the discovery of Parker's body over and over again like a film reel set on a loop.

James longed for some friendly but anonymous faces. He wanted the comforting din of background noise like outdated jukebox music or billiard balls being slapped together as they rolled across an expanse of green felt. Turning the truck south, James headed for the Woodrow Wilson Tavern, one of the county's few drinking establishments.

Sammy, the proprietor, was at his usual place behind the oak bar, wiping a pint glass to a high shine with a dishtowel. When he saw James sit down at the far end of the bar, he tipped his *Made in the U.S.A.* baseball cap and raised his eyebrows in expectation.

"What's on tap tonight?" James inquired in a low voice that belied his mood.

Sammy examined his patron's face and then began stroking his gray mustache as he tried to decide which brew would serve his customer best.

"You look a bit drained, Professor, so I reckon you could use some Presidential Ale to perk you up some. It's as full of flavors as some of them fancy wines." Sammy scratched at his unruly sideburns, which he wore as a mark of admiration for the Confederate Civil War hero, General Joseph Johnston. Sammy had been copying Johnston's image for as long as anyone could remember. It only required a Confederate uniform to complete the full transformation, and Sammy had at least two at home. In fact, he often closed his tavern to participate in reenactments and his clients were accustomed to arriving at the front door in hopes of a drink and finding a sheet of paper announcing the bar's closure instead.

But Sammy's eccentricities only enhanced the Wilson's charm. It was the only place within fifty miles that served up special beers from local breweries, some of which were made especially for Sammy.

Black and white photographs depicting the heroes and landmarks of the Old Dominion covered the walls, with the four Virginia-born presidents holding the place of honor above the bar.

"Which President is the beer named after this time?" James wondered. "Still serving up the Jefferson Amber Ale?"

Sammy began to fill a frosted pint glass. "No sir, we went through the Jefferson like a bear bingin' before winter. This here is Woodrow Wilson Pale Ale, and it'll set you straight." Sammy placed the foaming cup on a coaster bearing the state flag of Virginia and slid the beverage under James's chin. "You look like you're carryin' some weight this evenin', so I'll let you be. Just enjoy the Woodrow and give me a holler if you need somethin'."

James nodded thankfully but knew he would never need to call upon Sammy. The man was the perfect bartender. No one's cup ever ran dry without Sammy having a replacement prepared, and he didn't stand and chat unless it was clear that his presence was wanted.

Sighing, James picked up the coaster and examined the state seal. Within the white circle set on a deep cobalt field, a helmeted woman dressed in a blue toga placed a conquering leg squarely in the middle of the chest of her defeated victim. He read the Latin motto, *Sic semper tyrannis*, but couldn't remember what it meant. Holding the coaster aloft, he caught Sammy's eye.

"What's the English translation, Sammy?" he asked.

Along with his unique appearance, the barkeep was also famous for his knowledge of Virginia history. "It means 'Thus always to tyrants.'" He pointed at the woman. "That there is Virtue and about the purtiest woman I've ever laid eyes on, too." Sammy raised his eyebrows suggestively. "I wouldn't mind seein' her in a wet T-shirt contest, if you know what I mean."

James realized that Sammy was referring to the fact that Virtue's toga didn't quite cover her breasts, leaving one entirely exposed. She gripped a tall spear in her right hand and held a sword in the other, looking like a triumphant Amazon warrior. "She'd kick your ass if she heard you say that," James admonished Sammy, taking a deep pull of the pale ale.

The bartender grinned lasciviously. "Don't I know it? And that makes me like her all the more."

Ignoring Sammy, James drank more of his beer, savoring the taste of clean, crisp hops combined with a hint of banana and orange. "This is just what the doctor ordered," James said gratefully.

"And you don't need health insurance to be able to pay for it. Best medicine in the world, if you ask me." Sammy retrieved James's glass, even though it was only partially empty. "Lemme top you off, Professor."

Something in Virtue's determined countenance reminded James of Lucy. Feeling the need to unburden his troubled mind, he dialed her number at home and asked her to join him at the Wilson. Sounding groggy, she did not agree immediately. James then gave Lucy a brief account of what happened at the Caverns and hung up. Morosely, he sat wondering if she would have come if he hadn't been directly involved in a murder case. He brooded and consumed three beers before Lucy arrived.

Lucy burst in the door and put her arms around James. She gave him a quick hug, a sisterly pat on the middle of his back, and then asked Sammy for a glass of water. Thanking him, she drank half of it within seconds. "I'm trying to drink a minimum of sixty-four ounces a day," she explained. "Now," her cornflower eyes glittered in a manner James hadn't seen for months. "Tell me *everything*."

As no one was seated anywhere nearby, James told her all he could remember, down to the smallest detail. He knew that Lucy would be interested in every facet of the evening's events.

"Oh, I can't believe I wasn't there!" she exclaimed regretfully when he was finished. "I'm *so* bummed!"

"Why?" James asked with an edge to his voice. "Because now you're not involved in the investigation?"

Lucy shrugged. "I might have been able to help the police if I had been there."

"You *were* supposed to be there, Lucy. If you hadn't felt such a pressing need to get to your exercise class..." he began angrily.

Lucy shot James an irritated look. "Then what? Lindy wouldn't have needed to ask Kinsley for help and Parker would still be alive? Is that what you're implying?"

"Well, you did ditch Lindy at the last second, Lucy." He took a drink of beer. "Lately, it seems like you only have room for your classes and your strict diet and your job. What's happened to the rest of us?"

Lucy traced tiny circles on the outside of her water glass. "I'm so close to making it as a deputy, James. Can't you just support me? Lay off on the guilt a bit?"

"Support is a two-way street," he replied, irked. "Every time we have a date, things are all about you. Where you can eat, what time you have to get to bed, how I'd better not come inside." He finished his beer in two great gulps and wiped his mouth with the back of his hand. Exhaling, he asked Lucy the question he had wanted to ask her for months, finding that four beers had finally given him the courage to speak. "What's the real reason, Lucy?"

She turned her blue-eyed gaze on him, clearly perplexed. "For what?"

"For why we've never taken our relationship to the next level. It kind of feels like you're afraid your parents might come home and catch us or something." He spoke the words rapidly, before he could chicken out. "I feel more and more like your buddy than a romantic partner. If you want to go down the *just friends* road, then tell me so, but I've had enough of this limbo. I don't know what to think about us anymore!" All of the stresses of the past few hours boiled up inside of him, and he practically shouted the last phrase.

Lucy grabbed her purse and jumped out of her chair. James couldn't help but notice how agile the movement was and how her clothes seemed too big on her ever-shrinking body. Above all, he was aware of the haggardness of her face. Was Lucy pushing herself beyond her limit?

"Fine, James!" she spat. "If getting me into bed is all you want, then we're better off as friends." She tugged on her shirt, setting it to rest over her hips. It was a motion she habitually repeated when she was upset.

Anger flared inside of James's chest. "It's *not* all I think about, but it's a natural progression! It's what people do when they're a couple! *Why* don't you want us to move forward?" he demanded, throwing a twenty on the bar for Sammy.

"Not all people have to have sex to enjoy a fulfilling romantic relationship, James. There are still couples who wait until they're married."

The term "married" hovered over their heads like a cloud of noisy bees. Lucy seemed to regret having uttered it and James tried to pretend that she hadn't. One failed marriage was enough. If he were to ever stand in front of the altar again, he would have no doubts about the future of him and his bride. Right now, when it came to Lucy, all James had were doubts. Had he missed some clue over the past months regarding Lucy's feelings on their physical interactions? He didn't think her chastity was based on religious reasons—she didn't even go to church. Was he still too fat to be viewed as attractive? James turned away from his reflection in the bar's horizontal mirror.

He had never been so confused about a woman before.

James dug his index fingers into his temple, where a headache had sprouted and was boring deeper and deeper into his skull. He groaned as the pain increased. Unbidden, a vision of the ugly red and purple welts around Parker's throat entered his mind and he shoved his arms into his coat. It was time to retreat to the silence of his bedroom and escape in the fantastical realms of one of his books.

"That word scared you good, didn't it?" Lucy laughed harshly with no trace of humor. "Such a typical man. I knew I shouldn't have mentioned any kind of a long-term commitment."

"I don't have anything against long-term commitments, Lucy." James sighed. "But we haven't exactly been happy together lately, so how can I be thinking about the future? The only thing we've done well as a couple recently is argue."

"Oh, that's nice. Now it's clear how you feel about me!" Lucy shrugged on her own coat and slung her purse over her shoulder. "Fine then! We're done with dating. And since I won't be going to the next Fix 'n Freeze class, I guess I'll see you when I see you." Lucy turned and marched out the door.

Sammy came over to collect the empty glasses. He lifted a coaster and showed James the image of Virtue. "I can see a resemblance between those two women." He chuckled. "And I think you're lookin' an awful lot like this guy here with a woman's foot stompin' on his chest."

"Thanks a lot, Sammy." James ripped the coaster from the barkeep's hand and stormed out of the Wilson, muttering to himself as the realization of what had just happened sank in. He was unexpectedly, unhappily single again.

———————

"TGIF, Professor," Scott said the next morning at work. "And no offense, but you look like you could use the upcoming weekend to rest."

"Look, the next *Dune* book is out—it's part of the prequel trilogy by Frank Herbert's son, Brian," Francis chimed in, gazing at the hardcover in his hand with a kind of rapture. "I'll let you check it out instead of me, if you think it might keep your mind off ..." He seemed at a loss for words.

"What happened in the caves?" Scott finished his brother's thought.

James thanked them for their concern, patted each young man fondly on the back, and proceeded to spend the morning repairing the loose spines of the books that saw the most use. The work allowed him to distance himself from the library patrons, who streamed into the building, eager to hear an eyewitness account of Blue Ridge High's shocking field trip from their own head librarian.

James could only imagine how the phone lines must have been abuzz with gossip until late into the night. Now, with the new day, the story of Parker's death must have grown so elaborate that the townsfolk would be searching for a reliable source to provide them with some semblance of the truth. And if not the truth, then, at the very least, a few juicy tidbits to add fresh hues to an already colorful tale.

"I'm lucky," James reflected aloud as he glued down the back cover of the abused copy of *Sex After Sixty*. "I get to hide in my office. Lindy, the poor thing, has no refuge. The townspeople probably formed a line outside her classroom at six this morning."

Still, James was hardly chipper. As he worked in welcome silence, he kept thinking back to his heated exchange with Lucy. Why had their relationship fallen apart? Was he really a pig or a Neanderthal because he wanted to respond to his baser nature?

James capped the glue and set the restored books in neat stacks around his office to dry. Next, he printed out a group of postcards meant to remind patrons about their overdue books or fines, and as he stamped them, he ruminated on the value of calling Lucy. Part of him wanted to talk things over, but the other part reasoned that it was too late. He wanted sex and she didn't—not without a ring, anyway.

"I think that's just an excuse," he told the postcards. "I think she wanted an out and I gave her one." James felt his anger swelling inside his chest. "Marriage? Lord! No way! Lucy Hanover and I are done!"

Scott poked his spectacled face into the office. "Did you need something, Professor? I thought I heard you calling."

"Ah, no." James cleared his throat. "Why don't you take the first lunch today, Scott?"

The young man beamed. "Excellent. I'll have just enough time to read the last story in this Ursula Le Guin collection while I chow down on the fattest, messiest meatball hero this town has ever seen." He rubbed his flat stomach. "Made it this morning. It has so many meatballs that I had to use a rubber band to keep the bun from busting open!" Scott dashed away in gleeful expectation.

James shook his head in amusement. The Fitzgerald twins could pack away startling amounts of food without gaining an ounce. They were pin-thin and ate at every possible opportunity. Bulk bags of potato chips, sub sandwiches the size of footballs, packages of Hostess cupcakes, and liters of Coke would make up a single meal. James thought about the sesame chicken salad and small Granny Smith apple he had waiting in the break room and frowned. He popped half a dozen tic tacs in his mouth in order to stave off the hunger pangs for another thirty minutes.

After lunch, as James continued to avoid his patrons by working on the annual budget, a headache encroached upon his concentration. Pulling open the desk drawer where a bottle of Advil was found, James struggled with the childproof cap. Finally, with the aid of a pair of scissors, he managed to pop the top off, slicing his palm at the same time.

"Damn," he muttered and then, "Damn!" a bit louder when he realized that only a single tablet remained in the bottle. As he sucked on his bleeding hand, James was both pleased and horrified to see through his office window the figure of Murphy Alistair emerging from her car. For a moment, he stared at her animated face and trim figure and then remembered that she was a reporter, and an aggressive one at that. Plus, she was not alone. Another woman, clutching a legal pad, jumped out of Murphy's passenger seat.

"Two reporters! I think it's time to call it a day," James said, eyeing the clock. He gathered his belongings in haste and then tried to get the attention of the nearest twin.

"Pssst!" he whispered to Francis. "Murphy's coming! I'm going to hide in the bathroom and then make a break for my truck. Stall her for me?"

Francis grinned. "Sure, Professor, but I wish *I* had her chasing after *me*." Noting his boss's agitation, Francis grew more serious. "But I guess this isn't a social call. She's gonna want to pump you for info about the murder. Hey bro!" he called across the library. "We got a Special Op assignment."

Scott straightened his spine and pushed his heavily framed glasses back on the bridge of his nose. "Cool. What is it?"

"Mission: Media Evasion," Francis replied.

James raced to the bathroom, believing that he was safe in the hands of the overly imaginative, ever-loyal Fitzgerald twins. He was wrong. As he stood in front of the mirror, inspecting his teeth for any signs of salad remnants, the door swung open and a young woman carrying a notebook strode in.

"Ha!" she declared. "Ms. Murphy *said* you might be in here!"

"Yes, imagine that," James stated acidly. "A man in the men's room."

The plain-faced woman, who looked even younger than Scott and Francis, had the grace to back out of the restroom. James was right on her heels, and as she opened her mouth to hail Murphy, he cut her off by saying, "Tell your boss, as I'm assuming you are one of her reporters—though I don't recognize you—that I'm heading over to Goodbee's Drug Store. She can follow me, but I'm not in the mood to talk about that field trip. I've been featured in

The Star more than I'd like as it is." And with that, James hustled outside to the sanctuary of his beloved Bronco.

––––––––––

"I think your blood pressure machine is on the fritz," James told the pharmacist as a teenage cashier rung up two giant bottles of Advil.

Mr. Goodbee, the kind-faced owner of the drug store, frowned quizzically. As he did, his multitude of freckles seemed to draw into a line across his brow. "What makes you say that, Professor?"

"I just used it and got results like I've never seen before." James downed three Advil. "We're talking crazy numbers."

Mr. Goodbee stroked his chin. "Lemme watch you take another reading."

James slid his arm into the stationary cuff and then hit the start button. He watched in fascination as the gray cushion inflated with air, constricting his arm like a slow and deliberate python. He observed the red digital numbers in their field of black with wariness, but once again, his results were unlike any he had received before.

"See that?" James pointed at the screen. "One hundred ninety-nine over ninety. That's got to be an error."

"Mind if I try?" Mr. Goodbee took the seat and placed his own arm in the cuff. Within a minute, his reading turned out to be 112/70. "Same as I got this morning." Still seated, the pharmacist looked up at James with concern. "I believe you have a medical problem, son. You'd better see a doctor and soon. Those numbers were no mistake, but if your blood pressure is actually that high and you ignore it, *that's* a mistake that could cost you your life."

James rubbed his temples in alarm. "I think I'm going to need something stronger than Advil."

He drove straight home and flung open the back door.

"Pop!" he yelled into the house. "Where are you hiding that bottle of Cutty Sark?"

SEVEN

DOCTOR'S OFFICE LOLLIPOP

Sodium per Serving:

20 mg

"Yep, you're definitely hypertensive. Two hundred over ninety-five, James," Doc Spratt declared later that afternoon, clucking his tongue in concern. "These results don't surprise me, considering what happened to your mama."

James shivered as the cold metal from the stethoscope touched the bare skin of his back. "What do you mean? I thought she was totally healthy when she died. That's what made it so hard ... such a shock."

Doc shifted the stethoscope to his patient's chest. "Deep breaths, now." He listened to James's lungs and then straightened. "Your mama struggled with her blood pressure most of her adult life. You and your daddy may not have been wise to that because she kept it under control as long as she could by watching what she ate and by regular exercise." He sighed. "Sometimes we just can't cheat fate, son."

James nodded in resignation. "I wish I had the energy she had. She was always on the move."

Doc Spratt smiled. "Yessir. That woman loved a project. I can't tell you how many checks I wrote for her charity endeavors over the years." He hung his stethoscope around his neck and studied his patient. "You've got to start avoiding salty foods, young man. Are you still paying regular calls to the gym?"

"I'm not going as often as I did over the summer," James admitted.

"You'd better get back on the treadmill then. I'm going to write you a prescription for some pills. You start taking them pronto. I want to see you again in a month, and I'd like to see those numbers down, you hear?"

"Yes, sir."

Doc Spratt gave James a pat on the head. "Don't worry, son. With a little discipline, you'll be right as rain." And just as he had for thirty-five years, Doc pretended to pull a lollipop from behind James's ear.

"Nothin' wrong with a little sugar every now and then," Doc repeated the same phrase he always did when handing out treats. "Everything in moderation, except for fishin'." He chuckled and then left his patient alone to change back into his clothes.

On the way home, James unwrapped the translucent green sucker and stuck it in his mouth.

Upon entering the house, he found Jackson seated at the kitchen table.

"What's for dinner?" his father inquired eagerly.

James dumped his briefcase by the back door and slumped into the chair opposite his father. "Nothing with salt," he said, sighing heavily.

Jackson's fuzzy eyebrows drew into a line. "I hope this doesn't mean another damned diet," he muttered. When his son didn't reply, he pushed a piece of scrap paper covered with scratchy handwriting under James's nose. "That Lindy girl called. You're supposed to see some McClellan fellow before your cooking class tomorrow." Jackson's eyes suddenly glimmered. "I sure do wonder what you're makin'. I can't wait to eat your homework."

"Where's Lucy?" Gillian asked as she tied on an apron listing both the Latin and common names of the plants used in a wide variety of herbal teas.

"She's not coming," James answered, evading Gillian's piercing eyes.

"Again," Lindy muttered, most likely referring to the field trip.

Bennett sidled over, proudly displaying a new apron that read *Iron Chef of the Shenandoah.* "I designed it myself." He grinned and then immediately grew somber. "How are you guys? James? Lindy? I guess it would be an understatement to say you had a rough week."

Lindy nodded. "Let's just say I'm not going to be elected Teacher of the Year anytime soon." She lowered her voice. "I don't think the police have any leads about Mr. Sneed's real identity, either. James and I just met with them, and we just keep repeating our original statements. It doesn't help that we knew practically nothing about Parker except that she was a friend of Murphy's, a vet, and seemed like a sweet person."

"That poor girl!" Gillian clutched her hands into fists. "Who would do such a thing! And what about her *sister*?" She fanned herself as though she might swoon at any moment. "You know, they say that when a twin loses a sibling, they're never *really* the same again."

"I believe that," Murphy said from behind them. She had entered so silently that none of the other Fix 'n Freeze students had heard her. "Honestly, I doubt Kinsley will ever recover. She's racked with guilt over allowing Parker to take her place on the field trip." Murphy rubbed her forehead wearily. "I think that Kinsley feels as though she's the one who should be dead."

"But who would want to do either of those lovely girls harm?" Gillian wailed. "And how does the fake grandfather guy fit in? What kind of *person* could do that? It's like pretending to be Santa and then stabbing someone with a candy cane!"

No one could think of an appropriate comment to make following Gillian's bizarre comparison, so the five of them stood quietly, sadly reviewing the fate of Parker Willis.

As Murphy hung up her coat and began to tie on her apron, James took a long look at her. He saw the deep shadows encircling her bloodshot hazel eyes and the slump in her shoulders. He was used to seeing Murphy alert and filled with determination. Here she was, mourning the loss of a friend, and he had run away from her when she had come to see him at the library. Ashamed, he averted his face as she spoke.

"I can't make sense of any of this, Gillian. Parker and I were really close in college, but we haven't seen each other much recently. I just met Kinsley, so I couldn't say what skeletons were in either of their closets." James could feel Murphy staring at him. "Believe me,

I'm trying to gather as much information as possible, but at this point, I haven't uncovered anything useful."

James met her eyes. "I'm really sorry I didn't catch up with you the other day. I wasn't thinking about how much this must be affecting you." He felt like reaching out to her, but didn't. Instead, he simply said, "I'd like to help you."

Lindy touched Murphy on the arm. "Me too. What can we do?"

Murphy was clearly moved by the offer. "I'd like to hear every detail about the mysterious Mr. Sneed. He's got to be the killer. He's the only unknown out of the chaperones, and you all saw him that day."

Bennett nodded. "The five of us *have* solved a few murder cases together. Maybe we can join forces and help you figure out what happened to your friend."

"I'd really appreciate that, you guys. And Lucy? She seems to have a knack for detective work, too." Murphy turned to James. "Do you think she'd be willing to help?"

"Um." James couldn't think of a response. He didn't think Lucy would want to be within fifty feet of him at the moment. Luckily, he was saved from having to answer by Milla, who burst into the room bearing two enormous trays of hors d'oeuvres.

"Ready to eat, cook, and be merry, my dears?" she trilled as she deposited the trays on the center island. "Oh my. This class is shrinking." She looked crestfallen. "Were my chicken enchiladas that bad?"

"No, no," Lindy hastened to comfort her. "The class is smaller because ..." She cast a glance at Murphy.

"Because we've recently lost a friend," Murphy said softly, as if she were fighting to maintain a steady voice. "Sorry, Milla, but we're a bit downhearted. It may take us awhile to get back to normal." She looked back toward the door. "I don't think we can expect Colin tonight either. He's probably too ..." she broke off, unable to keep the tremors from her speech.

Milla wrapped an arm around Murphy's back and gave her a maternal hug. "Oh, my dears," she said gently, looking at her class. She then rubbed her hands together and smiled. "Let's hope that cooking will cheer you up a bit. And if that's not therapeutic enough, there's always eating!" She gestured at the trays. "For your snacking pleasure we're having a few Spanish tapas treats tonight. Try saying *that* a few times fast."

James inhaled the aromas of food fresh from the oven and immediately felt some of the tension stored from the past week melt away. He examined the beautifully arranged appetizers with interest.

"Tapas?" he asked. "I've heard the term before, but I'm not sure exactly what it means."

"Tapas are like a special snack," Milla replied. "You can just have a few like we're doing now, or you can serve a bunch of different tapas dishes and create an entire meal. Tonight we're sampling peeled almonds fried in olive oil and sprinkled with sea salt; rosemary bread sticks served with slices of Serrano-style ham; green olives in a bath of olive oil, garlic, and fresh parsley; and some mushroom fritters. Now, for our liquid refreshment." Milla disappeared and returned again bearing a bottle of wine and some pottery tumblers. "I think we could all use a glass of Spanish red tonight. This is an affordable and tasty Rioja called Monticello."

Milla poured everyone a glass of wine. "I love these pottery cups. No worries about spilling. Now, a toast." She raised her glass. "To healing."

"To healing," the rest of the group chimed in.

"I feel a bit better!" Gillian declared. "And it's so refreshing to have some vegetarian delicacies. Thank you for being *so* sensitive about our needs, Milla."

Milla beamed. "Well, I'm not all about the greens, my dear, and I hope you're not too disappointed, for tonight we are making Spanish pork chops and vegetable paella." She consulted a notebook and screwed up her lips. "Wait a tick. I forgot to put out the saffron. Back in a jiffy."

Her pupils munched on the tapas and sipped their wine. James sampled every dish with the exception of the fried almonds and green olives, concerned that Doc Spratt would disapprove of him selecting such salty snacks.

"That woman is a gem," Bennett commented as he chewed the flesh from an olive.

"These mushroom fritters are heavenly," Lindy said, dabbing her mouth with the corner of her apron.

While Milla was busy in the pantry, Murphy set her wine cup down and cleared her throat. "I want to start my own investigation into Parker's murder, and I'd like you to help me, if you're willing. I'd like to hear everything you remember about Mr. Sneed once our food is in the oven."

James spoke for the group. "We'll tell you everything we can remember, Murphy."

The students took their positions at the cooking spaces and listened to Milla's instructions on how to trim the fat from their meat. After chopping some tomatoes and garlic cloves, James began to slice a green bell pepper. He didn't plan to eat the flavorful vegetable, however, as it had given him terrible indigestion his entire life.

Setting his prepared vegetables aside in tidy piles, he recounted Mr. Sneed's physical details to Murphy.

"He had a short beard that was more gray than black, a pretty prominent hooked nose, a big forehead with lots of horizontal lines, and teeth as yellow as a daffodil," James said as he removed the browned chops from a frying pan coated with olive oil. Next, he poured some white wine into the pan and tossed in a few sprigs of rosemary, finding it difficult to concentrate on cooking and talking at the same time. "I shared every detail with the police. None of them seem to make a difference, especially since I couldn't see the man's eyes behind those sunglasses or much of his hair beneath that fishing hat."

"Did he ever take the hat or glasses off?" Murphy inquired sharply, dropping garlic cloves into her pan without even looking at what she was doing.

James shook his head. "No, not even inside the caves."

"What about his body? Anything exceptional?"

"Sneed seemed pretty padded around the gut—not unlike myself—but his arms and legs were on the thin side. He walked with a shuffle and, well, he walked like an older person, like a grandfather."

Murphy stirred the contents of her pan absently. "Nothing struck you as unusual then?"

"I thought his skin tone was odd," James answered. "It was kind of orange. It didn't seem to go with the wrinkles and the age spots." He paused. "I guess it's because around here, older people are pale in the late fall. I mean, this is a far cry from Miami Beach. And," he added, "the color looked kind of uneven."

"Sounds almost like a self-tanning cream." Murphy looked at her palms. "I tried that stuff once and the inside of my hands and my ear lobes turned a pale orange. Was it like that?"

"I don't know. I've never tried to tan myself before, using lotion, the sun, or those beds with the lights." He smiled at her. "There are fish that live miles deep in the ocean that have more pigment than my skin does. I pour on the sunblock by the bottleful and head for the shade with a book."

Murphy returned his smile. "I'm going to stop by the library on Monday with some of that tanning lotion and then you can tell me if it looks like Mr. Sneed's skin."

"But why does it matter if he used tanner?" James wondered.

"It might not have been self-tanner. Sneed could have been wearing makeup to cover up his real face and that would be *some* kind of lead." She placed her chops in the oven. "And right now, that's better than what I've got, which is nothing."

As James put his pork in the oven for the necessary ten minutes, the other supper club members provided Murphy with their own descriptions of Mr. Sneed. The most memorable things about him were his enormous sunglasses and the awful hue of his teeth.

"His clothes looked like thrift-store wear," Bennett stated. "I know that Sears put out that blazer in the late seventies. Shoot, it was on the cover of their 1978 holiday catalogue, and my mama kept every one of those things. For what reason I'll never understand. Women!"

Gillian looked thoughtful. "You know, I thought it *unusual* that he was only fat in the tummy. The rest of him seemed almost skinny. He looked like he was a pregnant movie star wearing a turtleneck. Maybe," she whispered, "it was a *disguise*! Like one of those baby bellies they try to get teenage girls to try on!"

"Actually, I think that's a possibility, Gillian." Murphy donned an oven mitt and pulled her finished chops from the oven. She then stepped away so that the others could follow suit. "I think this guy wore makeup, some kind of false belly, thrift store clothes, and possibly a fake beard and wig. Any markings on the hat?"

"Just a fishing fly," James said. "It was feathery. Looked like a red bug with black wings."

Murphy got excited. "That might be an important clue, James! I'm going to bring you a fly-fishing catalogue along with the tanning cream."

"Okay, my dears! Enough chitchat for the moment," Milla broke in. "We've got paella to make!"

For the next half an hour, James chopped vegetables and listened to Milla's lecture on the significance of saffron in making authentic paella. They were allowed to choose which vegetables they added to their rice mixture, and James was more than happy to avoid the heads of broccoli. He had never liked the feel of broccoli florets on his tongue.

At last, their main course was wrapped and ready to go home. After they spooned their paella into Tupperware containers, they each thanked Milla for teaching them two delectable new dishes. James felt as though their fragmented group had come together strongly as a result of Milla's positive influence and from sharing their thoughts with Murphy. It had felt like a genuine supper club meeting, even without Lucy's presence. Thinking of her caused a pang of misery in his gut, and he didn't hear Murphy speak until she tapped him on the arm.

"Sorry, I missed that."

"I said, how about dinner tomorrow night?" Murphy asked again as they headed to their cars bearing warm take-out containers. "You can tell Lucy that it's a working date."

James paused next to his Bronco. "I don't need to tell *her* anything. We broke up."

Murphy's face filled with concern. It was not the reaction James had anticipated. He thought she'd give him a dose of her flippant flirtation, but she was genuinely distressed for him. "On top of everything else that's happened lately?" She shook her head. "Man, oh man. Are you okay?"

Touched by her show of tenderness, James nodded. "I will be. Let's go to Dolly's tomorrow for dinner. I believe I've owed you a cheeseburger for almost a year."

"I believe you have," Murphy said with a smile, and then she waved goodbye.

Milla's Vegetable Paella

4 tablespoons olive oil, divided
1 large onion, chopped
8 garlic cloves, minced fine
2 cups long-grain brown rice
4 cups vegetable stock
1 pound tomatoes, coarsely
  chopped
1 medium red bell pepper,
  chopped
1 medium green bell pepper,
  chopped
1 small eggplant, cubed
1 medium zucchini, cubed
½ cup sliced black olives
1 teaspoon saffron
1 teaspoon sea salt
½ teaspoon black pepper

Preheat the oven to 400 degrees. In a large saucepan, heat 1 tablespoon of the olive oil and cook the onion over a medium heat, stirring until translucent. Add the vegetable stock, rice, and saffron. Bring to a boil, then reduce heat to simmer and cook, covered, for about 30 minutes. Remove from heat. While the rice is cooking, heat the remaining 3 tablespoons of the oil in a large saucepan and add chopped garlic, red pepper, green pepper, eggplant, zucchini, olives, sea salt, and pepper. Sauté until the peppers are tender (about 5 minutes). Gently stir the tomatoes and the rice mixture into vegetables. Transfer the mixture to a greased casserole dish. Cover with aluminum foil and bake for 10–15 minutes.

(If some of these vegetables aren't to your liking, trade one of them out for ½ cup sliced mushrooms, a carrot, a celery stalk, or a cup of fresh or frozen peas.)

EIGHT

BEEF BRISKET

Sodium
per
Serving:

470 mg
for 3 oz.

WHEN JAMES STEPPED INSIDE Dolly's Diner on Sunday night, he felt unusually serene. That morning, he had gone to church and three of his favorite hymns had been selected for the service. After lunch, he and his father had chopped firewood and enjoyed the fruits of their labor by drinking coffee in front of a crackling fire. For several pleasant hours, James was absorbed in Ron McLarty's *The Memory of Running*, and Jackson perused the paper. At the end of the long and relaxing afternoon, James told his father that he had dinner plans, but promised to bring home a dessert from Dolly's.

Jackson, who had been on the edge of a sulk over being forced to open a can of soup for dinner and a package of oyster crackers, perked up. "If ole Clint's made his pumpkin cheesecake pie with the graham-cracker crust, bring me two pieces."

Clint, Dolly's husband and the chief cook of Dolly's Diner, must have had pumpkin on the brain. The daily special board announced pumpkin soup, pumpkin mashed potatoes, pumpkin muffins, and pumpkin cheesecake pie. Fortunately, Clint couldn't work pumpkin into a meat dish, and his famous Sunday brisket was the featured entrée.

"Professor!" Dolly greeted him at the door with a strange mix of pleasure and alarm. Her plump cheeks were more flushed than usual, and she fanned her large bosom with a dishtowel. Reaching behind her head as if to restructure the loose bun of hair, she glanced over her shoulder and grabbed James by the elbow.

"Your favorite booth is free, hon. Come on with me." As they walked, Dolly was practically glued to his side. Her bulk forced James to graze all the booths to his right as they made their way to the back of the room. Twice, he knocked the elbows of other diners and had to apologize. Dolly chatted feverishly along the way, and though she was always loquacious, she was never in a hurry, so James knew that something was afoot.

"Here we are!" she trilled once they had reached the booth decorated with coconut shells, a grass skirt, some colorful leis, two small tiki torches, and a large poster of an inviting cobalt sea bordering a strip of gleaming sand.

Clint had traveled all over when he was in the navy and he and Dolly had collected unique souvenirs from every port. James preferred this booth because he liked to gaze at the poster of paradise and fantasize about going there one day. Normally, strolling on the beach alongside Lucy had been a part of that fantasy, but now he could only envision walking alone.

"I think I'll switch booths tonight, Dolly," he stated a touch morosely. "Change is good, right?"

Dolly's bosom fanning stopped abruptly. "But why? You always sit here." She gave him a little push into the seat that faced away from the rest of the dining room. "You can twist things in a knot next time you come, but I like things to stay nice and predictable-like, so take a load off and I'll bring you some diet root beer." She took the pencil from her bun and held it in the air over a blank pad. James had never known her to actually write down an order and it didn't look like she'd be starting any time soon. "Unless you're not on that diet anymore?" Dolly questioned.

"No, diet root beer's great. I'll order a bit later, Dolly. I'm waiting for a friend."

As she ambled off, James turned to watch her progress toward the kitchen, still curious as to why she was acting so peculiar. Then, he saw the reason behind Dolly's agitation. Lucy was seated between James and the diner counter. Even though he was looking at the back of her head, he knew it was her caramel-colored hair and the soft curve of her cheek. He recognized her round shoulder clad in her favorite deep blue sweater, the one that brought out her cornflower-blue eyes so that they sparkled like a moving stream.

Lucy was not alone. In fact, the person facing in James's direction was, without a doubt, the best-looking man James had ever seen. Despite himself, he stared at the individual who could have been an actor, a model, or the cover face for the "Sexiest Man Alive" edition of *People Magazine*. The stranger was probably in his late twenties and had a strong jaw, a straight nose, and shining golden-brown hair. His skin was clean-shaven and radiated a sense of good health. His sweater, which looked like a soft, touchable cashmere, was stretched tightly over a firm torso and muscular arms. He had pushed the sleeves up in order to eat, and his forearms rippled with each movement.

Suddenly, he laughed at something Lucy said, and James caught a glimpse of his captivating smile and the pair of dimples that had sprouted in his smooth cheeks. He then heard the man respond to Lucy's joke using a deep and masculine voice that resonated with confidence and warmth. Finally, the man noticed James staring and raised a hand in friendly greeting. Lucy swiveled around in her seat and red patches resembling raspberries quickly speckled her cheeks and neck.

She said something quietly to her dinner partner, wiped her mouth hastily with her napkin, and walked over to James, who was seething with jealousy.

"Hi," she said, sounding nervous. "Can I sit for a minute?"

James shrugged and Lucy took the seat across from him.

"That's my friend, Sullie. We're training together."

"I bet," James muttered.

Lucy's flush grew deeper. "We're not, uh, a couple or anything. We just work out at the gym and stuff. He's applying to become a deputy, too, and I've been helping him prepare for the written exam."

James couldn't control the anger boiling in the pit of his stomach. "Is that what you were doing all those nights you blew me off? And your friends? Hanging out with that slab of meat over there?" He jerked his thumb in the young man's direction.

Lucy's face darkened. "Don't call him that! He's a really nice guy. Not all of us have read half the books in the library, you know." Her eyes flicked back to Sullie. "Just because he doesn't have enough degrees to plaster a bathroom with doesn't mean that he's some mimbo!"

Taking a sip of water, James tried to clear his head. "A mimbo? That's a new one. That mimbo's the reason why we broke up, isn't he? It was never about you wanting to get married or about us not having sex before marriage." He lowered his voice, growing more and more enraged. "It was just about not having sex with *me*! Were you already banging Mr. Perfect? Is that why you kept pushing me away?"

"No!" Lucy shouted and then covered her mouth with her hand. She twisted her silver necklace around and around her index finger. "God, James! Give me some credit. But … I *do* have feelings for him." She looked down at her lap. "Actually, I have feelings for both of you, but then you seemed to want out, so you basically made the choice for me. I didn't plan for things to get this messy and I'm sorry. I should have been honest with you about how confused I was, and I shouldn't have mentioned getting married, either. God knows I'm not ready for a walk down the aisle."

"But everything's all cleared up now, right?" James hissed. "You've got your new man after, what?" he pretended to check his watch. "All of five minutes after quitting on us?"

Lucy glanced in Sullie's direction. "He doesn't know." She swallowed hard. "And I'm not *exactly* over you, James."

"Sure looks like you're doing a pretty good job to me." James could barely think straight. He looked around for some kind of escape. "Oh, here comes Dolly with more root beer. You'd better get back to your *date*."

Lucy shot out of her seat. "Fine! I won't keep you any longer." She turned away and strode smack into Murphy.

"Hi, Lucy." Murphy gave an awkward laugh as she pushed her hair back into place, as her headband had gone askew in the collision. "Where's the fire?"

Lucy ignored her and turned to James. She glanced at her watch and spat, "Five minutes, huh? You hypocrite!" She returned to her table and seconds later, she and Sullie the Beautiful left the diner.

Murphy studied James's face as she sat down. "You okay?"

"Yes." James nodded. "Starving for a piece of brisket, though. You still having a cheeseburger?"

"With a mountain of French fries in gravy, yep."

Dolly came over and took their orders, her eyes gleaming over having witnessed the scene between James and Lucy. James knew that her tongue would be wagging like a dog's tail until everyone in Quincy's Gap knew about their falling out.

"You don't have to talk about it if you don't want to," Murphy said. "It just seems like you could use a friend right now."

"I'd rather focus on Parker," he told Murphy. "Have you thought about motive at all?"

While they waited for their dinners, Murphy told James all she knew about the Willis sisters.

"Money could have been the motive, but I can't figure out how," she began. "Both Parker and Kinsley are heiresses. Apparently, their father was a real bioengineering wizard. He invented a strain of drought-resistant grain that most of the farms in the Midwest swear by, and he also made marked improvements to threshers and some other equipment I wouldn't know the first thing about. The bottom line is, both the girls are worth a few million each."

James sipped his root beer thoughtfully. "But they're both young and single, so if something happened to them, who would get their money?"

Murphy held out her palms in a gesture of helplessness. "That's one of the things I need to find out." She smiled as she saw Dolly approaching with their dinner platters. Dolly had barely set the heavy porcelain plate down when James picked up his silverware, hurriedly cut into his brisket, and took a large bite. He chewed eagerly, drippings from the meat trailing down his chin. Murphy dunked a steak fry into her cup of brown gravy and sighed contentedly. "I could eat here every night." Reaching across the table, she wiped at James's chin with her napkin. "Sorry. Just trying to save your shirt."

"Thanks." James slowed down, embarrassed by his piggish eating. Then he watched as Murphy ripped into her cheeseburger. She chewed rapidly and downed several fries before speaking again.

"I'm not the most delicate eater, James. You'll probably have to clean up gravy from the tip of my nose by the time we're done." She winked in her usual flirtatious manner and then immediately turned somber. "Anyway, I'm attending Parker's memorial service back in Kansas, and I'm flying out there with Kinsley. I know she's upset, but I'm going to ask her a whole list of questions on the plane."

"How about another motive, besides money?" James asked. "Jealousy maybe? Do both of the girls have a boyfriend?"

Murphy nodded. "Kind of. Kinsley told me that she broke off a pretty serious relationship back in New York with some fast-track trader named Gary. They worked together. From what she told me, which was brief, this guy was really sweet but also super ambitious. When Kinsley told him she wanted to lead a slower life, he said they were heading in different directions and should split. Apparently they still care about each other enough to talk regularly on the phone." Murphy sank her teeth into her pickle spear. "It sounds to me like she's still in love with him."

James debated over whether to sample the pumpkin muffin Dolly had put on his plate. He took a small nibble and then, relishing the taste, popped the remains into his mouth. "And Parker was involved with Colin Crabtree, right?" he inquired once he had swallowed.

"Right. You met him briefly at Milla's first class." Murphy gazed off over James's shoulder. "He's a real charmer. Runs a large-animal practice—you know, for treating cows and horses—just south of Harrisonburg."

"Do you think he had any reason to do Parker harm?"

Murphy's eyes grew round with surprise. "I don't know. I only talked to him the one time, and he seemed like a great guy." She paused. "Kinsley mentioned that Colin was helping out with Parker's practice until they could hire another vet. She also said that Parker's current partner, Dwight Hutchins, is fantastic with animals, but apparently shies away from dealing directly with animals' owners whenever possible. Parker used to complain to Kinsley about Dwight's quirks." Murphy pointed the remnants of her pickle spear at him. "James, you've got to go to Luray and check them both out."

"But I don't have a pet!" James protested.

"Oh, you should get one. They're such wonderful company. You could always adopt a kitten or a puppy and bring it up to Luray for shots."

James thanked Dolly as she cleared away their bare plates. "'Bout licked clean," Dolly said happily as she examined their dishes. "That's what I like to see."

"Murphy," James continued after Dolly was gone. "I'm not adopting a pet just to snoop on Parker's boyfriend and co-worker. Owning a pet's a big decision, a big commitment."

Murphy looked sheepish. "Yeah, I guess you're right." She grew thoughtful. "What about the other members of the supper club? Anyone have a pet?"

"Gillian's got a cat."

"Well, take her along. It's good to have a second pair of eyes when you're trying to get a take on someone."

James thought about Gillian's tabby, the Dalai Lama. He didn't seem like an easygoing character that would enjoy an unnecessary visit to the vet, but he couldn't think of any other way to investigate Colin Crabtree.

"You two want some decaf?" Dolly asked, reappearing from nowhere.

"Sure." James looked at Murphy. "Unless you've got someplace to be?"

"Nowhere better than here," she replied with a saucy smile.

Dolly gawked at the pair for a few seconds and then hastened off behind the counter where the coffee carafes were kept.

James felt warmth spread beneath the collar of his shirt. "I never know quite how to read you, Murphy," he confessed.

Murphy waited for Dolly to serve their coffee and reluctantly walk away to help another customer before she spoke. "Then I'll make it easy for you, James. I've liked you from the start. I have never cared about your weight, your ex-wife, or the fact that you live at home with a hermit for a father. You're smart, cute, and funny. When you and Lucy became an item, I was pretty bummed."

She broke eye contact and focused on stirring sugar into her coffee. "I know that I'm more aggressive than Lucy. I know that she and I are pretty different and that I'm probably not even your type. I also know that you're not over her and may not be for some time." She blew on her coffee before taking a sip. "But I'm still interested in you, James. When you and Miss Future Deputy are really done, I'll be waiting." She wagged a finger at him. "But not too much longer, Professor. First of all, I'm a catch. Second, I'm not a patient woman and I don't want to be the one to initiate things anymore. If you want me, you'll have to be mighty clear about it." She made a move to take out her wallet.

James recovered himself enough to reach for her hand and stop her from pulling out any money. "I've got this."

Murphy flipped her hand around and squeezed his warmly. "Whatever happens or doesn't happen between us—thanks for helping me, James." To his consternation, her hazel eyes glistened with tears. "This whole thing with Parker has really shaken me up and there's not much in this world that can do that." She blew her nose into her napkin and composed herself. "Okay, enough of that. We've got a job to do, James. You and I are going to find Parker's killer and after that," she finished her coffee and slung her purse over her shoulder, "maybe you'll be ready to take a chance on us. See you when I get back." She stood up to leave.

James stumbled to his feet, not knowing whether he should attempt to hug her goodbye, shake her hand, or do nothing. Murphy made it easy for him by stepping out of his reach in order to button her coat.

"Good luck," he finally said as she walked away.

He watched her until she had stepped through the front door and disappeared outside.

"My, my!" Dolly exclaimed as she collected the coffee cups. "Tonight's been better than a whole tootin' season of *The Bold & the Beautiful*. What in the world is going on with you, Professor Henry?"

James rubbed his temple and prayed that a new headache wasn't making itself known. "I'm not sure I can answer that yet," he responded vaguely and then ordered two slices of pumpkin cheesecake pie to go.

NINE

BANANA

Sodium
per
Serving:

0 mg

JAMES WAS UNPREPARED FOR the amount of noise one cat, trapped within the confined space of the Bronco, could create. The Dalai Lama howled from the moment Gillian covered his green eyes and shoved him into his purple carrier, and he didn't show any signs of letting up once they had gotten underway.

"He *knows* where he's going." Gillian said as she stuck her fingers through the narrow bars of the carrier's door in order to allow her tabby to smell her fingers. The Dalai Lama stopped mewling for a fraction of a second as he sniffed, then resumed his pathetic keening.

"I guess he doesn't like going to the vet too much," James observed and then turned off the radio. He couldn't stomach the combination of cat noise and country honky tonk, though some of the high-pitched fiddle sounds were indistinguishable from the strangled cries issuing from the Dalai Lama's throat.

"Don't say that word!" Gillian whispered urgently. "He's been throwing up his food a lot lately and he'll get an *especially* upset stomach if you say V-E-T!" Her face turned worried. "Oh dear, I think he might be on the edge of *distress* right now."

James looked at Gillian in disbelief. "How can you tell if a cat is going through a gastrointestinal event?"

Gillian took the question very seriously. "Well, he kind of scrunches up his face like this." She twisted her mouth sideways and squeezed her eyes shut. "Then he gives a few shallow coughs." She replicated the coughs, which sounded like someone clearing her throat. "And then he barfs."

"He *what*?" James eyed the cat in alarm. The Dalai Lama's cries increased in volume as he returned the stare.

Gillian slipped a cassette into the Bronco's tape deck. "I'm glad your truck's not too new 'cause some of the new cars only have CD players now. *This* is the Dalai's favorite mix tape. Yanni settles him down immediately." She turned up the volume knob. "Maybe it's a good idea that I'm taking him to get looked at. Just the other night, he actually threw up most of his can of Fancy Feast! He's *never* wasted the tiniest drop of wet food before." She poked her fingers around inside the carrier. "Here comes some soothing, Dalai."

As the calming strains of instrumental music piped out of the Bronco's speakers, James tried to think about what kinds of questions he could ask Colin Crabtree in order to get a sense of his personality, but his attempts at concentration were hopeless. Gillian added to the potpourri of noises already echoing inside the

Bronco by humming and swaying with the music, her rows of silver bangles tinkling as she mock-directed an orchestra.

"If I get a headache," James murmured, "it won't be related to high blood pressure."

Some twenty minutes later, as James wished that he had brought a bigger cup of coffee along with some earplugs, Gillian abruptly switched off the music. "Sorry, James, but I need to turn *inward* for a moment and focus on how I'm going to read this Colin fellow's aura."

Pulling her sequined peasant skirt over her legs, Gillian rearranged her body so that she was sitting Indian style. Resting her hands on her knees, she turned her palms upward and closed her eyes. Even as the Bronco rounded dramatic curves in the road, Gillian was like a statue. James was impressed by her balance. Maybe there was something to her yoga addiction after all.

Less than a mile south of the town proper, James turned into the gravel driveway marked by a white sign reading *Luray Veterinary Clinic*. Painted wooden cutouts of a variety of dogs, cats, and birds lined the parking lot. At the exact moment that James pulled into a spot marked by a wooden golden retriever, the Dalai Lama stopped howling.

"Good boy," Gillian cooed into the cage as though the cat's behavior throughout the trip had been precisely what his owner wanted. The tabby rubbed his cheek against the cage door and smiled, or at least it seemed that way to James.

As they entered the reception area, Gillian took the lead. She told James that she knew exactly how to handle the animal people and that if he left everything in her hands, they'd be able to gain access to Colin and Parker's partner Dwight.

"Good afternoon," the woman behind the counter greeted them with a pleasant smile. She was dressed in pink and yellow scrubs decorated with cartoon cats and dogs and was likely an assistant veterinarian rather than a receptionist. James was surprised to see another bird's nest head of hair in the same Bozo-the-Clown orange as Gillian's. The woman didn't have Gillian's dozens of bracelets on her wrists, but she had three-inch chandelier earrings bearing several tiny brass bells that played a chorus with every move she made. It seemed as though Gillian had discovered a kindred spirit.

"What a *perfect* shirt! Oh, and what a groovy mood ring!" Gillian exclaimed and then placed the purple carrier on the counter, facing the assistant. "Look, Dalai Lama. See the pretty lady?"

The woman leaned toward the carrier. "Oh my, what a handsome fellow! Do you have an appointment, you darling thing?" she directed her question at the cat.

"He does," Gillian answered, clearly familiar with the pampered-pet dynamic. As a professional groomer, she probably spoke in a similar manner all the time. "Tummy trouble," Gillian whispered conspiratorially to the assistant.

"Uh-oh," the assistant replied. "But we're not his regular vet, right? I would have remembered seeing someone *this* gorgeous before."

The Dalai Lama actually started to purr.

Gillian shook her head. "Our regular doc is at some kind of convention. Now, we *love* and *trust* him to no end, but the doctor who's filling in—" She threw an anxious look at James. "Well, we just don't feel that he *cares* as much. He doesn't see the animals as having their own *selves*. Do you know what I mean?"

The assistant pursed her lips. "I certainly do! Oh, I wish you could have met Ms. Willis, the woman who started this practice. She was just *magical* with animals."

"She's not here today?" Gillian pretended to be stricken.

"Oh, it's been all over the news!" the assistant seemed shocked that Gillian wasn't aware of the latest headlines. "*She* was the one found dead in the Caverns."

"*NO!*" Gillian swooned and James reached out as if to grab her, not knowing how far she would go to put on a convincing performance.

"Yes!" was the woman's rejoinder. "The police questioned the whole staff three times and tore this place apart looking for clues. It was very traumatic. The *chi* around here was completely destroyed for days!"

"I don't mean to sound selfish," Gillian whined, "but who will take care of my precious baby now?"

"Ms. Willis's partner, Dwight Hutchins." The assistant stood and handed Gillian a clipboard. "Don't worry. He's great with animals, too." She lowered her voice. "Dr. Hutchins is grieving over the loss of his friend and partner, so he might not be too talkative, but your cat will get the finest care from him."

Gillian paused and then turned to James. "Oh, I just don't think I can go back there. Will you take him, James? I'm going to chat with—" She turned back to the assistant. "What's your name, friend?"

"June."

"I think I need June's comforting presence right now," Gillian said, smiling warmly at the assistant.

Panicking, James eyed the cat carrier. "But I don't know what to tell Dr. Hutchins about his symptoms."

"Just tell him how he won't eat regularly and that he's puking up half his food!" Gillian wailed and then sank into one of the chairs in the waiting room as if it were all too much for her to take. "June? Do you happen to have any herbal teas?"

June leapt up from behind the counter. "Of course! It's all I drink. How would you like some Magic Mantra Mulberry?"

Gillian sighed with happiness. "Perfect. I *knew* my instincts were right when I made this appointment. Sometimes you just have to trust in a higher power."

June beamed. She then gestured impatiently for James to come to the back and wait in Exam Room Two. Without bothering to open the door for him, she scurried off to the kitchen, her earrings ringing in time with her animated steps.

Moments later, the Dalai Lama renewed his mewling. James didn't have the slightest clue as to how to comfort the animal, so he simply said *hush* over and over again and prayed that the vet would appear soon. As he whispered to the agitated tabby, he examined an oversized poster on the wall depicting different cat breeds. He was so fixated with the illustration of the Abyssinian that he barely noticed when a man in a white lab coat entered the exam room.

"Dwight Hutchins," he muttered by way of introduction. He did not shake hands but quickly turned to the carrier. Taking a look at the manila file in his hand, he cast a curious glance at the Dalai Lama. "Interesting name. What seems to be the trouble with him?"

The vet never made eye contact with James and seemed more focused on removing the cat from his carrier than connecting with his owner. However, Dwight's behavior gave James an open opportunity to study him. He was young to be a full-time vet and a partner in the practice. James didn't think Dwight was a day over thirty.

Of medium height with mud-brown hair, deep-set brown eyes, and a pointy nose and chin, Dwight was simply plain. There was nothing about him to make him stand out in a crowd. The man was average in almost every way except that he did seem to possess a unique, calming touch when it came to animals, at least in the Dalai Lama's case.

"Hey, boy," Dwight spoke softly to the nervous cat. "What's wrong, big guy?"

James realized that this was his cue to fill the vet in on the tabby's symptoms. "Um, he's not eating with his regular gusto. We're worried that something more serious might be going on than just fussiness. And he's throwing up a lot."

Dwight nodded, his gaze never leaving the Dalai Lama. He stroked the cat's fur gently and scratched him under the chin. The tabby responded by purring, rubbing at the vet's fingers, and finally, gazing up at Dwight with a look of pure adoration. Dwight smiled and, even though the smile was tinged with sadness, James saw genuine animation in the younger man's face. As the vet carefully massaged the cat's abdomen, he asked, "Is he up to date on his shots?"

James hesitated, but knowing how much the Dalai Lama meant to Gillian, he felt he could safely answer the question. "Yes."

Dwight nodded. "Does he seem to be drinking more water lately?"

"Uh," James began. He had no idea what to say. He decided to settle with honesty. "I really don't know."

"How about the vomiting? More than once in a while?"

Thrilled to be able to reply accurately, James practically shouted, "Yes! Quite often, actually."

The young vet ran his long, thin hands over the Dalai Lama's hips. "After eating?"

"Not right after," James guessed, "but yes, after meals."

"He looks pretty healthy to me," the vet stated in his quiet way. "Still, there are a few things we could check for. He could be lactose intolerant, but if he's throwing up after eating his regular food, then he could have inflammatory bowel disease."

"Cats get stuff like that?" James was amazed.

Dwight nodded. "I'm going to recommend you give him some Metamucil or try some canned pumpkin. He may just need more fiber in his diet."

James gaped. "Canned pumpkin?"

"Some cats really like it." Dwight scribbled something on Dalai Lama's chart.

"So your office must be pretty backed up these days," James said in what he hoped sounded like a sympathetic tone.

The young vet nodded without looking away from his paper, but James saw a shadow darken his features. "We are, but one of," he struggled to say the name, "Ms. Willis's friends—a large-animal vet—is helping out."

"That must be a load off your mind," James stated enthusiastically. "Ms. Willis seems to have had a great reputation for her way with animals. I hope her friend is just as good."

Dwight's face became stormy, and James knew that he had hit a nerve. The vet averted his eyes, but James could have sworn he saw them grow misty.

"Oh, he's *not* that good, huh?" he inquired innocently and then, when Dwight refused to answer, added, "Well then, I'm glad we got *you* instead."

"I'm not much of a people person," Dwight admitted after a long pause in which he struggled to get a hold of himself. It was clear that he also wished to move the subject away from Colin Crabtree. "I love all animals, though. They're very giving. They don't care that you're not charming. They want you around no matter what you look like or how much money you make." He clamped his mouth shut after that, probably regretting that he had revealed such private thoughts in front of a stranger.

"If this fellow is more of a large-animal doc, it must be a challenge to come in and treat small animals," James persisted.

Dwight nodded, but said nothing. Completing his notes, he closed the folder. "You can put him back in the carrier. I'm going to get you some literature on inflammatory bowel disease."

James eyed the tabby fearfully. He blocked Dwight's exit and gestured at the carrier. "He can be pretty persnickety. Mind giving me a hand?"

Wordlessly, the vet picked up the Dalai Lama and eased him into the carrier, cooing at him gently. The tabby offered up no resistance. As Dwight was fastening the door, James took the opportunity to ask him one last question.

"I've got a friend who'd like to start raising cows. Do you think I could get this other vet's card so that she could talk to him about which breed to get?"

Opening the door to leave, the young vet shrugged. "You could ask June if she's got any of his cards. Dr. Crabtree isn't here today."

"Uh-oh," James pretended to look disturbed. "I hope he didn't have some kind of emergency with one of his own patients."

"No, nothing like that," Dwight answered. "He's out of town for the moment."

James took a stab in the dark. "On a fishing trip?"

Dwight shot him on odd look but didn't respond. "I'll leave your paperwork with June. Goodbye." He let the door close behind him.

James was more than ready to get back in the truck and compare notes with Gillian. He hoped she had discovered something more useful from her new soul sister, June.

Back in the Bronco, the Dalai Lama remained strangely peaceful and silent, as if Dwight Hutchins had placed a spell of calm over him. Gillian, on the other hand, could barely sit still. She bounced around the passenger seat from the second James pulled onto the main road heading south to Quincy's Gap. Handing James one of the bananas she had brought along for a snack, she began eating hers with small, frenzied bites.

"I can't believe how destiny led me to June today! We're like sisters!" Gillian chewed the last bit of her fruit and then sighed blissfully. "She told me everything I asked her. What a *giving* soul."

"And?"

Gillian arranged her skirt, fluffed up her wild orange hair, and exhaled. "Parker and Colin have been an item for about six months. They met in the parking lot of a movie theater. Apparently, some *abusive* pet owner had left his beagle locked in the car with no windows open. It was a warm spring day and the sun had been beating down on that poor creature for over two hours." Gillian cooed to her cat. "I'd *never* neglect you that way!" She then returned to her narrative. "They both noticed the abandoned dog before their movie started and again two hours later as they were heading back to their cars. Parker, who was with another friend, was going to smash the window to free the beagle. Colin stopped her, went inside the theater, and demanded that the manager make an announcement to all the moviegoers that if the beagle's owner didn't appear by his car in five minutes, Colin would call the cops."

James was riveted. "What happened?"

"The man came out. He had tickets to a double feature and was aggravated at being interrupted. Can you imagine that kind of self-absorption?" she asked with indignation.

"Was the dog okay?"

Gillian grinned. "That's the best part! The owner shoved the helpless animal into Colin's hands and shouted at him to keep it. Well, Colin accepted the offer and Parker volunteered to give the unwanted pooch free check-ups for life." She put her hands over her heart. "Have you *ever* heard such a romantic story? It was love right from the start. And all because they both tried to rescue a dog! They named the beagle Sunshine as the film that they had both gone to see was *Little Miss Sunshine*."

James approved. "What a great movie." He digested the details for a moment. "Does June think Colin was just trying to impress Parker, or did she indicate that he acts like a hero all the time?"

Gillian shook her head. "According to June, Colin is *utterly* devastated over Parker's death. He came over here right away to help out with her patients, and June says he has a *very* warm and generous spirit." She pushed a fluff of hair off her forehead. "It would seem, that despite a childhood of *privilege*—the best schools, summers in Maine, help with setting up his practice—we are not dealing with a self-centered individual here."

"Well-meaning though he may be, how can Colin take care of two practices?" James wondered.

"I don't know, but he's very much at home around Parker's office. Colin and Parker regularly visited one another's practices to help out or just to watch the other one at work." She clasped her hands together. "June truly believes that they were *soul mates.*"

James was growing irritated by all of the references to love and romance. "Sounds like this Colin is too good to be true. Everyone has vices. What are his?" He cast an unfriendly glance at Gillian. "Is that all June had to say?"

"Patience, my friend." Gillian patted his forearm. "She even showed me two pictures of Colin that Parker kept on the desk in her office. Guess what he was wearing in one of the photos?" She bounced up and down on the seat in excitement.

James had no idea. "A tutu?" he said mischievously.

"Silly! Not a tutu, but a fishing vest, complete with hooks and lures and all that other stuff."

James immediately had a vision of the fishing fly on Mr. Sneed's hat. "That *is* interesting, Gillian. Still, he might just be an award-winning fisherman in addition to all his other talents," he added ruefully.

"Tsk, tsk," Gillian said, wiggling her finger back and forth. "You're not letting me paint you the entire mural. Colin Crabtree is *not* perfect."

Thinking back on how Dwight's face had clouded over when James had broached the subject of Parker's boyfriend, he felt a thrill course through him. "So he *does* have some vices."

"At least one. June really didn't want to tell me, either. I think she might be a teeny, tiny bit in love with Colin herself." Gillian leaned back into the seat and gazed dreamily out the window. "After all, good-looking, sensitive animal-lovers don't grow on trees."

"The vice, Gillian?" James redirected her.

"Well, he might have loved animals, but they didn't always love him back," Gillian spat out quickly, as if hating to criticize Colin. "June confessed, after a lot of prodding and three cups of ginseng tea, that Colin is *much, much* better with people than with animals."

James was confused. "What does that mean?"

"It means that he should have been a human doc. See, animals can only speak using their eyes and a kind of *hidden* voice. You need to be able to read their body language to understand what they're trying to communicate. *Some* of us have that gift," she preened. "Others do not."

"Have there been complaints?" James inquired eagerly.

Gillian nodded. "Parker's regulars are asking to see Dwight Hutchins instead of Colin. June also said that Colin's practice hasn't been doing so well. Some angry farmer named Ramsay out in Mt. Sidney has been complaining to all his friends about the last birth Colin attended."

James pressed down on the accelerator as his heart quickened in excitement. "So money could be a motive!"

"I guess so," Gillian responded glumly. She clearly wanted Colin to be innocent of Parker's murder. "Can you slow down a bit, James? The Dalai is looking a little peaked." She reached for the radio. "Better put his music back on."

Nothing came out of the speakers. Gillian tried to eject the tape but it had come unwound around the heads of the Bronco's cassette deck. Yanking it free, Gillian held the shredded black tape out in front of her.

Seeing the look of dismay on his friend's face, James tried to distract her from the ruined tape. "Before I forget, Gillian, I should tell you that Dwight said to start giving your cat Metamucil or some canned pumpkin. Apparently, he needs more fiber in his diet."

Gillian accepted the advice solemnly. "And that should help with his *digestive* issues?"

"That's what the man said. He seemed to connect with the Dalai Lama well enough."

"Poor Dalai!" Gillian wailed. "I had no idea that you've been living with this kind of *discomfort*. I thought you were simply being *finicky* over your food. Oh, oh! Can you *ever* forgive me?"

In response, the disgruntled tabby put his face directly against the bars of his cage, opened his mouth wide, and vomited all over the truck's center console.

TEN

APPLE STRUDEL

Sodium per Serving: 369 mg for 5 oz.

AFTER HER FLIGHT FROM Kansas City landed at Washington-Dulles, Murphy drove straight to the library. James knew the instant her car pulled into the parking lot: Francis practically leapt over the counter of the circulation desk in order to interrupt his boss, who was speaking to a young girl about the book report she wished to research. Her chosen topic was unicorns.

"This is supposed to be a report for science class, right?" James asked the girl.

She absently turned out the pockets of an enormous pink parka and nodded. "I really like unicorns."

"Alert! Member of the media in the immediate vicinity," Francis whispered urgently and then turned to the young patron. "You know, I like unicorns too, but your science teacher probably wants to you to pick an animal that lots of folks have had a chance to study." He leaned down and spoke quietly. "Only a few people have been lucky enough to see a unicorn, and they can't talk about it. It's a secret."

The girl's eyes were wide with amazement. "That makes sense," she responded seriously and then sighed. "But I wanted to pick something no one else would pick."

Francis was surprised to see that James hadn't moved from his place behind the desk but was watching his exchange with the young girl in amusement.

"It's okay, Francis. Ms. Alistair and I are working on a project together," James said. "But thanks for looking out for me."

"Let's get back to you then, my unicorn-loving friend," Francis said and then smiled. "If you want a special animal to write a report about, then how about one that's *almost* as magical as a unicorn."

The girl was doubtful. "What could be as cool as that?"

Francis gestured toward the computer workstations. "How about a soft, fuzzy, adorable kangaroo that can climb trees?"

"That *is* cool." Convinced, the girl hopped up and down in excitement, her purple backpack bobbing in time. "Let's go!"

As the pair moved away, another twosome approached the reference desk. Murphy had brought one of her reporters along. James immediately recognized the young woman that had confronted him in the men's room the week before.

"I'm glad you're back," James said by way of greeting.

Murphy looked haggard. "Me too. It's been a hard couple of days. I believe you know Lottie, one of my reporters."

"We've had the pleasure, yes," James answered wryly.

The young reporter issued a small smile but said nothing.

"Lottie agreed to be our self-tanner guinea pig. I thought we'd deal with Mr. Sneed's makeup riddle before our next get-together in which I share what I learned at the funeral and you can tell me what you found out at the vet's." Murphy signaled to Lottie. "Show him your arm."

Pushing up her sleeve, Lottie revealed a thin, almost hairless, and very orange arm. She twisted her limb so that James could see the brighter and more uneven hue of the underside of her forearm.

"That's the self-tanner," she said and then rolled up the sleeve covering her other arm. "I've got foundation on this one." Seeing the perplexed look on James's face, she explained, "Foundation is a base makeup that a lot of women use to cover imperfections in their skin. It's supposed to match your skin tone, but some of the cheaper ones can look a bit orange."

James thought back to the shade of Mr. Sneed's face. "It's not like the self-tanner. That's too orange." He pointed at Lottie's left arm. "The overall look was much more like that makeup stuff, but a bit more uneven."

"Maybe he didn't know how to apply foundation properly," Lottie suggested. "It goes on the most smoothly with a makeup sponge. He may have just used his fingers. Sounds like he didn't choose a shade that exactly matched his normal skin tone, either. He must have gone a shade too dark."

Nodding, James looked at Murphy. "He could have bought this stuff at any drug or grocery store, right?"

"That's right." Murphy was clearly disappointed. "We'll never get anywhere pursuing that angle, but let's think about what else might have been a fake. His wig? His beard? That stuff's not too easy to come by."

Hating to knock down her theory, James hesitantly said, "Except that Halloween was just two weeks ago."

Murphy looked like she was on the verge of tears. "Give us a minute, would you, Lottie?"

Lottie moved off and began examining the new fiction releases. Within moments, Scott appeared at her side and the two whispered animatedly while staring at the cover of the latest Tad Williams fantasy, *Shadowplay*.

"Did any clues turn up at Parker's office?" Murphy asked. Her face was filled with a trepidatious hope.

"Everyone seems to love Colin Crabtree. Especially women," James told her.

Murphy rubbed her swollen eyes. "Yeah, I kept an eye on him at the funeral. There's no denying he's handsome, yet he's remarkably down-to-earth as well. He seemed pretty broken up about Parker, but he could just be a great actor. Between Milla's class and the funeral, my impression so far is pretty favorable." She drummed her fingers on the countertop. "So no leads came out of your visit— just that everyone loves Colin?"

"Well, not everyone. There's a farmer named Ramsay who's been telling everyone that Colin's not worth his salt as a big animal doc. Even June, Parker's assistant, admits that Colin isn't at the top of his game in caring for animals. The other partner, Dwight, is taking care of the majority of Parker's patients right now."

"Ramsay, huh? I bet that's Ramsay's Beef Farm. My folks used to buy whole sides of beef from him when I was a kid. I'm from a pretty big family." Murphy rubbed her chin absently. James could almost hear the gears turning in her head.

"Let's pay this farmer a visit," she suggested. "I can pretend we're doing a piece on cattle diseases and promise him that we'll do a big spread that'll guarantee a lot of publicity for his farm."

"You want me to come along?"

Murphy smiled. "Absolutely! In fact, you're going to pose as my photographer."

James glanced down at his khaki pants. "What should I wear?"

"Jeans and some rubber boots." Murphy raised her brows. "We're going to be walking through barns and cattle fields."

"And you'll fill me in on your trip to Kansas in the car?"

Murphy tapped James affectionately on the temple. "You're a sharp one, Professor Henry." She caught Lottie's eye and waved her over. "I think we're onto something with Colin. He can't be as great as he seems."

"Maybe," James responded without conviction, as he didn't want to encourage her too much. "He does fish, too, but so do half of the men who live around here."

Clearly only listening to the first portion of his statement, Murphy grabbed James by the arm. "The fishing lure! We've got to nail that down. Another thing to add to our list." Her eyes glimmered. "If I can arrange for the interview to happen over the next couple of days, would you mind driving? My car's going in for service."

"I'll drive," James agreed, "but I can't miss any more work. Can you try to book the interview for Saturday or Sunday?"

"Sure. I'll call you as soon as I know."

"Murphy?" he held on to her arm. "Don't you think we should be investigating Kinsley's background, too? I mean, maybe the killer didn't realize that it was Parker on that field trip. After all, I didn't know it wasn't Kinsley until..."

118

With a shake of her head, Murphy dismissed this idea. "She just moved here, James. No, we need to focus on Parker's life. We're going to get to the bottom of this." After this declaration, she left with a visible spring to her step.

James watched her leave. He didn't honestly believe that Colin was a solid suspect. If he were, the police would have him in custody. According to all the major papers, no arrests had yet been made. Whoever had strangled Parker was still at large.

"Maybe we'll get lucky and just stumble on something," he muttered without conviction.

———————

"*What* is that smell?" Murphy held her nose as she jumped into the passenger seat of the Bronco early Saturday morning.

James glanced at the center console, which he had scrubbed using every type of cleaning agent he could find in his house. Apparently, none of the bleach, de-greasers, or odor neutralizers had found a way to vanquish the pungent scent of cat vomit. "The Dalai Lama got sick to his stomach on the way home from the vet," he said, scowling.

Murphy laughed. "The Dalai Lama? Man, that is *so* Gillian."

"So where exactly is Ramsay's farm?" James asked.

"South on I-81." Murphy consulted the Google map she had printed out off the computer. "Shouldn't take us long and then we can have lunch in downtown Staunton afterwards. There's this awesome little place called the Dining Room where we can get a seared and seasoned filet." She slipped her seat belt across her trim waist. "Might as well get a jump start on the Thanksgiving/Christmas gorge."

James drove through Quincy's Gap, which was still sleepy on a cold, November morning. One town employee, bundled up in coat, hat, and gloves, swept a scattering of shriveled brown leaves into a neat pile and tipped his cap at the Bronco as James drove past.

"I love this town," Murphy stated, sighing with contentment. "When I was in college, I always thought I'd move up to New York or D.C., be some hotshot journalist, live in an apartment twenty stories high, take the subway to cocktail parties, plays, and gallery openings, and dress in a lot of hip, black clothing."

"What happened?" James wondered.

Murphy shrugged. "I tried it for a few years, but I was no hotshot. Shoot, I never rose above the level of copyeditor, and my apartment was the size of an outhouse. I couldn't afford any of the hip clothes, and I spent the only cocktail party I went to trying to convince the other guests that I wasn't with the wait staff!" She pointed at the rolling hills outside the window. "Every time I came back here, to the Valley, to visit my folks, I'd feel more and more homesick. One day, when I had come back for a long weekend holiday, my mom showed me an ad calling for an editor for *The Star*." She smiled nostalgically. "That job had come vacant just for me. I felt it in my bones."

"Lucky for us," James said kindly.

"Not everyone feels that way." Murphy traced one of the lines on her map. "Reporters aren't always very well liked, James. We have to get in people's faces, get under their skin—even hide behind some bushes! We have to act sneaky and conniving and pushy all in the name of news. I remember rubbing *you* wrong more than once."

Chuckling, James nodded in agreement. "That's for sure. And I bet it was difficult to ask questions at Parker's funeral."

"It really was." Murphy's sigh was heavy with sadness. "I didn't learn anything of much significance, either. As I said before, Colin was there and seemed genuinely upset. I also met Gary Lowe, Kinsley's ex. I only saw him briefly, as he had to fly back to New York right after the service. I was surprised that they had once been a couple just because Gary doesn't look like someone that a smart, gorgeous, and wealthy young woman would date, but Kinsley clung to him the whole time like he was her life preserver."

James digested this information. "What about the money? That can't have been an easy trail to follow."

"No, it wasn't, but I was frank with Kinsley on the plane. I told her I was looking into Parker's death and wanted to know everything about the money. She was completely supportive." Murphy watched the landscape as it quickly changed from the heavily wooded, twisty road leading away from Quincy's Gap to the flat and crowded interstate. "You've got to realize that Kinsley is broken in two. She's a shattered person right now. I barely got her to talk, but she did tell me that the girls were required to make wills upon receiving their inheritances at age twenty-five. They each left their share to the other, with some of the money going to their favorite charities."

"Any idea which charities?"

Murphy shook her head. "Like I said, she was just too upset to talk much, and I didn't feel like I could push her any more than I did."

James noticed a sign for Mt. Sidney up ahead. "Is this my exit?"

"Oh! Guess I'm a better writer than a navigator. Sorry." She consulted the sheet in her hand. "We're going to head north on Route 11 for just a mile or so. We should see the farm off to the left."

121

Within minutes, the buildings dotting the roadside gave way to a view of an endless field in which dozens of brown and white cows munched on wiry, yellowish grass.

"I bet those are Ramsay's." Murphy pointed at the grazing herd.

The farm was a large one. James drove past one field after another until a white sign with green letters reading *Ramsay's Beef Farm* appeared on the right. Below the sign was was a rusty aluminum mailbox mounted on a crooked pole. Half of a weathered wagon wheel leaned against the mailbox pole and the remnants of a clematis vine stuck to the old rungs. A grouping of mums had been planted around the wheel, but their hues had faded from a perky paprika to a corrosive brown. Turning onto the dirt drive, James and Murphy were granted a view of a two-story white farmhouse with a tin roof and multiple outbuildings. A good distance behind the house were several mammoth barns and sheds, all painted a cheery apple-red.

Mr. Ramsay stepped out onto the front porch as James turned off the ignition. He was a compact man with rough skin and bearlike eyes, but he greeted them kindly enough and even offered them coffee.

"Maybe afterwards," Murphy replied in a businesslike tone, and James could see that she had transformed into reporter mode. "I thought we'd start off talking about diseases." She consulted her notebook. "Such as leptospirosis. You mentioned on the phone that you've had problems with that particular virus. Can you explain what kind of problems?"

Ramsay grunted. "With lepto? The worst kind. Gives ya cows that are terrible slow at gettin' pregnant and then lose the calves they're carryin'."

Murphy nodded as though she understood the full effect of the disease. "You mean, the calves are born before they're ready?"

Another grunt. "Way before."

"So they're dead at birth?" Murphy sought clarification.

Ramsay looked at her like she was simple. "Well, they ain't runnin' around lookin' for their mama's teat, that's for sure."

James blushed, but Murphy calmly made a note of Ramsay's answer. "So you had them vaccinated with this stuff called Spirovac?"

"That's right. The five-way wasn't protectin' my herd no more."

"The five-way is the vaccine that's always been used for fighting lepto." Murphy had clearly done her homework. "Why change to Spirovac now?"

Ramsay puffed out his weather-roughed cheeks. "Wasn't workin'. There's a new strain of lepto, and it's meaner than the other one."

"But I've read that Spirovac is an expensive drug." Murphy's tone turned sympathetic. "Isn't that hard on your budget?"

"'Course it is!" the farmer declared. He glanced at James as if to say *Is she really this much of a moron?* Out loud he added, "But it beats the hell out of not havin' healthy calves born. Can't sell any meat if you don't have calves to grow up into rib eyes and flank steak, now can you?"

Murphy kept her expression even as she gazed off into the fields where a cluster of cows was gathered near a shallow creek. The muddy water wound its way through the grass and into a copse of trees far off in the distance.

"How do you vaccinate so many cows at once?" James asked curiously. Murphy shot him a warning look, and he remembered that he was only supposed to be the photographer.

"We got a system. When it's time to give 'em their shots, Doc Crabtree brings in the drugs and stays to help out." Ramsay suddenly made a pained face but said nothing further.

"Colin Crabtree?" Murphy inquired, her pencil suspended over paper.

"Yep. Helps me give out shots, and I buy lice powder and the like from him." He cast a tender look toward the fields. "We can take care of most things 'round here ourselves, but I do need a hand with the shots and Crabtree's fees are fair. I'll say that much for him."

Murphy cleared her throat and said carefully, "I've heard some folks say that Mr. Crabtree isn't a very skilled animal doctor. Have you ever had any problems with the way he treated your animals?"

Ramsay hesitated. James knew that there was a difference between a farmer complaining to his fellows and defiling a man's name on record to a reporter.

"Don't worry. I won't print what you say," Murphy quickly assured him. "I just want to know what happened."

Undecided, Ramsay stood and stuffed his rough hands into the pockets of his denim overalls. "I gotta check on some feed," he said, pulling on the black and red flannel jacket that had been draped across the porch banister. "Walk with me down to the barn."

The farmer walked with a strong, heavy stride, and James felt himself struggling to keep up. He was thankful that he had worn his rubber boots. Patches of soggy grass and wet mud squelched beneath his feet as the three of them made their way to one of the barns. Ramsay led them to a straw-lined stall and leaned on the door.

"When Crabtree was here last, he saw one of my heifers have her very first calf." He stared at the clean, dry hay. "That girl was ready. She had had her lepto vaccine, was a picture-perfect weight of eleven hundred pounds, and had been eatin' high on the hog for months. That heifer had the best—fescue, alfalfa, corn. Even some barley. *All* my heifers havin' their firsts get treated like queens," he said with pride.

"Why do they need such special treatment?" James wondered, unable to stop himself, but this time, Murphy didn't seem to mind.

"By the time she gets to her delivery day, a knocked-up heifer's cost me over a thousand dollars in expenses. I gotta do everythin' right to make sure that her calf comes out kickin'." He pointed out in the direction of the field. "My Herefords are mated with an Angus bull. That combination makes the best-tasting, most marbled meat you've ever sunk your teeth into." He coughed into his hand. "But the calves gotta grow up first or I don't make a dime."

Murphy smiled. "You're right about your meat. My folks used to order from you when all of us kids were still living at home."

A light appeared in the farmer's eyes and he looked at Murphy as though she was suddenly a completely new person. "Well, I'll be. Your pa ain't Mike Alistair, is he?"

"One and the same."

Ramsay chuckled. "You tell ole Mike that he can split a side of beef with a friend. He doesn't have to buy store meat just 'cause his kids have growed and flown the coop."

"I will," Murphy assured him and then gestured at the stall. "So, did you have a bad calf delivery?"

"Yep." His face darkened. "Crabtree was here, helping me vaccinate the older cows. We'd already done the pregnant ones a few weeks back. Anyhow, I'd been keepin' a watch on one of my heifers who started her labor just after dawn." He looked back at the hay again. "They gotta give birth someplace real clean, so I brought her down to one of the lower fields and left her to it while Crabtree and I worked. By the time we were done and headin' back to the house, I could see she was havin' trouble."

"How could you tell?" Murphy was fascinated.

Ramsay shrugged. "I've lived on a cow farm my whole life. This heifer's labor was takin' far too long, so I asked Crabtree to look her over. He got his hands inside that poor, scared heifer and turned the calf. It was good and slick, and it took both of us to pull it out. That's when the real work started, but that's when Crabtree froze up on me."

Murphy was utterly alert. Pencil poised eagerly, she queried, "In what way?"

"That calf was half dead when it came out. Had the cord wrapped 'round its neck so it looked like a noose for a hangman." He shook his head in disgust. "I thought Crabtree would get the cord off lickety split and work on gettin' that calf to breathe, but that sonofabitch just sat there, starin' and starin'."

James and Murphy exchanged glances. "He didn't try to save the calf at all?" Murphy was incredulous.

"Nope. Just sat there, lookin' like a ghost himself. All white and frozen. Shoot," Ramsay flicked a piece of mud from his pants. "Can't have been the first time he'd seen an animal born like that. Happens all the time. Cows, horses, pigs, you name it. Nature's got her share of faults, believe me."

"What happened next?"

"I got the cord off and locked lips with that slippery little calf," Ramsay stated flatly. "It came 'round sure enough. My youngest son and I moved the baby and its mama into this stall, because that calf hadn't started off too well, and I wanted to make sure it wouldn't have to work too hard to get its first meal."

Murphy looked relieved at learning the calf had survived. "And Crabtree?"

Ramsay glowered. "I told him to get the hell off my land. Told him he wasn't worth his weight as a cow doc and he should think about quittin'. Haven't seen nor heard from him since and that's fine and well by me!"

"Your feelings are certainly understandable." Murphy turned to James, a mischievous glint in her hazel eyes. "Let's get some photos now. Mr. Ramsay, do you think we could get close enough to that bull of yours to get a picture?"

Pleased, Ramsay nodded. "Sure thing. But you'd better stay on this side of the fence, boy," he said to James. "That ole bull ain't called El Diablo for nothin'."

Murphy laughed as the color drained from James's face.

"And after that, y'all can come on up to the house for some good, strong coffee." Ramsay closed the stall and stepped out of the barn. "The missus made one of her famous apple strudels, too. It'll melt on your tongue like a pat of butter."

"Yum. Sounds like heaven," Murphy rubbed her hands together in anticipation. "Doesn't it, James?"

But James had caught sight of El Diablo and was having trouble moving one foot in front of the other. Looking down at the camera hanging from his neck, he felt like whimpering. The lens didn't seem nearly long enough. As El Diablo noticed his visitors, he raised his dark head, glared at them in defiance, and trotted brazenly over to the fence. Eyeing James, he snorted and pawed the ground with a lethal-looking hoof.

James fumbled nervously with the camera. "This thing better have a zoom function!" he whispered in agitation and then began shooting photos without remembering to first remove the lens cap.

ELEVEN

KITCHEN SINK NACHOS

Sodium per Serving:

2590 mg per plate

ON THE RIDE BACK home from Ramsay's farm, Murphy decided to persuade Colin to join them at that evening's Fix 'n Freeze class.

"We need to study him in a relaxed environment," she claimed. "The event with the calf happened *before* Parker was killed. It seems strangely coincidental that he wigged out because a newborn cow was being strangled and then his girlfriend ends up being murdered the same way." She flipped through the pages of her notebook with a furious determination. "I bet the police don't know anything about the calf incident."

"If they don't see Colin as a suspect, he must have a solid alibi," James suggested. "That Sergeant McClellan doesn't seem like the type to leave any pebble unturned."

"An alibi? Hmm, that's a good point," Murphy conceded. "I think I'll ask Colin all about that important detail tonight. If I do my best to seem sympathetic about his being questioned by the authorities, he may open up to me a little."

James pushed down on the Bronco's gas pedal as they began the ascent over one of the mountain roads. "That's *if* he decides to come to class."

Murphy leaned back against the headrest and sighed, watching the valley below as it became swathed in late afternoon shadows. "When I get home, I'll just call Milla and tell her that Colin will be rejoining our class," she added softly, and then turned away so that James couldn't see the tears in her eyes.

———

When James returned home, it was almost dark and the late afternoon air carried a sharp chill. Burying his neck deeper into his wool scarf, James hustled from the truck to the back door, seeking warmth. Inside, he called for his father, but the house had an empty feeling to it. No lights burned and the fireplace was laid with a small stack of wood, but had not yet been lit.

"Pop?" James yelled at the foot of the stairs but received no answer. He poked his head into the dining room and then mounted the stairs and headed for his parents' bedroom. Turning on one of the lamps, James noticed that his father had finished stripping the metallic wallpaper in the bathroom and had prepped the walls for their first coat of primer. The light fixtures, switch plates, outlet covers, and towel racks had been removed and were strewn about on the bed. On the nightstand, a pile of screws of various sizes was sitting in a wobbly and shallow pinch pot that James had made in the second grade.

Jackson was not working in the bathroom, so James headed outside to the shed. Trying the door, he found it locked, as usual. But this time, the padlock had been taken from the outside latch and undoubtedly reattached inside.

James rapped on the door. "Pop?" he called. "Are you in there?" No one answered. James began to grow cold and irritated. "What do you want me to leave you for dinner? I've got cooking class tonight so I need to fix it *now*, before I go."

There was no reply. "Come on, Pop! Answer me or you're going to get a tuna fish sandwich!" James knew this was a solid threat, as Jackson disliked tuna fish, especially when it was made with low-fat mayo.

After another full minute of waiting, James turned away from the door. Just as he did so, the sounds of a key turning in a lock and a bolt sliding free caused him to stop. His father's glum face appeared in the crack of light that escaped from the interior of the shed. It gathered around Jackson's head like a halo.

"I don't give a damn what I have for dinner!" Jackson spat and shut the door again. This time, he didn't bother locking it. In fact, he had slammed it so hard that it had bounced backward, leaving a space big enough to peer through. James hadn't been inside the shed since his father had begun working on his wildlife paintings, and Jackson had made it more than clear that no one was invited within his private refuge. Unable to quell his curiosity, James pushed tentatively on the door.

As it swung inward, James froze. There was his father, sitting as still as a stone on a metal folding chair as he stared at a piece of plywood that had been painted a uniform white. A pile of similar rectangles of wood was stacked neatly against the far wall and

Jackson's paints and brushes were laid out in a fanlike pattern on his orderly workbench.

James stepped inside the shed and quietly sat on a low step stool next to the door. "What's wrong, Pop?" he asked gently.

Without taking his eyes from the board in front of him, Jackson muttered, "I can't do it no more."

James also gazed at the blank canvas. "You can't paint?" he asked cautiously.

Jackson nodded. "That gallery lady, Mrs. Perez, told me that my pictures weren't sellin' too well." He looked down at his work-worn hands. "Says the last batch was *flat*." He turned to face his son. "What does that mean? 'Course they're flat. I paint on damned boards."

"I think she means they're not as lively as the first group of paintings. Um," he proceeded carefully, fearful of hurting his father's feelings, "like they need more movement or more feeling coming through, so that when someone looks at them, they react."

Jackson eyed James as if he was speaking a foreign language. "I don't *feel* anythin' about them. They're birds, for cryin' out loud." Uncreasing his brows, he sighed. "She thinks I should paint somethin' different. I'd sure like to, but I don't know what. I want new fixtures for the upstairs and I want to get goin' on your bathroom, but if I can't sell some of these pictures…" he trailed off. "Birds was all I could do. I had them up in my head," he tapped on the side of his skull, "and then they just kind of flew onto the board. What am I gonna do now?"

At a loss, James struggled to find a solution to his father's dilemma, but he couldn't think of a single idea. He had been amazed by the beauty and exquisite detail his father had infused into the dozens of paintings that had quickly leapt off the walls of the D.C. gallery owned by Lindy's mother. Jackson wasn't interested in fame, but the thousands of dollars he had earned from the sales of his work had restored his battered pride and lifted him from a state of listlessness and depression.

"Let me think about it, Pop," James replied solemnly. "You've got more in you than those birds. We've just got to figure out what." He absently touched one of his father's brushes. "Don't you worry, we'll think of something."

Jackson nodded mutely and then stood, his body slow and stiff, as though his artistic failure had suddenly aged him beyond his years.

"I think you need some comfort food." James put a hand on his father's scrawny shoulder. "How does a grilled cheese and bacon sandwich with a side of mustard potato salad sound?"

"Better than tuna fish," Jackson grumbled and then reattached the padlock on the door. "But not as good as rib roast with mashed potatoes and a bucketful of gravy." He sighed morosely and shuffled into the house.

James had had the foresight to call Gillian, Lindy, and Bennett and tell them why Colin had been encouraged to come to their cooking class. They were only too happy to buddy up to Parker's boyfriend in order to get a better impression of his character.

When Gillian heard the details of Colin's visit to Ramsay's farm, she was distraught. "How could he allow such *suffering*?" She wailed so loudly into the receiver that James had to move the phone away from his ear. "It is his solemn duty to care for all animals. It's the credo by which he should live *every* moment of his life! That *poor, innocent, suffering* calf!"

Before Gillian could rupture his eardrum with her keening, James assured her that the calf had come out of the ordeal unscathed. Undeterred, Gillian argued that the animal was probably suffering post-traumatic shock and should be seen by an animal psychologist at once.

"Why don't you suggest that to Colin?" James remarked facetiously. Unfortunately, Gillian thought that was a brilliant idea and planned to call Colin and encourage him to return to the Fix 'n Freeze class. Her intention was to invite him to share her cooking space so that she could read his aura and probe him about his feelings regarding the delicateness of an animal's psyche.

Milla greeted her students by leading them to an oval platter bearing a veritable mountain of nachos.

"I call these my Kitchen Sink Nachos," she laughed. "If you can think of something to add to my black beans, guacamole, Chihuahua cheese, homemade salsa, scallions, cheddar cheese, sour cream, seasoned beef, jalapeños, and black olives, you just let me know."

Colin greeted Milla warmly and then helped himself to a loaded nacho, handing out napkins to the others as though he had been in the class all along. It was only the second time James had seen their prime suspect in person, and he still found him extremely likeable. Colin was friendly and polite without being overbearing, and every expression on his pleasant, attractive face seemed to be sincere.

With gentle brown eyes, sandy hair, and a winsome smile, Colin had no difficulty striking up conversations with the women. He even hugged Gillian and thanked her for motivating him to come.

"I really needed a reason to get out of the house," he told her gratefully.

As James joined in the chitchat around the nacho platter, allowing himself only a single taste, as he feared the amount of sodium hidden in every tortilla chip, he also found himself at ease in Colin's company.

Even Murphy, who stood on the outskirts of their little group taking tiny nibbles from a cheese-laden chip as she eyed Colin warily, seemed to delay her quest to interrogate Parker's boyfriend in favor of Milla's raspberry margaritas. Since the rims of the wide, hand-blown glasses were coated with sugar in lieu of salt, James happily partook of the sweet cocktail as well.

Just as the group arranged themselves about their cooking stations, the door to Fix 'n Freeze opened, letting in a gust of frosty air. In came Lucy, trailed by her dashing training partner. Everyone immediately fell silent as she hung up her coat and then placed a proprietary hand on Sullie's solid bicep.

"Hello!" Milla marched forward to greet them. "We're just getting started on the tortillas for our tortilla soup. I got your message on my machine, and I'm *so* glad you decided to come back, Lucy." She winked at Sullie. "And with such charming company, too."

Spying the mound of nachos, which the rest of the group had been unable to finish, Sullie beamed. "Now, *this* is the kind of school I could get used to." He innocuously stepped out of Lucy's grasp and headed toward the appetizers, waving at James as their eyes met.

"So that's who she left you for, huh?" Murphy grumbled to James. "Nothing but a pretty face." She shrugged. "Well, her loss is hopefully going to be my gain. Forget about them. Let's focus on our tortillas."

James knew that Murphy was trying to soften the blow of his having to witness Lucy and Sullie arriving together to class, but his mood had turned sour nonetheless. They had joined Fix 'n Freeze as a supper club and now their original group of five was completely splintered. James resented the tension Lucy had created by simply entering the room.

He took his frustrations out on the tortilla dough, roughly grinding the vegetable shortening, flour, and warm water into a soft, supple lump. He angrily ripped pieces from the chunk of dough and began to form small balls between his palms. He dumped about a dozen of these on a small plate to let sit for the ten minutes Milla suggested and strode off to the center island to refill his margarita glass.

Within seconds, Lucy appeared by his side.

"Hi, James. How are you?" Her voice was soft, almost hesitant.

"Fine," he responded shortly without looking at her.

She took a minuscule sip of margarita. "So Parker's boyfriend made an appearance, huh?" She stared at Colin over the rim of her glass. "Are you guys trying to get a read on him?"

James was stunned by her intuitiveness. "What makes you ask that?"

"Gillian's been laying it on pretty thick." She smiled. "I've seen her in action before, you know."

Gillian was practically draped across Colin's cooking space as she gestured theatrically and kept her gaze locked upon his face as she spoke. James was grateful that all the noise from the oven fans masked whatever she was saying. Watching her, he felt himself start to chuckle. Lucy broke into a grin and soon they were both giggling uncontrollably.

Lucy was the first to stop laughing. "I miss you guys," she said sadly, her smile evaporating. "I know everyone probably thinks I'm a jerk. They're probably one hundred percent on *your* side about our—"

"I haven't told them anything about us breaking up," James interrupted. "If they're mad at you, it's for dropping them like hot coals as soon as Sullie walked into town. That's got nothing to do with you and me."

Lucy fixed her blue eyes on the beautiful man and said, "He's my friend, but he can't replace the rest of you."

James was tempted to say something nasty to Lucy, but he found that he didn't want to hurt her after all. In fact, looking at the familiar curve of her smooth cheek, he found that he only wanted to assure her that everything would turn out all right. "Tell the others exactly what you just said," he counseled. "Besides, we could use your help tonight, Lucy. We're trying to find out if Colin fly-fishes or would recognize the fly from Mr. Sneed's hat. I've got a catalogue in my coat pocket that has a picture of the exact red and black fly I saw the night Parker was killed."

Lucy's face became animated. "Sullie is into fishing big-time! Leave it to me, James! I'll tell Sullie to bring up the subject and somehow we'll find out if Colin knows one fly from another."

"Thanks."

She touched his arm, briefly and tenderly. "Thank you, too, James. Now I'm going to go over to the cooking spaces and kiss some major butt. Well, three of them, actually. I owe my friends a big apology."

A timer sounded and James realized that it was time to roll out his balls of dough and place them into the griddle. When he returned to his cook station, Murphy was smacking her dough onto the floured circle in front of her as though it had committed some kind of terrible trespass against her. She glared at James and then slapped one of the discs of dough into the hot griddle. He decided to ignore her childish behavior and concentrate on the hot pan in front of him. It only took a few seconds to cook each tortilla, and he took great delight in flipping each circle and examining the speckled brown spots that appeared on the cooked side of the dough.

Milla directed the group to place the stockpots on their front burners and begin sautéing the small bowls of garlic and onion.

"Seems like we start with this step in every class," James said to Milla. "Not that I'm complaining," he added hastily. "I love garlic."

"That's all the slaves who built the great Egyptian pyramids ate," Bennett stated. "Garlic, bread, and water. So we oughta be able to perform some high and mighty feats after graduating from your class, Milla."

"What else do you know about garlic?" Colin asked Bennett.

Bennett shrugged modestly. "About ninety percent of it's grown in good ole California. And if aphids are troublin' your roses, spray those little bugs with some garlic water and watch 'em run!"

Colin's eyes widened. "That's really interesting! You know, I'm into trivia, too. Do you watch *Jeopardy!* at all?"

James could see that Bennett was going to have a difficult time viewing Colin as a murder suspect. He and Colin exchanged facts on onions as Lindy and Gillian listened with amusement. Lucy and Sullie took the opportunity to have a hushed exchange in the vicinity of the coatrack. James could tell that they were plotting out the details of their fly-fishing ambush. He felt assured that Lucy would handle the operation skillfully.

Turning to Murphy, he had to smile as she violently emptied a can of tomato puree into her chicken soup stock. Moving over to her side, he removed the can from her hands and scraped out the remains with a wooden spoon.

"Easy does it," he whispered to her.

"What were you two cutting up about over there?" she demanded testily.

James explained and then they both fell silent as Sullie began to ask Bennett what he knew about fly-fishing.

"Not much," Bennett answered, reading the situation perfectly. "I can drop my pole in the water, but that's about it." He turned to Colin. "You?"

Colin nodded. "I know a bit. It's one of my hobbies, but I'm not too good at it, to tell the truth. What would you like to know?"

"My sister just gave me a set of flies for my birthday," Sullie explained. "But I don't know which flies to use with which fish. I have the catalogue in my coat. Can I show you what she got me?"

"Sure," Colin replied pleasantly and then turned his attention to slicing an avocado.

Sullie hustled back, holding out the catalogue. "See this red and black one? She gave me that fly, but I have no idea what fish it's supposed to catch."

Colin's expression was one of mild curiosity and it remained unchanged as he answered, "I've never seen that particular fly before. But there are specialty flies for every fish out there." He held out his hand for the catalogue. "May I?"

"Ah, yeah." Sullie handed it over.

Colin studied the fine print below the photo of the fly and then shrugged. "You'd better return that one, my friend." He pointed at the description. "Unless you plan on learning to fly-fish on the West Coast."

Sullie was clearly confused. "Huh?"

"This is a fly for salmon fishing." Colin smiled. "As far as I know, we don't have salmon in Virginia. If you've got a receipt, exchange yours for this bass fly here or this fly here. That one will attract catfish, and there's nothing as tasty as fresh grilled catfish."

"Except for my Mexican wedding cookies!" Milla argued playfully.

As they cleaned up the debris created from making the tortilla soup, Murphy whispered to James, "I don't think he recognized that fly."

"Me either," James agreed. "You still going to ask him about his alibi?"

Murphy pulled a bowl of confectioners' sugar in front of her and dipped her finger into the white powder. "I will, but not tonight. We're probably going to have to go back to the drawing board, and that's too depressing to think about right now." She licked her finger. "I'd rather concentrate all of my efforts on dessert."

Milla's Mexican Wedding Cookies

1 cup powdered sugar (divided—you'll need some for rolling cookies in afterward)
1 cup butter, softened
2 teaspoons almond extract
1 teaspoon vanilla extract
2 cups sifted all-purpose flour
¼ teaspoon salt (except for James)
½ cup finely ground pecans

Preheat the oven to 325 degrees. In a large bowl, beat ½ cup powdered sugar, butter, and extracts until fluffy. Stir in the flour, salt, and pecans. Mix until dough forms. Shape the dough into 1-inch balls. Place them on an ungreased cookie sheet. Bake at 325 degrees for 15–20 minutes until the cookies are set but not brown. Remove them from the cookie sheet, cool them slightly, and roll them in powdered sugar. If you prefer, allow the cookies to cool completely and then roll them for a second time in powdered sugar.

TWELVE

GLAZED MINI CAKE CRULLER

Sodium per Serving: 190 mg

ONCE AGAIN, THE FITZGERALD twins were waiting for James as he pulled into the library parking lot Monday morning. Surprised, he checked his watch. He was ten minutes early. Francis, who was pacing back and forth liked a caged cheetah, couldn't seem to wait for his boss to reach the set of steps leading up to the front door. Bounding down the cement stairs, the two ends of his brown scarf trailing out from his neck like a little girl's pigtails, the twin gripped a small rectangle in his outstretched hand.

"It's the lottery ticket!" Francis shouted breathlessly. "The one from the book box! And," he sucked in a deep breath of crisp air, "it's a winner!"

Scott couldn't contain himself either. Within seconds, he had leapt down the steps as adroitly as a mountain lion and snatched the ticket from his brother's fingertips. "It's worth a ton of money, Professor!"

James stared at the green, orange, and white ticket in awe. "How much are we taking about?"

"Well." Francis exhaled in relief as though being the keeper of such a significant fact was causing him physical pain. "No one won the week before, so the pot was held over until last Friday. It's for $150,000!"

"And *this* lucky number," Scott tapped the black numbers printed on the ticket, "was an *exact match* for the winning numbers announced on the news." He looked over at his brother. "We were watching just in case."

"Yeah!" Francis pushed on his drooping glasses. "We wrote the numbers down so we could check first thing this morning. But then we couldn't wait. We came over here on Saturday just before closing and took the ticket out of the *Lost But Not Yet Found* box."

Scott pointed toward the sky. "We felt like we were in some other dimension or something. We just stared at the ticket, thinking that someone from our town has just become rich and doesn't even know it yet!" He raked his hands through his bushy hair. "It was a total Ray Bradbury moment."

"Why didn't you call me?" James wondered, though he wasn't angry in the least.

Francis looked sheepish. "You seem to have a lot on your plate lately, Professor, so we thought we'd try to solve this mystery by ourselves."

James glanced at his watch again. "Let's finish this conversation inside. It's a bit brisk out here."

Scott and Francis, who didn't have a spare inch of body fat between them, were too animated to notice the chill. Once inside the library, they followed him like frisky puppies as he hung up his coat, put his lunch in the fridge, and began to brew a pot of coffee.

Rinsing out his *Will Catalogue for Food* mug that the twins had given him for Christmas last year, James said, "So who are our possible winners?"

Francis pulled out a notebook from his coat pocket and eagerly turned the pages. "The books in our outside box had been returned by the following patrons," he began in a secretarial tone. "Stuart Matthews returned a James Patterson and a Vince Flynn, Wendy Carver returned two Nora Roberts paperbacks, Danny Leary brought back an audio tape biography of JFK, and Ruby Pennington returned a book called *Get Rich Cleaning Out Your Attic: An Introduction to Internet Auctions.*"

James listened thoughtfully. He knew all of those patrons. Stuart was a military man and had recently been deployed to Iraq, so it was likely that his wife returned his books. Wendy worked in the cafeteria at the elementary school, Danny owned the town's only liquor store, and Ruby was the organist at James's church.

"Were you able to rule anyone out?" he asked, pouring himself a large mug of coffee. He stirred in some fat-free half-and-half, a package of Sweet'N Low, and a sprinkle of cinnamon and took a grateful sip.

Scott shrugged. "Only the Matthews family. Mrs. Matthews told us that they don't have money to waste buying lottery tickets." His eyes turned sad as he looked at his brother. "We felt bad that they weren't the winners. Seems like they could use the money."

James pointed at the names on the list. "With the exception of Danny, who seems to do pretty well for himself, I'd say all these people could use the money."

"We made the phone calls on Sunday," Francis explained. "On Saturday, we kind of had to calm down and think straight, and before we knew it, we had watched four back-to-back episodes of *Star Trek: Voyager*. Then, it was too late to call anyone."

"Mr. Leary never answered, so we asked him to call the library on Monday. Ms. Carver can't remember if she bought a lottery ticket or not. Sometimes she does and sometimes she doesn't."

James took another sip of coffee. "Does she always pick the same numbers?"

"We asked her that, too!" Scott answered, pleased that they were all on the same wavelength. As he rummaged around in his backpack, he added, "She said she picks her birthday every time and unfortunately, her birthday hasn't been too lucky. Wasn't this time, either."

"And Ruby?" James stared at his coffee and longed for a glazed donut from Krispy Kreme to dunk into the warm liquid. As if by magic, Scott pulled a small, white bag from his pack and shook out a half a dozen mini crullers onto a paper plate. James stared at his employee and wondered if the young man was clairvoyant in addition to being wise and generous.

Francis helped himself to a donut as he shook his head. "We never reached her and she doesn't have a machine." He popped the pastry in his mouth, chewed enthusiastically, and reached for another.

"So you've got some work to do this morning," James stated, giving in to temptation and taking a cruller. "Danny won't open until ten, so you may as well call the church and try to get a hold of Ruby. I know she does administrative work there, like the deposits and weekly bulletins and such. She may already be at work." He dunked the donut into his coffee and then bit into the soft, sweet dough, moistened with milky sweet coffee. The combination was heavenly.

Scott practically ran for the phone as a disappointed Francis volunteered to empty the book bin and, afterwards, boot up all the computers. James finished off his coffee and then moved around the library, turning on lights and walking through the stacks, his fingers lovingly brushing the multicolored spines of orderly books. He replaced a few strays from the reshelving cart and then straightened the slightly disheveled fiction section in the recently improved audiobook area. As he watched Francis switch on the computers and printers in the newly expanded Technology Corner, James felt a surge of pride flow through him.

He had always thought that resigning his professorship at William and Mary would spell the end of any chance for career fulfillment. Now, however, as he surveyed his kingdom of books and computers and saw the first patrons of the day step into the warmth of the vestibule, he knew that he was more at home in this library than he had ever been in a lecture hall. His fiefdom was small, but he could see the changes that had been enacted since he came onboard as head librarian, and the positive proof of his hard work and devotion was a richer reward than a title or a higher salary could offer.

"Good morning, Professor," an elderly woman greeted him as she settled herself at one of the computer terminals. "My daughter said she posted pictures of the grandkids at the pumpkin patch on this web site." She dug out a grocery store receipt from her crocheted handbag. "The name's written on the back. Can you help me figure out how to look at the pictures? I miss all of them so much. They're growin' like weeds and this is the only way I can keep up."

"Of course, Mrs. Woodman. It would be my pleasure."

As James helped his patron view her photos, he peered over the computer screen and noticed Scott holding a conference with Francis behind the circulation desk. After helping Mrs. Woodman print out several color copies of the photos, James headed over to join the twins.

"We're in a bind, Professor," Scott whispered. "Ms. Pennington says she bought a lottery ticket but doesn't want anyone to know. She says it's her secret vice."

"That's not the only problem." Francis looked forlorn. "Mr. Leary called here. Seems he bought a ticket, too. Neither he nor Ms. Pennington remembers what they did with theirs. What are we going to do?"

"Let me think about it for a moment." James busied himself with some paperwork while his thoughts flitted from one subject to another like a hummingbird zipping from bloom to bloom. He saw his father's downtrodden face as he sat outside in the shed and then envisioned Murphy's eyes filled with tears as she spoke about Parker. Added to these unpleasant thoughts was the image of how two townspeople would react when informed that they needed to prove that a lottery ticket worth a ton of money was rightfully theirs.

Pushing the paperwork aside, James dialed Danny's number at the ABC store.

"Howdy," Danny answered.

James identified himself and then said, "How are those anagrams going these days?"

"You must've known I was downright stuck," Danny replied as James listened to the sound of the liquor store proprietor rifling through the newspaper.

"This week's theme is state birds," Danny explained. "I've been doin' good, but I just can't get this one."

"Let me have it." James poised a mechanical pencil above the memo pad next to his phone. As Danny recited the letters, James copied down the following: *adalcrni*. "Okay, give me a chance to stare at it a bit while we talk."

"What's on your mind, Professor?" Danny inquired pleasantly. "You callin' about the lottery ticket, too?"

James took a deep breath. He knew what he was about to do was a big gamble, but he had known Danny Leary for years and felt confident that he was an honorable gentleman through and through. "Yes sir, I am. I'm calling to tell you that the lottery ticket in question was found in the book return box outside. It either belongs to you or to another fine citizen of Quincy's Gap. We've ruled out all the other possibilities."

"Yeah?" Danny seemed intrigued. "Who's the other person?"

"I can't mention that individual's name, but I'm going to be completely honest with you, Danny. The ticket is a winner. A big winner."

There was a pause and then Danny asked softly, "How much are we talking about here, Professor?"

"One hundred and fifty thousand dollars," James answered flatly.

"Wow." Danny whistled. "That would buy a lot of things." He whistled again. "A whole lot of things."

"That money rightfully belongs to one of you, and I'm asking you to think about whether you might have dropped your lottery ticket into our book box along with the audiobook you returned." His voice firm, James pressed on. "I'm asking you to think real hard, Danny. If neither of you two can remember your actions clearly, then I'm going to suggest you split the money."

Danny sighed on the other end of the phone but said nothing. James listened to the silence and stared at the word jumble in front of him.

"God's truth, Professor. I can't think straight right now."

James nodded even though he knew Danny couldn't see him. "That's understandable, my friend. Why don't you try to recall what you did the day you returned those tapes? Look at the calendar. Think about your whole day. Call me back when you think you know."

"I will do my very best," Danny promised him.

"I know it. And Danny?"

"Yes?"

"The answer to your jumble is *cardinal*. It's our own state bird."

Danny laughed. "You sure are good at these, Professor. Thanks."

When James hung up with Danny, he dialed the church's number and went through the same routine with Ruby.

"I'll think and pray and think and pray, Professor," Ruby assured him. "I know my mind was an awful mess that day, because I broke a vase at my mama's house that she'd been given as a brand-new bride. It was mighty precious to her and I felt so awful!" Her voice sounded as though she was on the edge of tears. "That's why I bought the ticket! I prayed that I might get lucky and win so that I could buy an old vase like mama's off the Internet. I planned to give any extra directly to the church, just so's you know."

James asked her to spend the rest of the day pondering her movements on that first Friday of November. He then turned his thoughts away from lottery tickets and focused on his job.

By four thirty, the library was abuzz with groups of high school students using the computers or simply hanging out in the magazine section as they took turns reading the more sexually themed quizzes in the latest issue of *Cosmo*. This happened several times a week, and though his only part-time employee, Mrs. Waxman, a former teacher, could settle the kids down within seconds, James liked to hand over the reigns to her at five o'clock and every Saturday with the library in a state of order and quiet.

Scott and Francis did their best to settle the rowdy teenagers down, but James finally had to intervene. He admonished a few of the more boisterous young ladies and forced them to begin the homework they had been sent to the library to complete. Once the room's customary whispered hushes had been restored, James headed back to his office to phone Danny and Ruby. Just as he removed the receiver from the cradle, he saw Danny step up to the circulation desk and mutter something to Francis. Unable to control his curiosity, he hustled out front.

"Did you remember something?" he asked, surprised to see Danny standing on the other side of the desk. He must have left work a little early to get there before James headed home.

Danny looked glum. His thin, shoulder-length white hair was tied loosely at the neck with what looked like a twist tie for a garbage bag, and his oval, silver-rimmed spectacles were covered with spots. Though James had often compared Danny's looks to those of Ben Franklin, the liquor store owner tended to look more relaxed than portraits of the famous American statesman. Today, however,

Danny looked as weathered as the likeness of Franklin printed on one-hundred-dollar bills.

"It's not my ticket, Professor." Danny sighed. "I keep all the losing tickets in a stack in my TV room," he explained. "I figure if I play long enough, the statistics are bound to let me be a winner sometime." He shrugged. "Maybe not a big winner, but just something to show that the odds are right. Anyway, I like to keep count of how many I've bought for when I finally do win."

Francis leaned over the desk. "So was your ticket for this drawing in that stack?"

Danny shook his head. "That's the thing. It wasn't. I thought maybe it had got stuck in that audiobook since I would have had both the ticket and the book on the front seat of my car." He looked at James. "But I did what you said and tried to recollect the whole day. I remembered that just as I was about to leave work for the day, the word jumble that had been scramblin' my brain all day like an egg shakin' in its shell made itself clear to me. I grabbed the lottery ticket to write on, and then opened the newspaper to check the answer."

"Were you right?" Scott asked, having appeared from nowhere.

"Yeah," Danny's lips curved into a hesitant smile. "But I threw the paper back in the trash bin and the ticket must have still been in the pages. That's the last place I saw it."

James rubbed his temples. It had been days since his last headache, but ever since his phone calls to Ruby and Danny, he had been sensing that he was only a stressful thought away from getting a whopper. "Still, Danny. You're not sure. That ticket could still have ended up in the book bin."

"No, Professor. That ticket..." he trailed off as Ruby Pennington approached the desk.

Ruby's face was blotched with red and her eyes were puffy with recently shed tears. Her brown hair, which was streaked with gray, had been hastily braided and hung down her back like a fraying rope. She reached out both her hands, calloused from playing both the organ and the piano on a regular basis, and grasped James's.

"I tried, Professor. I tried to remember about—," she glanced at Danny quickly and then continued, "—that piece of paper. Thing is, I just can't say what I did with it, so I want you to go on and let that other man have the money. My mama will grant me forgiveness, and that's all the wealth I need in this world."

Danny's eyes widened. Before anyone else could speak, he removed Ruby's hands from James's and took them in his own. "I'm the other ticket holder, ma'am, and that money sure don't belong to me. I threw out my ticket with my newspaper. Danny Leary at your service." He squeezed her hand. "It's your money, ma'am."

Ruby's face slackened as she realized what he was saying. Gently removing her hands, she turned back to James. She opened her mouth to say something but only her expired breath was able to escape.

"I think this lady here needs to sit a spell," Danny suggested, taking Ruby's elbow.

James led her to the break room and all of them sat down. Scott and Francis were beaming, apparently thrilled to the core that the mystery had been successfully solved.

Ruby removed a tissue from her purse and blew her nose with such a sharp honk that all four of the men had to smile. Catching their grins, Ruby relaxed as well. "Okay then. Okay. Since you say so, it's my ticket. And if it's my ticket, I'd like to claim the money."

She put her tissue down on the table and sighed in relief. "And if it's my money, then I can spend it however I see fit. Is that right?"

James was perplexed. "Yes, Ruby. However you like."

Ruby pulled on her braid. "It's the season of thankfulness, Professor. I have many things to be grateful for, and I would be grateful to you if you would help me out with…" She trailed off and glanced at Danny again. "Mr. Leary, I have an idea. It involves you, and I sure hope you'll help me."

It was almost six by the time James finally left the library. His heart was full after he listened to Ruby Pennington's plan. In fact, it had given him a plan of his own. Bursting through the back door, he startled his father, who had just come inside from sweeping the porch.

"You tryin' to kill me, boy?" Jackson barked.

"No, Pop." He gave his father a quick hug. "I want you to live to a ripe, old age."

Jackson gave his son a bewildered look. "What's gotten into *you*?"

"Pop!" James announced. "We are *not* having Dolly's 'Housewife-on-Strike Thanksgiving Dinner to Go' this year."

His father was alarmed. "Why not? There's not a soul on this earth who can make a sweet potato casserole like that woman."

"Oh, I think there is," James said mysteriously, winked, and then bounded up the stairs to his room, clutching the portable phone is his hand. "And I'm going to invite her to our house to cook it!"

THIRTEEN

OYSTER CORNBREAD STUFFING

Sodium
per
Serving:

576 mg
for ¾ cup

THE DOORBELL OF THE Henry home rang shortly after one o'clock. It was such an unusual sound as the house was located at the end of a long, gravel drive and anyone familiar with the Henrys knew that they came and went exclusively through the back door. Even the mail carriers had learned that if a letter or package needed to be signed for, a light rap on the door leading to the kitchen would produce the best result. So the only time the door bell was brought to life over the course of the year was on Halloween, when a handful of zealous trick-or-treaters, likely in their early teens, made their way down the rough drive, waded through piles of leaves blanketing the cracked front walk, and forced the slumbering door chimes into life.

When Mrs. Henry was alive, she'd greet the enthusiastic candy gatherers with a warm smile and a bag of homemade chocolate-chip peanut-butter cookies tied with an orange ribbon. Since her passing, the kids now had to settle for Dum-Dum lollipops and many of them felt that the trek to the Henry house was no longer worth the effort.

Jackson looked up from the television as the ringing echoed through the downstairs. Turning down the volume, he listened carefully to determine if the sound of the doorbell was a figment of his imagination. When it wasn't repeated, he restored the volume of his show about the day's big football game to a deafening level.

As James ran a comb through his hair and examined his appearance in the mirror, he noted that his pants weren't quite as loose as they had been last month.

"How am I supposed to concentrate on fat, carbohydrates, and salt content all at once?" he demanded of his reflection. "I should just eat lettuce. Seems to be the only safe food." Cocking his head, he thought he heard the doorbell again. Knowing that his father would never get out of his recliner in order to see if someone was at the door, James hastened down the stairs with eager steps.

"Happy Thanksgiving!" Murphy said from beneath the layers of a plaid scarf that had worked its way over her pointed chin. Standing on the threshold, she leaned over and kissed him quickly on the lips. Her arms were laden with a white box bearing homemade dill rolls from the Sweet Tooth, a bouquet of ochre-colored roses, and two bottles of dry champagne.

"Come on in," James said, recovering from her demonstration of affection. Fleeting as the kiss had been, it was the first time a woman other than Lucy had brushed his lips with her own, and he felt a twinge of irrational guilt. "I'm so glad you could join me and Pop today," he added warmly as she put her packages down on a small table in the hall.

He helped her shrug off her brown leather coat and hung it on one of the heart-shaped hooks lining the wall outside the kitchen. As he turned to gather up the champagne bottles, the doorbell rang again.

"Aha!" James rubbed his hands together with glee. "Our chef has arrived!"

Murphy gave him an odd look but said nothing. Her view of the next guest was blocked by James's broad back, but she recognized the exuberant voice immediately.

"You are *such* a dear boy to include me in your holiday!" Milla planted a maternal kiss on his cheek, leaving a dimpled oval of rosy lipstick behind. "I've got the sweet potato casserole almost ready for the oven, but the turkey's out in the car along with my delicious cornbread and oyster dressing and the fixings for dessert."

James ushered her into the hall. "You come in and make yourself at home. I'll get your things from the car."

It took three trips to bring in the cardboard boxes filled with food, spices, pots, pans, and kitchen gadgets. When he was done, James joined the two women in the kitchen as Milla rearranged everything in the refrigerator and rummaged through the cabinets in order to get a complete assessment of what kind of kitchen she had been invited to take control over.

"What do we have here?" Milla peeked under the lid of a Tupperware bowl.

"Cranberry-orange relish," James replied proudly. "I also made green bean casserole. I told you I wasn't going to let you cook the whole dinner." He pointed at a pie cooling on a wire rack on top of the fridge. "That's just a regular pumpkin pie. You're going to make a dessert on top of the sweet potatoes, turkey, and stuffing?"

"You bet your boots I am!" Milla put her hands on her hips and then smiled at Murphy. "Why don't you visit with James? I'm going to put the *other* man of the house to work. It's well past time he learned how to use some of the tools crammed in these drawers." Her eyes twinkled. "Send him in here, James."

James hesitated.

"Go on," Milla ordered. "I can hold my own. Besides, I doubt he bites."

"He just might," James mumbled and then took Murphy's arm and led her into the lion's den.

Jackson barely glanced away from the television screen as James introduced him to Murphy. He grunted something that might have been the word "hello," but that was the extent of his hospitality. Murphy, nonplussed as always, didn't try to force Jackson into conversation. Instead, she spied a battered Monopoly box on one of the bookshelves and carried the game over to the room's only table, which was cluttered with magazines and stacks of books.

"How about a little game of vicious capitalism before dinner?" she asked James, her eyes sparkling with mischief. "Monopoly used to bring us kids close to blows during most of our family holidays."

"Well *I'm* not playing some kids' game," Jackson grumbled, and James knew that despite his gruffness, his father was doing his best to deal with two strange females invading his home for a holiday that had only been special while his wife was still alive.

"That's right, you're not, Pop." James switched off the TV set and jerked his thumb toward the kitchen. "You're wanted in there."

Jackson's eyebrows almost merged with his hairline. "What?" he growled in surprise. "A man's supposed to stay out of the way 'til it's time to carve the turkey. Don't you know the first thing about women, boy?"

"*This* woman wants *your* company," Milla stated from the doorway. She wore an apron covered with turkeys being chased by a fat chef wielding a cleaver. Smiling, she marched over to the recliner, grabbed Jackson's hand, and led him from the room. "We two widows need to stick together," James heard her say. "Plus, I've got some heart-warmin' bourbon that I'm going to mix into the sweet potatoes. My thinkin' is we'd better try some first. Make sure it's good enough to serve to everyone else!"

James didn't hear Jackson's reply, but whatever he said sent Milla into peals of laughter. Tuning the radio to a light classical station, James settled down across from Murphy and spent half of the afternoon trying to coax her out of charging him the required rent as he landed on property after property dominated by her hotels.

"I never win when I play with the dog piece," he said sulkily as she directed her own playing piece, the top hat, straight to Free Parking. "I can't believe it! You've won that three times!"

Murphy laughed. "Why do you keep playing with the dog if you never win with it?"

James shrugged. "There's a first time for everything."

"That's what is so endearing about you." Murphy reached across her mountain of paper money and squeezed his hand. "Your optimism. It's infectious."

"You're just trying to make me feel better about getting my butt kicked two games in a row. I surrender. You're too much of a real estate tycoon for me to handle." He eyed the bookshelves. "How are you at Scrabble?"

She gave him a lopsided grin. "I *am* in the business of words, so I'm not bad, but I haven't played in decades."

"Good, then maybe I stand a chance." James rose and replaced the Monopoly assemblage with an equally ratty Scrabble box. "Can I get you anything while I'm up?"

"Let's break into that champagne," Murphy suggested.

As James cautiously entered the kitchen, he was amazed by both the nostalgic aromas floating out of the oven and the sight of his father, seated across the table from Milla, happily peeling Granny Smith apples.

"You cannot be a novice, Jackson Henry," Milla teased. "No true beginner can get the peel off in one whole piece. I believe you've been fibbing to me all afternoon long about not knowing your way around a kitchen."

"When I tell a fib, ma'am, it's a whopper!" Jackson stated proudly.

Was his father flirting? The thought froze James in his tracks. Milla spied him and shook a flour-encrusted rolling pin his way. "No interfering with my tutoring lesson."

"We have some parched throats back in the den," James explained. "Am I allowed to open some champagne?"

Milla stepped out of the way. "Why didn't you say so? Your father and I are already feeling nice and warm from sampling the bourbon, so you go on ahead without us."

After James popped the cork on the champagne bottle, he realized that he didn't own the appropriate glassware for a sparkling beverage. Settling for highball glasses, he first peeked into the oven at an unbelievably plump and browning turkey before returning to the den.

"We're having a feast fit for royalty," he told Murphy as he handed her a glass.

The pair had only consumed several sips of champagne and completed two highly competitive rounds of Scrabble when Milla ordered them to relocate to the dining room.

"Nice spread, Professor," Murphy praised James as she looked over the table setting.

Earlier in the week, he had driven to a gourmet kitchen store in Charlottesville and purchased mustard and cranberry-hued pottery plates and a set of wire napkin rings in the shape of pumpkins. He had taken out the good silverware, which hadn't seen the light of day in years, and buffed his mother's set of crystal water goblets to a high shine. Milla had cut Murphy's flowers short and arranged them in a woven basket. The small chandelier cast a soft light overhead and two tapers in deep red illuminated the center of the table. James realized that he should have ironed the tablecloth, but he doubted much of the surface would be visible under such a vast array of food dishes.

Jackson carried Milla's sweet potato casserole with bourbon in one hand and James's green bean casserole in the other. Milla trailed behind him bearing a bowl heaped so high with mashed potatoes that James felt the weight of the dish might cause the older woman to become unbalanced and pitch forward. In her other hand was a napkin-lined basket containing the fragrant dill rolls from the Sweet Tooth and a butter dish. Whispering orders to Jackson, who complied with a nod and a shy smile, Milla laid out the food and surveyed the table.

"Let's see. Your daddy's getting the cranberry-orange relish, the oyster cornbread dressing, and the gravy, so I guess it's time to bring on the main attraction."

The turkey had shrunk several sizes during its long roast in the oven, but its skin had been burnished a golden brown. Milla had lovingly coated it with high quality olive oil, sea salt, fresh ground pepper, and sprigs of fresh rosemary. She had also stuffed the cavity with more rosemary and fresh thyme. Jackson's eyes shone with lascivious greed as he surveyed the bird, and James knew that his father was secretly fantasizing over claiming both drumsticks.

"You'd better sharpen that knife, Pop," he cautioned his father upon seeing the carving set appear next to the platter bearing the regal turkey.

"Shoot, boy. I had these ready to go days ago." Jackson pointed at the knife, preferring not to look any of his guests in the eye. "This blade's so sharp it'd cut through a piece of lead pipe just like jelly. Watch and learn, son. Carvin' is a man's job."

"Truer words were never spoken," Milla declared, winking at Jackson as if they shared a secret.

As a slight grin tugged at the corners of his mouth, Jackson deftly sliced off pieces of tender breast meat and made a big show of serving Milla first. "You always pay respect to the cook," he said, presumably for James's benefit, though James was certain it was his father's way of paying Milla a compliment.

When everyone was served and the glasses set before them were filled with fizzing champagne, Milla raised her hands and said, "I'd like to say a blessing, if I may."

James shot Jackson a worried glance, as his father had never been big on saying grace. He had avoided attending church service his entire life outside of his own wedding and the baptism of his only child. James and his mother had always gone to church together, but Jackson claimed he was suspicious of all churches and didn't need anyone to tell him how to talk to his Maker.

"He's talking to his Maker with his fishing pole," James's mother would joke as they'd settle into their regular pew. That was often all she'd have time to say before the sound of Ruby Pennington pouring passion into the ancient organ—whose reluctant pipes seemed unable to keep pace with Ruby's flying fingers—would explode inside the church. The image of Ruby seated on her bench in front of the organ reminded James that he had an important task to complete before the night was through, but for the moment, he took Murphy's outstretched hand and bowed his head.

"Lord," Milla prayed. "Thank you for bringing us together and for the bounty before us. We are so grateful for the friends we have held close to us as we have grown older and to the friends we have lost along the road of life." She paused for a fraction of a second as her voice caught. Next to James, Murphy's eyes had filled with tears, as she was undoubtedly thinking of Parker. Milla inhaled and continued. "And we are grateful for new friends. It is the people in our lives that define us and I couldn't be happier to be holding hands with such wonderful people as the friends seated around me. Amen."

"Amen!" Jackson declared and then immediately added, "Tuck in!"

Over the next hour, the foursome traded innocuous gossip and small talk while interjecting exclamations over the sumptuousness of the food. James was pleasantly amazed at how comfortable Jackson seemed to be with the two women who had invaded his home and forced him to speak more sentences over the course of the past few hours than he had uttered during the whole of the past two months.

During the dessert course, which consisted of pumpkin pie, apple crisp with fresh whipped cream, and decaf coffees, the foursome grew lethargic. Their bellies were so full that it was an effort to even swallow a sip of water. Pushing themselves away from the table, they unanimously declared that the meal was done.

James and Murphy volunteered to clean up. After clearing the table, they loaded the dishwasher and then began scrubbing the dozen pans, pots, and bowls that Milla had brought over.

"Why don't I come back tomorrow to collect all of my things?" Milla quietly asked Jackson as he held out her coat. James stiffened, wondering what his father would say. He even put down the pan he was drying and spied on the couple as they stood in the hallway. "We can have some coffee."

Jackson hesitated for a moment, but then he nodded his assent and walked Milla to her car.

"They are so sweet together," Murphy whispered as she watched them leave. Drying her hands with a paper towel, she put an arm around James. "Thanks for having me over. With my family away at my older sister's, I would have felt so lonely today."

James could sense an air of expectation descend upon their shared space. Turning to Murphy, he stared at her pretty face and saw the gratitude in her hazel eyes. Without pausing to dissect his feelings, he leaned over and kissed her, drawing her trim body into his. He kissed her warmly for almost a minute and then slowly released her, smiling tenderly as he did so. James didn't want to admit it, but he was still experiencing some conflicting emotions about

Lucy, and he didn't want to begin a serious relationship with Murphy until his confusion had been completely resolved.

"Hey," he said to her as Jackson came back inside, rubbing his cold hands together. "How would you like to witness the unfolding of an incredibly heartwarming news story?"

A gleam appeared in her eyes. "When? Right now?"

"Yes." He handed her a pen and paper. "Follow me to the phone, Brenda Starr."

James removed a memo pad from his backpack that he had taken notes on during his meeting with Ruby Pennington. He had two phone numbers written on it, and he dialed the first one eagerly.

"Mrs. Matthews? Hello, this is James Henry from Shenandoah County Library." He paused. "I know this is Thanksgiving, ma'am, and I don't want to take up too much of your time." He took a moment to find the right words. "It's just that I have some good tidings to pass along, and I promised to do so before the holiday was over."

James went on to explain that an anonymous library patron turned out to be the owner of a winning lottery ticket worth a great deal of money. "This person doesn't believe in coincidence, Mrs. Matthews. This person felt that there was confusion about who owned the ticket for a reason. This person feels that was there was a specific purpose behind there being three other library patrons' books in the book box. Because of this, I have been directed to tell you that a check for twenty-five thousand dollars is waiting for you at the library. It is this person's way of giving thanks for the realization that they are already living a rich and fulfilled life."

Mrs. Matthews didn't respond. James was certain she was in shock.

"Ma'am? Did you follow what I said?" He waited. "Mrs. Matthews? Are you okay?"

She started crying. "Are you serious, Professor? Because if you are . . ." She trailed off. "You don't know what this would mean for our family."

James smiled into the phone. "I wouldn't pull your leg, ma'am, and I've got the check to prove it. Stop in tomorrow when it's convenient."

Sniffling, Mrs. Matthews tried to catch her breath. "How can I thank this person, Professor? I just can't take the money without expressing my deepest gratitude!"

"He or she especially wished to remain anonymous, Mrs. Matthews. They just wanted to spread a little cheer on this special day."

"I can't believe there is really someone like this out there, Professor! It's like finding our own personal angel."

James smiled. "I believe Quincy's Gap is chock full of them. Good night and Happy Thanksgiving."

Murphy's mouth was hanging open, though her hand was working furiously. "Are you going to tell me who this person is?"

James shook his head. "Nope. Danny Leary was also given the same amount, and I'm now going to call Wendy Carver, a woman who has worked in the elementary school cafeteria for over twenty years, and tell her about her windfall. She makes the third person whose books were in our box." He narrowed his eyes. "And don't try to get anything out of Scott or Francis, either. They won't tell you a thing."

Fingers trembling with excitement, he dialed Wendy Carver's number.

Wendy's reaction was to shriek like a maimed hyena for over two minutes. James put her reaction on speakerphone as he and Murphy giggled gleefully, waiting for the cafeteria worker to calm down.

"Bless you, Professor!" Wendy yelled joyfully over and over again.

"Don't bless me. I'm just the messenger," James answered happily when he could finally get a word in edgewise.

James could almost visualize Wendy shaking a finger at him. "Don't you tell me who I can bless! I say bless you and yours and that angel from heaven who's given me this crazy gift and ... and everyone! Yessir! Bless everyone!"

"Can I ask you a personal question, Ms. Carver?" James interrupted.

"Sure, hon. But better do it quick, 'fore I have a heart attack."

"What do you plan to do with the money?"

Wendy chuckled. "That's an easy one. I'm goin' on one of them cruises where they have those buffets of nothin' but chocolate. After twenty-two years of servin' out school food, I'd like someone to serve *me* for a change." She chuckled. "And I'm gonna take Mildred along. She's been mopping floors in that place for just as long as I've been dishin' out macaroni and cheese and has never stepped foot outside of this town. Besides, it's no fun eating desserts alone."

James looked at the remains of the pumpkin pie sitting on the counter and then back at Murphy's face, which was aglow over witnessing such a bounty of happiness. "You got that right," he said to Wendy in agreement.

FOURTEEN

HERB-CRUSTED ROAST BEEF

Sodium
per
Serving:

82 mg
for 4.5 oz.

THE WEEKS FOLLOWING THANKSGIVING drifted away like the leaves chasing one another in circles across the brown and brittle grass in front of the library. James was alternating between watching their dance and working on the staff's holiday vacation schedule. It was growing dark when Scott scurried into James's office, closed the door, and faced his boss. Panic was etched across his pale features and he was breathing fast.

"Scott? Are you okay?" James got to his feet, concerned.

"She's here," Scott whispered, removing his heavy-framed glasses and wiping them with the bottom of his shirt.

"Who?" James was about to open the door to investigate but Scott stopped him.

"Lottie. The reporter for *The Star.*" He resumed cleaning his glasses.

James cracked the door and peered out through the opening. Lottie was busy examining a display on heart-warming holiday reads. She then wandered over to the shelf bearing the staff's recommendations and selected all four books listed under Scott's name. Her plain face lit up as she skimmed the jacket of one of his all-time favorite fantasy books.

"She's so cool," Scott murmured behind James, a dreamy look in his eyes. "Did you see that? She's getting the first book in the *Memory, Sorrow, and Thorn* series." He was so fixated on the young reporter that he didn't notice that he had leaned so far forward that his boss was now supporting almost all of his body weight. James, on the other hand, was acutely aware that he was practically giving Scott a piggyback ride.

"Scott!" he barked, causing the twin to jump backward in surprise. "What exactly is the problem? It seems as though you like her. Do you?"

Scott nodded dumbly.

"Then go talk to her. You've talked to her before. What's different now?"

"Now I *really* like her," Scott muttered miserably.

James started to smile, but then realized that it would be insensitive to mock the young man's anguish. "If you really like her, ask her out."

"I want to, Professor. I really do. I'm just no good at this kind of thing."

James nodded. "It's not easy, that's for sure."

Scott went on as though James hadn't spoken. "I ... I even made her something for Christmas."

The twins were extremely handy. Last year they had built a float for the town's annual Halloween parade and had won first prize. Naturally, James was curious as to what Scott would have created for the girl he wanted to date. "What did you make her?"

Scott shrugged. "It's nothing. Stupid, actually."

James glanced at the oversized calendar tacked to the wall behind his desk. Christmas was only a few days away. He noted the red circle around Christmas Eve. Murphy had asked him to come to her house for a late dinner. He had originally planned on showing up with a bottle of wine and red roses, but now he wondered if those gifts were too clichéd. Perhaps Scott's handcrafted gift would spark some creative ideas. "Really, Scott. You can tell me," he pressed.

Scott shot a quick look at Lottie, who was still floating around the library. "It's a Battlestar Galactica birdhouse," he said as he stared at her. "She's watched all the old episodes a million times and loves the new ones airing on the Sci-Fi Channel."

Unable to think of a suitable reply regarding the gift, James gave Scott a paternal pat on the back. "She's going to love it, son. Just go out there, tell her you've got a surprise for her, and plan on someplace private to give it to her." He propelled Scott out of the office. "She's a strong-willed woman. Just give her the opening and she'll take the lead. Trust me. She's a reporter. They are *not* a shy breed."

"Somewhere private," Scott uttered to himself, clearly lost in thought. James continued to gently shove the young man forward until he had practically collided with the object of his desire. Subtly, James veered away from the pair and ran smack into Mrs. Waxman.

"Sorry!" he apologized to the older woman and retrieved her handbag from the floor. "Um, may I ask you a strange question?"

The older woman shrugged. "You always do. Even as a student you'd stay after class to ask me oddball questions. But after twenty-five years in the classroom, I've heard it all, so out with it, Mr. Henry."

"What's a good gift to give a woman when you're just getting to know one another?" James blurted. "You know, at the beginning of what may become a long-term relationship."

Mrs. Waxman frowned in thought while patting her puffy hair. "I'd go with chocolate. In a fancy box. Lets her know that you plunked down some good money for the high-quality stuff. Not that waxy junk they sell at the drug store, mind you." She shook her finger at him for emphasis.

"Thank you," James replied and then slunk back to his office. He didn't think that chocolates were the perfect gift. He heard Mrs. Waxman enter the break room, whistling "Santa Claus Is Coming to Town" and felt his anxiety over Murphy's gift increase.

With clammy fingers, James dialed Lindy's cell phone number, his eyes riveted to his wall calendar. Lindy picked up, sounding especially weary.

"Long day?" he inquired.

She sighed. "I've had to repeat the whole story behind the threatening remark I made to Kinsley to that Sergeant McClellan *again*. I can't tell you how much I wish I didn't have my mother's temper." James could hear the crinkling of a candy wrapper being opened in the background. "He even insists on coming to my New Year's Eve party. Undercover. Pffah! Like everyone doesn't know who he is! The man's a skyscraper with legs."

James listened to this news with interest. "Did he ask you to invite anyone else?"

"Yeah. The whole staff from Parker's office! Can you believe it? And all of the adults on the field trip to the caves, of course." She paused. "And Kinsley, if she'll come. She hasn't been back to school yet. Luis says she's going to try again after Christmas break. I feel bad, James. I keep meaning to call her, but I don't know what to say."

"Call and invite her to the party instead of mailing an invitation," James suggested. "You can always small talk with her about kids from school if she doesn't feel like talking. After my mother died, it was nice to listen to people without having to say anything."

"That's why you're a librarian." Lindy's mood seemed to instantly improve. "You just know how to help."

"Well, maybe you can help me, too." James proceeded to ask Lindy's advice on a gift to bring Murphy.

"I'm still recovering from the news about you and Lucy!" Lindy scolded. "How am I supposed to think about you and Murphy as a couple now? I just can't picture you with a different woman!"

"Murphy and I are not a couple," James protested. "But she's invited me over for Christmas Eve, and I can hardly go empty-handed."

Lindy was silent for a moment. "You're right. Good manners must prevail. Hmmm. You could bring over a plant, like a poinsettia. Or maybe a pretty scarf. A woman can never have enough scarves, or gloves for that matter."

James thanked her, but decided that Lindy's suggestions seemed more directed toward the type of gift one would give to a piano teacher or a mother-in-law, not something unique enough to impress an intelligent and attractive reporter.

After some internal debate, James decided to call Gillian at work.

"Is that you, James?" Gillian shouted over what sounded like a blow-dryer. "Just hold on! I've got to put Angus Rex back on his leash."

James waited, wearing an amused smile as the variety of noises coming through the earpiece created a comic image of Gillian struggling with Angus. After a series of barks and the screech of nails on a slick floor, he heard Gillian trying to verbally coax the canine to allow her to reattach his collar.

"Come on, big boy," she cooed to the dog. "You are *so* handsome now. You don't want to mess up your beautiful bath because you're distracted by Zsa Zsa, do you?" He heard Gillian making *tut tut* sounds as though she were rebuking the dog. "I *know* she is a very, very alluring and sophisticated French poodle, but perhaps you should remember that you have a *wife* of your own back at home. Remember her? Agnes Rex?" Gillian grabbed the phone once more. "Sorry, James! Angus is a Great Dane with a *very* strong personality!"

James quickly explained his predicament so that his friend could answer his query and then return her attention to Angus Rex.

"Why, that's *such* a simple issue! I know *just* the thing!" Gillian exclaimed.

"Thank goodness someone does." James felt relieved and then remembered that Gillian's idea of a perfect present might border on the bizarre. He held his breath and hoped for a stroke of brilliance to inspire his friend.

"Listen carefully," Gillian instructed. "You should find out what her element is. Then, get her a gift that matches the very core of her being. For example, *my* element is fire." James could envision Gillian fluffing her flame-colored hair as she spoke. "I'd love a candle in yellow and orange shades, perhaps some sunflower-scented body oil, or a lemon-eucalyptus face spritzer. *Everyone* can use a nice spritz, and winter is especially harsh on our delicate skin."

Thanking Gillian for her creative ideas, James hung up and uttered an exasperated sigh. He packed his bags, said goodbye to Mrs. Waxman, and headed to the Custard Cottage to get a gingerbread latte. Inside the cozy eatery, he was pleased to note that Bennett must have had a similar craving. James ordered a skim-milk version of the holiday treat, asked Willy to hold off on the whipped cream, and sank down next to Bennett.

"You look like a man with some things on his mind," Bennett commented. "I'm awful sorry that none of us have come up with any solid notions about Parker. Is that what's weighin' on you?"

"Partially," James said. "Though it sounds like McClellan's got some kind of plan. He's asked Lindy to add a bunch of names to her New Year's party list."

"Interesting." Bennett's eyes gleamed. "Gettin' all of the suspects together to see if they create a reaction. Very scientific."

"Very Agatha Christie, too." James took a sip of his latte and scorched the tip of his tongue. "Wow! That's hot!"

Willy sat down beside James with an enormous cup of hot chocolate. "Now, this ain't McDonald's. Don't go suin' me, friend."

"Willy, that looks like a cereal bowl," Bennett said, gesturing at the proprietor's snowflake-decorated mug.

"I call this my hot chocolate crater. It's made with real chocolate syrup, cream, and chocolate shavings." Willy stirred a peppermint stick around the frothy surface of his drink. "I never told y'all about it 'cause you're tryin' so hard to be good."

"Listen, men." James put down his cup. "You're both smart and innovative individuals. Maybe you can help me solve my problem."

"We'll sure give it a try." Willy winked.

"What's the perfect Christmas gift to give a woman that … ah … you think you're starting to like as more than just a friend?"

Bennett plucked his toothbrush mustache as he thought. "Women like romance. How about one of those date movies? You know, *Sleepless in Seattle* or *Love, Actually*. They go wild over that stuff. She'll think you're *so* sensitive. I hear that's the thing to be these days," he added sarcastically.

Willy shook his head. "You don't need to get so worked up about this, Professor. You just gotta tailor your gift to the girl. Tell me something. When you two are alone, what do you do together?"

James shrugged. "Mostly we've been working on investigating Parker's death, but Murphy did come over for Thanksgiving. We played board games and … it was really fun." His cheeks grew pink as he related their banal activities.

Willy nodded. "If you ask me, folks should spend more time sittin' across a table from one another. In my family, it was always Chinese checkers and Parcheesi. What did you play with Murphy?"

"Monopoly and Scrabble, but we never finished the Scrabble game."

"That's it!" Bennett declared. "There's a cool Collector's Edition of Scrabble. Get her that and say you want to finish the game. It would be kinda like wrapping up the next date."

"He's right on with that one," Willy agreed, and he and Bennett exchanged high-fives. "Add a bottle of wine to that and you're gonna work yourself some magic with that woman."

"Why did I think the women I know would have all the answers?" James said to his friends. "Two of the three wise men are apparently sitting right here with me. Where'd you guys park your camels?"

"I haven't heard such flattery since I created my Sweet as Sin custard," Willy laughed. "Vanilla custard with ribbons of chocolate and caramel, topped with a shell of chocolate fudge and a generous coating of toffee chips. It'll bore holes in your teeth just lookin' at it!"

"Willy, you sure know how to make a man feel what he's missin'," Bennett said morosely.

"Cheer up, my friend!" Willy clapped him on the back. "At least you're not outside running around in the dark like that pair." He pointed out the front window at a couple dressed in matching jogging suits.

"They're crazy. It's damned cold out tonight," Bennett observed.

James said good night and hustled out to the Bronco, trying to prevent the frosty air from permeating his down coat and wool scarf. As he drove out of town, he noticed that the joggers had turned around and were now running back toward Custard Cottage. There was a man and a woman. The man seemed to be running effortlessly, while the woman was clearly struggling as she pumped her arms vigorously and her breath burst out of her mouth in white clouds, reminding James of a dragon exhaling smoke.

He stopped at a red light and stared at the runners, as something about the pair was familiar. Just then, the twosome ran beneath a streetlamp and James recognized the brown baseball caps embroidered with the Sheriff's Department logo. Lucy's chestnut hair glowed for a brief moment as she ran through the pool of light, striving to keep pace with Sullie. Suddenly, she looked right at James and though her steps never faltered, her expression was clearly pained.

In a flash, the light turned green and James drove past her, but her blue and wounded eyes haunted him all the way home. Did she look miserable because she was running, or was something deeper troubling her? James would have liked to believe that it wasn't his business, that he no longer cared about how Lucy Hanover felt, but he couldn't deceive himself. It was likely that he would always care. Even though she had hurt him, he still wanted her to be happy.

James dressed in a cheery red sweater and freshly ironed black pants before heading over to Murphy's house for their Christmas Eve celebration. He was nervous. He had seen Murphy several times over the last few weeks as they tried to discover more and more about how Parker spent her free time. Aside from going to the movies and restaurants with Colin, Parker and Dwight also volunteered at several area animal shelters during their off hours. Murphy got Kinsley's permission to snoop around Parker's house, but they found nothing out of sorts in her modest home.

In fact, everything about the young woman's home was warm and inviting. Even empty, it had a comfortable aura about it and it was pleasantly cluttered with books, animal art, photographs, and the usual mundane objects of day-to-day living. There were no incriminating videotapes, threatening notes, or the slightest indication of the violence that would creep along and steal the young woman's life.

It was obvious that Parker had loved her family and her patients. There were almost as many photographs of cats, dogs, and birds posing with their owners as there were of the Willis clan. As James flipped through piles of photo albums, Murphy went through Parker's bank statements. Again, there was no strange or suspicious activity. Parker had a job she loved, a nice, good-looking boyfriend, plenty of money, and her closets seemed to be completely free of skeletons.

James was impressed by the level of artistry displayed in the dozens of scrapbooks he found. Paging through the most recent album, he noticed a photo labeled *Gary and Kinsley on Broadway*. It showed Kinsley and a short man standing next to her. The man held up a pair of play tickets and was gazing at the camera with a look of satisfaction on his face. Kinsley, who was at least four inches taller than her boyfriend, beamed excitedly. Behind the couple, a poster of *The Phantom of the Opera* lit by a frame of bright bulbs made it clear which show the couple was scheduled to see.

"Here's Kinsley's boyfriend in New York." James showed Murphy the photograph. "It's like you said when you got home from Kansas. Not the kind of guy you'd expect to see Kinsley with."

"He sure is short, too," Murphy commented. "He's wearing a mighty smug expression in that photo. I couldn't really get a read on him at the funeral. Everyone was totally subdued." She flipped the page. "He looks much friendlier in this picture."

Peering over her shoulder, James stared at a snapshot of the couple skating at Rockefeller Center. It looked as though Gary had just fallen down and was grinning as he sat on the ice. Behind him, Kinsley was doubled over, her mouth open mid-laugh. Another photo showed the pair in business suits seated on the edge of a marble bench. In the background, a large sign read *Solmes Investments*. Gary's face was turned slightly toward the sign and his eyes looked veiled and unreadable. Kinsley seemed to be smiling automatically for the camera, and James noticed that the couple's bodies were turned away from one another.

"Looks like the beginning of the end here," James observed and then finished looking through the book. "Colin and Parker are the only pair of lovebirds left in this album. Here they are throwing a lobster dinner for the volunteers at the local food bank."

"Guess Gary must have had a great personality," Murphy stated unkindly and then sighed in disappointment. "There's nothing in this house to report to McClellan."

Murphy had been in contact with Sergeant McClellan. She had shared her belief that the killer had worn makeup and a wig and defended her theory that the false Mr. Sneed may have had some experience in the theater. She and James had stopped by every costume store within one hundred miles, looking for a similar beard and wig ensemble, but never found a match. Simultaneously, McClellan searched for a clue among the local theater companies, but his pursuit led him nowhere. Then, two weeks before Christmas, a local boy went missing and McClellan's priority shifted from seeking justice for a dead young woman to recovering the eight-year-old while he still lived.

Late in the afternoon of Christmas Eve, James found the Collector's Edition Scrabble game at the Barnes & Noble in Harrisonburg and carefully wrapped it using the holiday paper he had bought to support the middle school's fundraiser. Rolling a bottle of 2003

Cakebread Cabernet Sauvignon in sheets of red and green tissue paper, James gathered Murphy's gifts and pulled on his coat.

"No need to rush on back home," Jackson said by way of good night. James noticed that his father had donned a button-down and a coordinating sweater vest along with an ancient clip-on bow tie.

"Did you get Milla a gift?" James wondered.

Jackson scowled. "I made her one and that's all you need to know about it. Now git. I wanna have a shot of Cutty before she gets here. Give me some courage." He widened his eyes in an exaggerated gesture of amazement. "Lord Almighty, but that woman can talk!"

James smiled, knowing full well that his father enjoyed Milla's company and had been pacing around the house all week as if the days couldn't pass by quickly enough until she would return, bearing trays of food and filling the house with boundless energy and enthusiasm. Ever since Thanksgiving, Jackson had spent a great deal of time back in the shed, and James wondered if he had discovered a new subject to paint. He thought about the art books he had purchased for his father for Christmas and whether Jackson would be disappointed in the giant book on Van Gogh or the coffee-table tome stuffed with colorful plates illustrating a myriad of twentieth-century paintings.

"Can't worry about that now," James muttered to himself as he headed off to Murphy's.

Murphy actually lived in an apartment directly above the offices of *The Star*. She had placed electric candles in her front windows and had hung pre-lit wreaths from the top of each frame. Soft light emanated from her apartment and as James walked up the back stairs, the aroma of roasting meat greeted his nostrils.

An antique set of sleigh bells hung down the front of Murphy's apartment door. James knocked lightly and as she opened the door, the bells rattled merrily. Murphy wore a long, off-white turtleneck sweater that clung to her trim hips and a pair of black velvet leggings. James had to smile as he took note of her slipper socks, which were red and white striped and seemed completely incongruous with the rest of her polished look.

She followed his eyes to her feet. "My apartment floors are so cold," she said by way of explanation and then led him into the kitchen. "I thought I'd open a bottle of wine. Do you prefer white or red?"

James offered her the tissue-wrapped package in his right hand. "How about this one?"

"I like a man bearing gifts," she grinned and tore open the tissue. "Yum! I can't wait to try this." She handed him a corkscrew. "Will you do the honors? I've got to check on the roast beast."

As James opened the wine and poured two glasses, Murphy chatted about the trials of Christmas shopping for her large and widely dispersed family. The tales of her siblings made James wish that he had had a brother or sister. Now that the Henry family had shrunk from three to two, he realized how empty the house seemed, especially during holidays such as Thanksgiving and Christmas. He was grateful to Murphy for postponing her trip home so that she could spend Christmas Eve with him. As she removed the roast from the oven, he told her as much.

"Trust me, I'll see plenty of my crazy family tomorrow. It would take all the spiked eggnog in Virginia to calm that group down." Digging through one of her cabinets, she pulled out a hand mixer and began whipping together a bowl of boiled potatoes, butter, sour cream, and milk. "I'm happy you're here, too," she added over the whir of the beaters. "And it's so nice that Milla is over at your place. Do you think she and your pop are going to get hot and heavy?"

James felt his face grow warm. "I don't think so. I'm just happy that they enjoy each other's company."

Murphy stopped the beater and dumped the potatoes into a large ceramic bowl. She put her hand on her hip. "We enjoy each other's company, too." She plunked a wooden serving spoon into the steaming white mass and sprinkled pepper over the top. "Does that mean we can never get hot and heavy?"

Without waiting for an answer, she moved into the great room and set the bowl down on the table, where a plate of asparagus drizzled in hollandaise and a basket of crescents already waited. James felt his throat go dry as he mulled over her comment, staring at the candlelit table and listening to the moving strains of Chopin tripping out of a pair of hidden speakers.

As Murphy carried the roast beef to the table, she elbowed him playfully in the side. "Don't go all analytical on me, Professor. Can't a girl tease a guy anymore?"

Taking a gulp of wine, James relaxed. "Do you want me to carve the meat?"

"Slice away!" Murphy handed him a knife and went back to the kitchen in order to grab the bottle of wine and the butter dish.

The meat was covered in a fragrant herb crust and was very warm. James had trouble directing the knife into making a straight slice. He had thoroughly butchered two pieces by the time Murphy sat down across from him.

"You're supposed to let it sit a bit before you cut it," she explained why he was having difficulty, "but I'm too hungry to wait. Just rip some off of there and let's eat."

Over dinner, James told Murphy about the additional guests invited to Lindy's New Year's Eve party. They exchanged theories as to what McClellan was planning and then discussed the varied resolutions that their friends had made for the coming year.

"What's your resolution?" Murphy asked.

"I haven't thought about it too much," he answered. "Maybe to keep my blood pressure low so I don't die at forty. You?"

Murphy swirled the wine around in her glass. "I'll get back to you on that one. This cab is delicious, by the way. Thank you." She pushed her plate away and clasped her hands together. "Are you ready for *your* presents?" She jumped up and refilled their glasses with the remainder of the wine. "We can have dessert later. Come on!"

James wiped his mouth with his napkin and followed her over to the sofa. She had placed a small Christmas tree in the far corner of the room and a pile of expertly wrapped gifts lay beneath the twinkling white lights. Murphy pulled out two small boxes and handed them to James.

"You go first," she ordered.

He carefully ripped the paper off the first box and was delighted to see a new pair of shear-lined leather slippers inside. "How did you know?" he asked her, thinking about the ratty slippers lined up on the floor next to his bed. "I've needed a new pair for about ten years now."

"I saw them when I used the upstairs bathroom on Thanksgiving. It's always good to do a little snooping if you're getting a Christmas gift for a new friend." She winked. "At first, I thought it was such a lame present, but everyone needs to have warm feet. Now, open the second one. This one's much better."

James laughed as the second box revealed a new Monopoly game. "This is more of a gift for you!" he reprimanded her. "Do you really think I want to play this with you after you annihilated me so many times before? Let a man have his dignity."

"It's not your run-of-the-mill Monopoly." Murphy gestured at the box lid. "Look closely."

"Quincy's Gap Monopoly," James read the text aloud in astonishment. "How did you do this?"

"There's a make-your-own game set, so I used Quincy's Gap." Excitedly, she removed the game board and showed James some of the real estate squares. "See? There's the library and here's *The Star*, and there's the Sweet Tooth, Dolly's Diner, and I put the Custard Cottage on the Free Parking space because it's as good as money."

"I can't imagine how much time and effort this must have required." James was in awe. He looked into Murphy's hazel eyes. "What a special gift. No one's ever made me something before."

"Oh my, you used the word 'special.' I'd better go open a new bottle of wine." Murphy sprang up and returned with another bottle of red. "Good thing we had the Cakebread first. I don't know much about this wine. I just liked the name *Matriarch*." She poured two glasses and then gestured at the gift James had brought for her. "And what's in there?"

"It's for you," he stated miserably. "But I had a terrible time thinking of what to get for you, and I'm afraid I haven't made a great choice."

"Let *me* decide on that, okay?" She reached over him and grabbed her gift and as she did so, he caught her clean scent of baby powder and lavender mixed in with a slightly fruity perfume. "Oh, how fun!" she exclaimed when she revealed the Scrabble box. "And do you know why I love this present so much?"

James shook his head.

"It implies that you want to keep spending time together," she said softly and then brushed his cheek with her lips. "Let's play a round right now."

Over the course of the next hour, James and Murphy finished the second bottle of wine and began spelling nonsense words just to test the other person's vocabulary skills. The wine made it difficult for James to focus on diction, and Murphy's nearness tempted his thoughts away from winning the game and more on taking her in his arms.

Finally, he decided that it was time to make a move. Murphy had said that she would not be the one to initiate a romance between them, but she had already done her best to ensure that they had spent time together over the past two months. Banishing thoughts of Lucy into the farthest reaches of his mind, James suddenly swept all the Scrabble tiles off the board and onto the rug.

"What are you doing?" Murphy demanded, giggling. "Are you throwing a tantrum?"

"See if you can tell what this means?" James gathered a few tiles and spread them across the board until they read "I W-A-N-T T-O K-I-S-S U."

Murphy read the message and immediately stopped laughing, though a smile still played around the corners of her mouth. She inched closer and James put his hand behind her neck and drew her into his chest. She felt so much slighter in his arms than Lucy, but she was soft and warm and James could feel his body respond to her touch.

After a few minutes, Murphy broke away and, after taking another sip of wine, began spelling out a new message on the board. When she was done, she got up and walked down the hall into a dark bedroom.

James watched her in surprise and then looked back at what the Scrabble tiles read:

W-A-I-T O-N-E M-I-N-U-T-E

T-H-E-N C-O-M-E B-A-C-K

After a brief moment of hesitation, James drained his wine glass and also finished off the dregs in Murphy's and then tiptoed down the hall. Murphy appeared in the doorway to her bedroom, dressed in a silky white robe stitched with tiny red roses. Though the robe was long, it fell open to reveal one of Murphy's shapely legs. He wanted to stop time and drink in the image of her—the curve of her breasts beneath the thin fabric of her robe or the way the moonlight illuminated her hair and robe until she practically glowed.

"You're beautiful," he whispered and then she was against him, wrapping her arms around his back. He didn't think beyond the moment as Murphy pulled off his sweater and unbuttoned his shirt. His mind concentrated only on her iridescent skin, the feel of her lips, and the faint sounds of Chopin's Prelude in C Minor.

"Beautiful," he whispered again and then drew her down onto the bed.

FIFTEEN
CHILI CON QUESO

Sodium per Serving:

1062 mg for 3 oz.

AT THE FINAL FIX 'n Freeze class of the year, Milla announced that she had been in bed most of the day nursing a bad cold and the evening's menu was going to reflect her need for simple, comforting fare.

"Seems as though our friend Colin's still down and out with this nasty bug, and I sure hope none of you get it." She pulled a large bowl from the oven and, with the aid of a thick pair of potholders, carried it across the room to the center island. "I made us a nice bowl of fresh *chili con queso*," she said and then hid a rumbling cough behind a corner of her apron. "And since Lindy wants to serve this delicious Mexican dip at her New Year's Eve party, I thought I'd give you the basic recipe and then show you how to jazz it up, should you care to." Gathering her class around the butcher block, she gestured at a new painting hanging to the left of the large front window.

"Before we start, I wanted to show you the most splendid Christmas gift I've ever received. What do you think?"

The class oohed and ahhed over an oil painting of a woman's hands. One hand firmly grasped a carrot, while the other was frozen in the act of driving the blade of a wide knife into the end of the vegetable. A scattered pile of paper-thin carrot slices lay to the right of the hand doing the chopping. That was it. James stared and stared at the image, dazzled by the hues chosen to highlight the veins, knuckles, minute lines, freckles, age spots, and shadows of what were undoubtedly Milla's hands. The artist had captured grace, strength, and a sense of culinary giftedness in this focused snapshot of a woman at work in the kitchen. Simply entitled *The Cook* in block letters on the bottom left-hand corner, the painting was unframed and hung from a crude wire on a single nail.

"It's wonderful!" Lindy exclaimed.

"The *emotions* captured in this plain activity," Gillian breathed and moved closer to the painting. "People say the soul is in the eyes, but I think *this* artist is perfectly aware that the soul can reside in many parts of our body. The feet, for instance, are most revealing."

Bennett threw Gillian a perplexed look. "Who did this, Milla?"

"Jackson Henry," she declared. "And I think he's working on a whole pile of hand paintings as we speak."

Lucy had arrived while the class was busy studying the painting. "Wow. James, you must be so proud," she said as she moved to his side.

"I had no idea," he told her without meeting her eyes. With Murphy standing to his left and Lucy on his right, he felt torn between the past and the present. "He stopped painting altogether for quite a while, saying that he was completely stumped and needed fresh subject matter."

"Well, I'd say he found it." Lindy thumped James on the back. "I'm going to have to report this success to my mama, James. She'll want to fill the gallery again, I'm sure of it."

"And I hear more congratulations are in order." Gillian rushed to Lucy and threw her arms around her friend. "You've scheduled your physical exam for Monday, right?"

Lucy blushed. "Yeah, that's right. I think I'm finally ready."

"Where's your training partner?" Bennett asked innocently. "Sullie."

The color on Lucy's cheeks deepened a shade. "He ... um ... he passed both exams last week. He's been officially hired as a deputy in Albemarle County. I helped him pack his stuff earlier this week."

"So he's moved already?" Milla sighed. "I'm so sorry, my dear. But I'm sure you'll see a great deal of him once you're a deputy, too," she added brightly.

The room fell silent as everyone examined Lucy's dejected face.

Lindy, ever the cheerleader, grabbed Lucy's hand and held it tightly. "You're going to pass that test on Monday. And after you do, you're going to be the guest of honor at my party. That means you're going to get the first whack at the adult-themed party piñata!"

"Intriguing." Bennett edged behind Lindy. "What are the contents of said piñata, exactly?"

Lindy winked at Lucy. "You'll just have to wait and see."

Milla waited for this exchange to conclude before she clapped her hands together. "Now, my dears, let's continue with tonight's appetizer."

Once more, Milla was interrupted as the front door was opened, allowing frigid air to seep inside as a couple scurried into the toasty room. James was surprised to see Kinsley alongside a short man. The man helped Kinsley out of her coat and then appraised the group with interest.

"I think that's Gary, her ex," Murphy whispered to James.

Wordlessly, Milla moved toward the pair and enfolded Kinsley in a maternal embrace. Kinsley returned the hug and then smiled hesitantly at her classmates. "Everyone, this is Gary. He took a leave of absence from his job to keep me company for a while. Tonight, after a lot of urging, he finally convinced me to give leaving my house a shot."

"That's for sure," her companion said in a scratchy voice heavy with a New York accent. "No way I could take another episode of *Dr. Phil!*" He nodded and grinned. "I could do that job, anyway. You just tell every guest that they need to *get real* a few dozen times and then plug your latest book. Easy!"

Bennett sniggered. "You better watch it, man. You're in a room packed full of women. Never met a woman who didn't like Dr. Phil."

Gary pretended to bow in apology. "Too true. Still, I think the guy's got a cake life. But don't worry, I won't go trashing Oprah. I'm not *that* stupid. Even Princeton let me graduate. Heeeey!" He put his prominent nose in the air. "What's that awesome smell?"

As the newcomers joined the class by the butcher block, Milla showed her pupils an array of ingredients used to make *chili con queso*.

"Just promise me that you'll never make this with Velveeta." Milla attempted to sound stern. "None of you are so lazy that you can't melt real cheese in a saucepan for a few minutes. I like a combination

189

of Monterey jack and cheddar, but you can also use mozzarella. This recipe also calls for a cup of dry white wine, but you can use a quarter cup of half-and-half if you prefer a nonalcoholic dip."

"What are these?" Gary plucked two peppers from a plate and held them in front of his earlobes. "Look, I'm still wearing my Christmas bulb earrings," he lisped and then pretended to walk like a fashion model down a runway. Everyone laughed. James was pleased to see Kinsley laughing, too.

"Your earrings are Serrano peppers, dear." Milla pointed at the other foods before her. "Jalapeños, an onion, chopped tomatoes, garlic, salt and pepper, olive oil, and ta-da! you've got your base."

"Another meatless dish," Gillian clasped her hands over her breast. "I am so thrilled that our destinies aligned with the help of Lindy over here. I am going to have a fatter recipe box after meeting you, Milla."

"Well, I'm going to have a fatter ass!" Gary exclaimed as he helped himself to an oven-baked tortilla chip coated in Milla's warm *chili con queso*. "Man, this is too damned tasty to be healthy. Reminds me of a lobster dip my mom used to make every summer. 'Course, we had lobsters so fresh they were practically jumping out of the pot, and you gotta eat a pound of butter with every lobster." He toasted Milla with his half-eaten chip. "You must have a pound of cheese in this stuff. Nice work."

After sampling the dip, which was a combination of salty, spicy, and creamy goodness, James had to agree with Gary. It didn't take much wisdom to sense that the Mexican dip was too salty for his blood pressure, so he gloomily restricted himself to one more sample.

"It's certainly not a food for dieters," Milla agreed. "But it's great to eat in small amounts and to serve at parties." She turned to Lindy. "You can add a cup of champagne to yours instead of the wine, since you'll be serving it on New Year's Eve."

Lindy's eyes widened. "Cool."

"And for you carnivores, a nice helping of crumbled sausage will fill your bellies." She poked at Bennett with a wooden spoon. "Just make sure to cook the sausage first. When you're done with your snack, head over to your cook stations. We're making beef tamale pies this evening."

Realizing that he had forgotten his apron, James returned to the coatrack and began rifling through the jackets and scarves to discover that his apron was tucked away beneath both Kinsley's and Gary's coats and sundry accessories. As he began to remove Kinsley's red wool trench, Lucy appeared by his side.

"Want some help?" she asked.

He handed her the red coat. "Sure, thanks." After depositing Gary's leather bomber jacket in her arms, he finally met her eyes. "How are you, Lucy? I mean, with Sullie moving and all."

Lucy shrugged and replied in a defensive tone, "He's not that far away." Then, she seemed to change her mind. Sighing, she frowned and said, "Actually, it wouldn't matter if he lived right next door. He's not interested in me romantically, James. Turns out he never was."

James paused in the act of tying on his apron. Sullie was the reason that he and Lucy broke up, and yet, the man had been undeserving of all the negative vibes James had sent his way. "But it seemed like … you spent so much time together."

"He didn't want to hurt my feelings, and apparently he enjoyed my company, but that's it." Lucy cast her eyes on the floor. "I know I really screwed up what we had, James." Her face was a mixture of anguish and hope as she faced him once again. "Can you forgive me?"

James didn't know what to say. He shot a quick glance toward Murphy, but she was busy browning beef while chatting with Bennett. "I'm not angry with you anymore, Lucy." He didn't want to tell her that he was involved with another woman, especially one that Lucy had been jealous of in the past. "I'm your friend and I'm here if you need me."

Lucy looked as though she might cry at any moment. "So we can't..." She gulped. "We can't just start over? Go back to how things were before?"

He shook his head. "Too much has changed since then. I'm sorry." He knew he was being cowardly by not telling her that he was dating Murphy, but he didn't want to cause her any more pain.

Lucy nodded mutely and returned to her cooking area with a defeated slump to her shoulders. Watching her, James felt as though his heart might break all over again.

"Nothing's ever easy," he muttered and then forced himself to concentrate on his beef tamale pie.

The class flew by and before Milla's students knew it, their pies were being packed into cardboard boxes and their bodies stuffed into parkas, hats, scarves, and gloves. Kinsley and Gary were the first to leave. As soon as they were out the door, Murphy turned to her classmates with appeal in her eyes.

"We could really help Kinsley heal if we allowed her some closure," she said softly. "Just seeing her out tonight made me realize that I haven't done enough to help." Her eyes were mournful. "Parker would have wanted her sister to be surrounded by friends. Right now, she's only got Gary."

Lindy nodded. "I agree, but my party's in two days and McClellan will be there. He must have something up his sleeve. What else can we do?"

The group fell silent as they pulled on gloves and tied thick scarves in knots to protect their exposed necks. James watched as Gillian wound a flimsy red scarf stitched with gold thread around and around her throat until she resembled a male robin. He could hear running water coming from the back kitchen as Milla loaded pots and pans into a commercial dishwasher.

"I think we need to know more about *all* the men in the lives of the Willis sisters," James suggested. "Including the recently arrived Gary."

"And the other vet at Parker's practice," Gillian jumped in. "Though I don't see how anyone who is gentle with animals could be a murderer."

Murphy turned to Lucy. "How could we find out background info on these fellows: Gary Lowe, Colin Crabtree, and Dwight Hutchins?"

Lucy was clearly pleased that the group saw her as the expert in information gathering. As they all began to overheat in their winter outerwear, she pretended to consider the problem carefully, though James sensed she knew exactly what could be done from her desk at the sheriff's department. "I *could* sneak in a few background checks," she offered. "At least we can find out if any of them have criminal records or any other red flags."

Bennett pulled on his mustache. "The police would have done that right away. We need to know more personal things."

"I doubt the police investigated Gary," Lucy countered. "And the more complete a picture we can paint of all three men, the better chance we have of finding a clue." Giving Murphy a sympathetic look, she added, "Strangling another person is very personal. I think this Mr. Sneed must be one of these guys. But which one?"

"Gary's too short," James said quickly. "Unless he was wearing some serious height-enhancing shoes, it couldn't have been him posing as Adam's grandfather."

The group began to shuffle uncomfortably, torn between their desire to solve the riddle and the wish to call it a night.

Lucy edged toward the door and then turned to face her friends. Her face was determined. "We still need to follow through—peek under every rock when it comes to these three. If we keep looking, we might find something the police have missed. So, who can pay Dwight a visit? Gillian?"

Gillian groaned, but reluctantly agreed to take the Dalai Lama back to Parker's practice for a teeth-cleaning session. Apparently, hers was one of the few veterinary clinics in the state practicing dental cleanings without the use of anesthesia. According to the clinic's website, which Gillian had read over quite carefully, the professionals employed a technique they dubbed "the proprietary hold" when handling the fully conscious animals.

"I never even discussed Dwight with June. We were *so* caught up with Colin. Oh, I *am* going to enjoy visiting with her again. I should bring her some of my homemade facial cream. She says the winter weather brings out the *worst* in her skin! I make my own remedy out of all-natural ingredients right from the grocery store. Ground coffee, oatmeal, grape seed oil, juice from the aloe plant in my kitchen—"

"I'll call Kinsley first thing tomorrow and invite Gary to the party," Lindy interrupted before Gillian could thoroughly delve into the specifics of her homemade skin care recipes. "I can slip in some questions about her ex while I've got her on the line."

"And I'll try to do a follow-up interview with Colin regarding his behavior at the Ramsay farm." Murphy quickly explained how Colin had frozen during the difficult delivery of the calf as James had forgotten to tell the group about their discoveries there. He was worried that Lucy might ask questions about why James had accompanied Murphy on the outing, but she seemed particularly interested in the detail of the umbilical cord around the calf's neck.

"What about Colin's alibi on the day of Parker's death?" she asked Murphy.

"Apparently solid enough," Murphy replied ruefully. "He had cases and worked until late in the afternoon. Same story with Dwight." Murphy shrugged. "Of course, we don't know what kind of cases, and both of their assistants were gone before the last job was completed. The assistants leave at closing time, which is five o'clock at both practices."

"But the killer only needed an hour to eat with us, get down to the caves, and wait for the lights to go out," Lindy said. "Mr. Sneed met us at the restaurant, so either Colin or Dwight could have gotten changed and applied the wig and makeup in his car."

Lucy zipped up her down coat. "So even if the police suspect these two, there's obviously not enough proof to make an arrest. I say they could use our help now more than ever." Her eyes lit up. "That must be why McClellan wants everyone at your house, Lindy. He's hoping one of the culprits will make a mistake and say something revealing."

"Seems like a long shot to me." James pulled on a pair of lined leather gloves. "Still, I think you're on the right track, Lucy. We can't give up on this case, even though we've met with dead ends so far. We need to divvy up, investigate, and share what we know at Lindy's, before McClellan and our three suspects get there. Then *we* can watch them just as carefully at the party."

"Well, team." Bennett held the door open for his friends. "Sounds like this is going to be a New Year's Eve to remember. Who knows what's gonna happen by the time the ball drops!"

Milla's Chili con Queso

2 teaspoons olive or vegetable oil
1 medium onion, diced
6 garlic cloves, peeled and finely chopped
8 jalapeño chilies, seeded and chopped
1 Serrano chili, seeded and chopped (or a green chili, if you prefer the taste or can't find Serrano chilies)
2 tomatoes, diced
sprinkle of salt and pepper
1 cup dry white wine
8 ounces shredded Monterey jack cheese
8 ounces shredded sharp cheddar cheese
tortilla chips

Heat the oil in a large skillet. Add the onion, garlic, chilies, and tomatoes. Sprinkle with salt and pepper; sauté over medium heat until the onions are soft and translucent (approximately 5 to 7 minutes). Add the wine. Reduce heat. Add the cheese and stir the mixture until the cheese is completely melted. Serve with tortilla chips warmed in the oven. For a more festive presentation, mix blue and yellow corn tortilla chips or serve tri-colored chips such as those made by La Canasta.

SIXTEEN

MOCHA PROTEIN SHAKE

Sodium per Serving: 250 mg

LUCY ARRIVED AT THE library as James's shift was drawing to a close. James watched her approach from his vantage point on a ladder near the audiobook section. He almost didn't recognize her at first, for the confident posture of her body and the brisk walk seemed to belong to some other woman. Lucy had always been a bit tentative, almost as though she was trying to avoid having others look at her. Now, it was apparent that something had changed. She carried herself like a new woman.

The physical! James suddenly remembered. *It was this morning.*

"It seems as though congratulations might be in order," he said to her as he descended the ladder. "Unless I am reading the look of joy on your face totally wrong."

She smiled and opened her arms to be hugged, and James did not hesitate to do so, though he didn't draw her in as closely as he once would have.

"I passed!" Lucy said exuberantly as she disengaged from the quick embrace. "I brought us a protein shake to celebrate. Plus, I've got some info on our suspects."

James gave her a quizzical look. "Oh? Better come on back to my office."

As Lucy settled herself in one of the chairs across from James's desk, James retrieved a notepad from his top drawer and uncapped a pen. He didn't actually intend to take notes, but he wanted something to distract his hands in case their dialogue turned uncomfortably intimate.

"Tell me about the test first," he said, taking a sip of the protein shake. It tasted like mocha-flavored sand with an aftershock of soy, and he did his best not to grimace.

"It's kind of like an obstacle course," Lucy explained. "It covers 150 yards and it must be completed in one minute and thirty-six seconds or you fail."

"That seems like a lot of ground to cover in a small window of time."

Lucy slurped her shake. "You have no idea. First, I had to sprint for twenty-five yards, and then jump a distance of three feet." She paused to grin. "You know me, James. I've got legs the size of one of the seven dwarves. If you step on the rope marking the distance on either end of the jump, you fail. I think this whole town has seen me jumping over sidewalk cracks and leaping like a deranged lunatic across big puddles after every thunderstorm."

James smiled, trying to imagine her bounding around Quincy's Gap like a ballerina, except that her tutu was replaced by a blue down parka.

"Don't go getting any visions about me as the Sugarplum Fairy," Lucy teased as though she had read his mind. "Next, I had to climb a five-foot fence. That was easy. I've been practicing that at home with my dogs. They pretend to chase me like an attack dog would, and I have to get over the fence before Bon Jovi has the opportunity to nip me in the rear! After the fence, I had to go all commando and crawl under a low rope bridge, fling myself through a window opening, go up and down a set of stairs a few times, and then pull the trigger on a gun within a stationary border. If you jerk the gun into the border, you fail. You must hold perfectly still, even though you're huffing and puffing like a marathon runner who's just crossed the finish line."

James found that his mouth was hanging open. "All of this in a minute and a half? That's ludicrous!"

Lucy seemed pleased by his amazement. "*And* I forgot to mention that I had to drag that stupid one-hundred-sixty-pound dummy five yards, sprint between each and every obstacle, *and* identify the suspect described to me before the timer ever started." She examined her nails. "Guess that's what they'll be expecting me to do as a deputy."

"I am really impressed with you, Lucy." James thumped her on the back as though they were two men in a bar celebrating a football team's victory. "You have worked hard for this!" He smiled warmly at her. "It must feel so good to set a high goal for yourself and then achieve it. Not many people finish what they start. Good for you, Lucy. Good for you."

Lucy blushed and then gazed out the window at the barren trees bordering the library parking lot. "But look what it cost me, James. I almost alienated my truest friends and ... and I *did* lose you."

Made instantly uncomfortable by her candor, James tried to be flippant. "I'm right here, aren't I?"

"You know what I mean," Lucy replied darkly.

A heavy silence pervaded the room, and James occupied himself by sipping on his shake as though he were desperately thirsty. Lucy followed suit until both were sucking on dregs. They toyed with their straws until they had each drained every drop of mocha shake.

Putting her cup down, Lucy cleared her throat as though she were trying to banish the gloom that had taken over their conversation. "I have other big news to tell you." She tossed her cup neatly into the garbage can in the corner of the room, even though it was at least four feet away. "Colin Crabtree's office was burglarized late Saturday night."

"The night of our Fix 'n Freeze class?" James exclaimed, relieved to be able to shift gears. "What was taken?"

"From what I heard over the wire—you gotta remember that Crabtree practices in a different county—all of the petty cash, a few sedatives, and his entire supply of some other drug. Hold on, I have the name written down."

She pulled a piece of tattered notebook paper from her purse. As she did so, several gum wrappers, two used tissues, and a flurry of grocery store recipes rained onto the carpet. James shook his head in unpleasant surprise over the amount of clutter Lucy managed to cram into her bag, car, and every room in her house. He expected her to gather up the assorted papers and place them in the trash, but she simply shoved them back into her purse and then examined the crumpled paper left in her hand. "Here. It's called Wildnil. Can you look that up on the Internet? I didn't have a chance."

"Sure." James turned his attention to his computer and, within seconds, had a basic definition of the drug. "Let's see, its ingredients are carfentanil citrate, and it's used as a tranquilizer for large animals." He paused. "Oh man. It's also extremely potent to humans. This site goes on and on about the dangers."

He and Lucy exchanged worried looks. "And Colin was conveniently sick on Saturday night." Lucy screwed up her lip as she thought. "Maybe he staged the burglary and plans to use Wildnil on someone."

"Who?" James wondered, feeling a headache coming on. He realized that he had forgotten to take his blood pressure medicine that morning. Settling for two aspirin, he gulped them down with the remnants of a warm, flat Diet Coke that had been on his desk since lunchtime.

"I don't know." Lucy pointed at her piece of paper. "That's not all my news, either. I called Solmes Investments today, just to take a shot at finding out more about Gary, and guess what?"

James rubbed his temples. "Do I even want to know?"

Lucy's eyes gleamed. "They told me that no one by that name works for their firm."

"But Murphy said he was talking about his job at Solmes during our cooking class. It's where he and Kinsley met." His mouth grew dry. "Oh Lord, do you think Kinsley even knows that he's been lying about his job?"

Lucy glanced at her watch and then stood up in alarm. "James! It's after five! I wanted you to call the company pretending to be one of Gary's clients and demand to know what happened to him. We've got to know more before we go to Lindy's party tonight!"

James felt panic surfacing in his belly. "First the robbery and now this news about Kinsley's lesser half. Still…what difference does Gary lying about his job make?" He stared at the phone number Lucy had shoved in front of him. "McClellan will be at Lindy's, so we don't have to worry about anything bad happening tonight. I can always call Solmes after New Year's."

"Come on, James!" Lucy pleaded. "See if someone is still there answering the phones. I think we need to know *now*."

"I'm no good at this kind of stuff," James protested. "Who could I pretend to be?"

Lucy had turned pink with frustration. "Just think of some snobby name from your stint at William and Mary. Some of your students must have been from rich, blue-blood families. Put on a drawl and act angry that your money manager isn't returning your calls. Just do it! Now!" she barked at him.

Responding to the command in Lucy's tone, James's fingers began dialing the New York number. Strangely, he felt a calm fill him as the phone began to ring, and he cast a quick glance at Lucy. He was surprised to realize that despite everything that had happened between them, he still wanted to impress her.

"Solmes Investments," a nasal voice answered after three rings. "May I help you?" The woman sounded as though she would prefer to do anything but.

"Gary Lowe," James stated in an elongated drawl, deliberately omitting the word "please."

After a pause, in which James could hear the sounds of murmuring and glasses clinking in the background, the woman tiredly said, "Mr. Lowe is no longer with this firm."

"What!" James thundered. "What are you talking about? I go to Europe for a few months and come back to hear *this*! Where the hell is he?" James could feel his heart drumming against his rib cage as he shouted into the phone.

"I'm not at liberty to say, sir. Actually, we're closed at this time, so if you could call back after New Year—"

"DO YOU KNOW WHO I AM?" James hollered at the top of his lungs. "THIS IS RANDOLPH OLIVER THE FOURTH!" He gulped in air. "You get me someone who can tell me where my broker is or so help me, I will have your job, missy!"

"Um…" James had finally rattled the woman's icy composure. "I'm pretty new here, sir, but if you can just hold…"

"Oh, give me that phone!" another voice dictated from the background. "Whatdoyawant?" a woman lisped as though she was well on her way to becoming drunk.

James spoke excruciatingly slowly as if the person on the other end of the line wouldn't comprehend him otherwise. He was as condescending as he could possibly be. "I would like *someone* with half a brain in their little heads to tell me where in the Sam Hill Gary Lowe has gone. Why is he not sitting there at his desk *right this very minute* making me more money?"

"Because he was fired for front running, you arrogant piece of shit. Happy New Year!" The woman giggled, hiccupped, and then slammed down the phone.

Replacing the receiver, James immediately returned to Google in order to search for the term "front running."

"Wow!" Lucy shuffled her chair closer. "I didn't know you had that in you, James. You should join the Shenandoah Players."

"No teasing." James was relieved to return to his quieter tone of voice. "Gary was fired, Lucy. For something called front running. I'm checking out what that means. Aha, here we go."

Lucy picked up her chair and moved it alongside James's. "What did you find?" she asked eagerly.

"I don't know much about the financial world, but according to this definition, it's when a trader makes his own order before executing a big order being placed by the company or a customer he works for. Because of the big order, he knows how the market is going to be affected and tries to make a nice bundle for himself in advance."

"I'm totally confused by what you just said." Lucy shook her head. "Can you explain *exactly* what Gary did in *Stockbroking for Dummies* terms?"

James reread the definition on the computer screen. "I'll do my best. Okay, so Solmes Investments decides to buy ten thousand shares of stock for, ah ... Meaty Treats Dog Food."

"Meaty Treats!" Lucy laughed. "You're making that up, right?"

"Right. Now, Gary sees the order for ten thousand shares and thinks the purchase will drive up the price of Meaty Treats stock. So he buys a bunch of stock at the current price, executes the order for the ten thousand, and then sells his shares at the higher price. He makes a lot of money in just a few minutes."

"How much money?"

James shrugged. "Could be thousands every time."

"But he got caught and then fired because of this front running."

"Apparently," James continued in a voice laced with sarcasm, "he was fired and then magically appeared in Quincy's Gap to stand by Kinsley in her time of need. How touching."

"Doesn't hurt that Kinsley's worth millions, either." Lucy was angry. "We've got to tell her, James! That poor woman has been through enough pain. I'm not going to let some greedy, cheating, lying, pig scum cause her any more grief!"

"That's the Lucy I know and love," James said fondly and then, watching Lucy's eyes alight with happiness, realized that he had chosen the wrong words in which to compliment his friend's loyalty and desire to see justice done. He made a big show of examining the time on the wall clock over Lucy's head. "Uh, guess we'd better part ways for now. I'll see you at Lindy's. I know she wanted to meet up and share information before the other guests arrive. What time are we supposed to be there?" he asked, even though he knew the answer.

"She wants us all there at eight—including Murphy, who seems to have become an unofficial supper club member," Lucy said with a trace of acerbity.

James didn't reply and he couldn't move, as he was trapped between Lucy and the far wall of his office. "Are you dressing up, since you're the guest of honor?" he inquired, hoping to stir her into action by addressing her vanity.

Lucy wore an enigmatic expression as she stood. "I sure am. You won't believe your eyes tonight, James."

Following her to the door, James had a feeling that Lucy was absolutely correct, and that many unpredictable and eye-opening things might occur at Lindy's party.

SEVENTEEN
CHAMPAGNE &
CRANBERRY JUICE

Sodium
per
Serving:

9 mg

MURPHY CALLED JAMES TO tell him she was running late and he should head over to the party without her. He arrived at Lindy's small bungalow ten minutes early and was delighted by the sight of her outdoor decorations. In lieu of white or multicolored Christmas lights, Lindy had strung the straggly azalea bushes flanking her front door with dozens of glowing chili peppers.

Lindy opened the door, kissed him hello, and thrust a paper hat into his hand. "It's a dress code requirement, Professor." She grinned and gestured to her own fuchsia tiara bearing the words *Happy New Year* in silver glitter. "Unless you want one of these."

James popped the weightless lime-green cone on his head, admiring how sharp Lindy looked in a silver blouse, large silver hoop earrings, and a flowing black skirt made of some kind of shimmer-

206

ing fabric. "No thanks, I'll settle for the annoyance of having a string irritating the underside of my chin all night. By the way, you look fantastic, Lindy. Luis Chavez doesn't stand a chance."

"I'll drink to that! Can I get you some fiesta punch?" she asked, leading James into the kitchen. She dunked a soup ladle into an enormous ceramic bowl and filled a hot-pink plastic tumbler to the brim with pale red liquid.

"What are we drinking this evening?" he wondered as he took in the other decorations. Lindy had strung a group of red, yellow, pink, and lime-green balloons across the doorways leading into her kitchen and living room. A piñata shaped like the children's cartoon character Dora the Explorer dangled down from an eyehook at one end of the living room ceiling while a disco ball hung from the other. Rainbow-colored streamers were strung across all the light fixtures in each of the four downstairs rooms. Small tables covered with striped plastic cloths were arranged throughout the living room and a range of delicious smells were emanating from Lindy's oven and stovetop.

"It's champagne and cranberry juice," Lindy answered James's question. "Very refreshing, isn't it? Oh, there's the doorbell." She grabbed some hats and tiaras and hustled to greet Gillian and Bennett, who both gushed over the transformation of Lindy's house.

"The colors are simply *pulsing* with life and spirit!" Gillian shouted brightly. "I can just *feel* the renewal that a new year brings!"

Bennett mumbled something in agreement and then said, "What's with the kid piñata?"

"She's a Spanish-speaking cartoon," Lindy replied, directing her new guests into the kitchen where James was already ladling two glasses of fiesta punch into pink tumblers. "This is a Spanish-themed party, remember?"

"Hello?" Lucy's voice called out from the front door. "Can I come on in?"

"Oh!" Lindy marched into the hall and exclaimed "Oh!" again.

When Lucy joined them in the kitchen, James could see why Lindy had been at a loss for words. While Gillian's outfit was typically eccentric in that she wore an electric orange poncho stitched with green llamas over a gold lamé tank dress, Lucy was wearing a purple ruffled dress that could have been featured in *Sixteen Candles* or a Bangles video.

"What's with the eighties getup?" Bennett queried and turned to Lindy. "Were we supposed to dress in some kind of special way tonight?"

"No," Lucy quickly answered and then fluffed a tier of absurd ruffles. "This was the dress I wore to my senior prom. My *high school* prom. See? It fits again!"

All four of her friends examined her figure as she pivoted in a circle. There was no doubt that Lucy looked terrific and had toned her body into far better condition than it had been in during the previous New Year's Eve, but she was still a bit voluptuous to be wearing this particular style of dress.

"I figured since I was the guest of honor," Lucy continued, yanking at the hem of the dress, which was riding up both of her thighs, "I should break out something I wore when I was in good shape."

James tore his eyes from the row of wrinkled fabric across her hips and around her waist where the dress was clearly too tight. "You look great," he assured her kindly, and she beamed in response.

"A toast to our future deputy!" Lindy hailed her friend while raising her glass. After they drank, Lindy gestured toward the living room. "Let's get talking before the others get here. I've got some tapas for us to enjoy while we're trying to unravel Parker's mystery."

As they settled themselves in the next room, the doorbell rang again and Lindy ushered Murphy inside after handing her a yellow tiara. "Help yourself to some punch in the kitchen and then come join us. We're about to share our latest findings."

"Good," Murphy said. "I have a feeling that this is our last shot to figure things out."

"Why?" Lindy wondered in concern. "No, never mind. I'll find out when you tell everyone else."

Murphy entered the living room with a glass of punch and a dazzling smile. James locked eyes with her and tried not to let his gaze wander all over her body, which looked incredibly sexy in a pair of off-white suede pants and a tight, black top with a low neckline. She wore high-heeled black boots and a wide belt with silver studs. Like Lindy, she had also added a pair of saucy hoop earrings to her ensemble.

After exchanging kisses on the cheek with the supper club members, Murphy took a seat in a folding chair next to where James was perched on the end of the couch. With Lucy on his other side, he found himself wishing that he had sat in the leather chair next to the television, but Bennett had claimed it first.

"Let me hand out some snacks while I tell you what I figured out, which isn't much," Lindy said as she began to place an assortment of finger food on paper plates. "I've been racking my brains over how someone could have learned Adam Sneed's name, that he was a student in one of my art classes, and that all of my students were taking a field trip to Luray Caverns."

"I don't mean to disturb your train of thought," Gillian interrupted, "but these mushrooms are absolutely *inspired*."

"Thanks. Milla gave me a bunch of recipes for tonight." Lindy grinned. "Anyway, I realized, after rereading my daily planner, that the school had hosted Parents' Night a week before the field trip. My students were showcasing their work, and I was begging for chaperone volunteers at the time. Any Tom, Dick, or Harry could have learned Adam's name and all the details about the trip that night. I handed out fliers to everyone I could. And I saw so many people that night—parents, grandparents, third cousins once removed— the killer could have been there in disguise and I would never have known."

"Nothing about the fake Mr. Sneed looked familiar to you when you saw him at Johnny Appleseed's?" Lucy asked. Lindy shook her head no.

"I'll go next," Gillian volunteered. "I dragged poor Bennett with me to get Dalai Lama's teeth cleaned, which my sweet darling did not enjoy in the least, the poor soul."

"Him or me either," Bennett grumbled. "I had to sneak into Dwight's office while Gillian drank tea and ate cookies behind the front desk. And I was out of sight for so long that Gillian told June I had diarrhea and was locked in the men's room!"

Gillian smirked. "Well, I had to think of something. June was *very* sympathetic, too. She offered to brew Bennett some wild blackberry tea to assist with his *healing*, but he insisted on leaving as soon as he was done investigating. Rushing about is so *stressful* on the bowels, Bennett."

"Can we keep in mind that I didn't actually *have* diarrhea, Gillian?" Bennett fumed.

"June also told me that the reason Dwight moved to our gloriously beautiful part of the country was that Parker was one of a very small group of veterinarians practicing animal dental cleanings without the use of anesthesia. Dwight wanted to be trained by such an avant-garde thinker and, indeed, Parker taught him all she knew." Gillian sighed. "June is very impressed with how Dwight learned to look an animal in the eye, speak to it in calm and gentle tones, and calm its fears."

Bennett rolled his eyes. "Anyway, while those two nut jobs gabbed away about kitty dentistry and whether fruit flies have a soul, I learned that Dwight went to Princeton. That's curious because it's the school where Gary went, too."

Murphy leaned forward in her chair. "Did you follow that trail? Did you call Princeton?"

"*First*, we waited for the moment to feel right," Gillian stated while fluffing her hair, which was dusted with some sort of glitter. "We needed a very lucky time of day, so we phoned the Alumni Office just before sundown. Bennett pretended to be calling on behalf of the Luray Post Office. He said that a postal box belonging to Dwight Hutchins had just been switched over to a Mr. Gary Lowe and wanted to know which one should be receiving the Princeton alumni mail. Once Bennett was told the two men graduated the same year *and* both belonged to the same fraternity, we felt that there was just too much coincidence in this picture."

The group fell silent. "It's clear to see how Dwight benefits from Parker's death," Murphy finally said. "He has full control of a successful practice now."

"What does Gary gain?" James wondered aloud. "Is he planning to help Dwight with his future investments or is he up to something more devious?"

"Devious?" Lindy was bewildered until James explained the discovery he and Lucy had made about the former stockbroker.

"Deceit can cloud much *deeper psychological issues*," Gillian breathed and then shuddered.

Lucy absently pulled a piece of chicken from a kebab and plopped it in her mouth. "There's more," she said when he was finished chewing. She told the group about the burglary of Colin's office.

"That's where my story enters the picture." Murphy waved a kebab at Lindy. "These are almost savory enough to distract me from what I have to share, but it's not much of a tale. As soon as I heard about the burglary from a friend of mine at *The Harrisonburg Herald*, I met up with Colin at his office where he was going over everything that had been taken. He's really concerned about the missing ampoules of Wildnil. He and the local law enforcement officials think some kids or even some crazy hunters plan on using the drugs to go after hibernating black bears."

Gillian leapt to her feet. "That would be monstrous!"

"Well, I'm not convinced their logic is correct," Murphy told Gillian in a soothing tone. "It seems odd that this burglary occurred at the same time Gary showed up in Virginia."

James tried to absorb all of the information he had heard thus far. Suddenly, he remembered an important detail. He turned to Murphy. "Did you ask Colin about his lack of action at Ramsay's farm?"

She nodded. "He said he thought the calf was already dead and was upset because he couldn't do anything about it."

"That sounds like a pile of crap if you ask me," Bennett remarked. "I'm going in for more punch. Helps me wrap my mind around all of this. Who wants some?"

As Bennett refilled glasses, Murphy finished her narrative. "I have to admit that I wasn't sure if I believed him, either. It's hard to get below that suave surface level and catch a glimpse of the real Colin Crabtree."

"Perhaps he's a skilled actor . . ." Lindy let her thought hang in the air.

"But what's *his* motive?" Lucy broke the spell. "Dwight's the only one with a clear motive as of this point. Add in opportunity and I'd say he's looking more and more like our guy."

"Wait a minute," Bennett countered. "We've got no idea where Gary was when Parker was killed. I highly doubt the cops have checked *his* alibi either."

"But Gary couldn't have doubled as Mr. Sneed," James reminded the group. "He's too short."

Gillian drained her cup in three gulps. "I'm more confused than ever!" she wailed and then flopped back onto the sofa. James felt the same way.

Suddenly, the doorbell rang. Lindy glanced at her watch. "Our powwow time is up. I can see two teachers from Blue Ridge High outside and four more coming up the walk."

"Just keep your eyes and ears open," Lucy ordered. "I'll fill McClellan in on what we've learned and see if he'll share any new information with me. Since he and his men found that missing boy and returned him to his family safe and sound, he ought to have plenty of free time to help us solve *our* case."

"Wait just a minute!" Murphy frowned as Lindy moved to open the door. "*I'm* the one who's been in touch with McClellan since day one. Parker was *my* friend, so *I'll* relay our recent discoveries to the sergeant."

Lucy scowled at Murphy, and James was certain a catfight was about to erupt. Fortunately, Lindy had enough sense to put an end to any more arguments by inviting her co-workers inside.

A half a dozen women of all ages burst into Lindy's house, accepted tiaras, and squealed with delight over the festive balloons and streamers. Soon, a dozen party guests were eating and drinking as though they had lined up at a trough. Principal Chavez had also appeared and didn't seem to be paying Lindy any more attention than any other members of his faculty. As a result, Lindy alternated between smiling in front of the teachers and sulking in the presence of the supper club members.

Sergeant McClellan sauntered in at half past nine, wearing jeans and a maroon sweater, but even if he weren't the tallest man in the room, his authoritative presence would prevent him from ever blending in. Murphy allowed him to fill a plate and pour himself a cup of 7UP before leading him off to a quiet corner of the kitchen. As they did their best to whisper over the sounds of salsa music blaring from a boom box in the living room, their heads close together as though they were exchanging endearments, they noticed Colin and Dwight arrive and join the partygoers.

They had not entered at the same time, but James watched them closely as they shook hands and held a short, polite conversation. Eventually, a cute blonde in a beaded sheath struck up a flirtation with Colin and dragged him reluctantly away to dance with her in the living room.

By the time Kinsley and Gary appeared at ten, the party had grown a bit raucous. Few of the supper club members even noticed their arrival.

Lindy was perspiring as she replenished the punch bowl once again. She then arranged a tray of steaming garlicky shrimp onto an empty platter bearing the crumbs of what were once an assemblage of ham croquettes. People flitted in and out of the kitchen, offering to carry out plates refilled with scrumptious food.

"Oh, I completely forgot about the *chili con queso!*" James heard Lindy declare as he searched in her pantry for the garbage can. Turning up the heat on one of her stove burners, she turned to James. "Can you keep an eye on this? I see one of the PE teachers going after the piñata, and I don't want to break it until just before midnight."

James took the lid off the stockpot and sniffed. The simmering cheese dip smelled exactly like Milla's.

"James," Murphy beckoned from the doorway leading to the hall. McClellan stood like a sequoia behind her. "Join us for a moment. The sergeant plans on checking out Gary Lowe's alibi. The ones given by our two vets are pretty weak, but there's no way to prove when they left their offices. Man, my throat is getting hoarse. One second." She nipped into the kitchen, filled two tumblers with punch, and handed one to McClellan. He smiled at her appreciatively, and James felt a prick of jealousy.

The sergeant took a small sip and grimaced. "All right, I'm going to chat with Ms. Willis and her friend—"

A collective hoot followed by energetic applause eclipsed the remainder of McClellan's sentence.

Lindy suddenly appeared before the trio, her brown eyes even rounder than usual. "They got married!" she whispered in shock.

"Who?" James asked.

"Gary and Kinsley! Yesterday!" Lindy blinked slowly. "They flew to Vegas Sunday morning and just came back today. Kinsley says they came to the party right from the airport." She shook her head rapidly as though trying to clear her mind. "I've got to get the stuff off the stove."

James watched Lindy dish *chili con queso* into a half a dozen cereal bowls. She grabbed random guests and ordered them to disperse the dip around the house. She then ripped open bags of tortilla chips and, without bothering to warm them in the oven, dumped them onto paper plates and distributed those as well.

James, Murphy, and McClellan were still absorbing the stunning news.

"Guess there's no prenup if they went to Vegas," Murphy mumbled, her expression troubled.

"Wonder if he's told her about getting fired from Solmes," James worried as he felt his anger rising. "Of course, that little detail might have hurt his chance of becoming a multimillionaire."

McClellan handed his full cup of punch to Murphy. "Excuse me, folks. I think I'll go congratulate the newlyweds."

As McClellan moved off, James noticed Kinsley heading in their direction, a smile igniting her lovely face. She pointed at the white T-shirt she wore beneath a black blazer. The text, in block letters, read *Bride*. "That's me. Mrs. Kinsley Lowe. The bride! Crazy, huh?"

Murphy elbowed the frown from James's mouth and gave Kinsley a brief hug. "Which one of you came up with this wild scheme?" She laughed with forced gaiety.

Kinsley, who was holding one of the bowls of *chili con queso* in one hand and a plastic cup stuffed with tortilla chips in the other, set the bowl on a nearby table and began eating with gusto as she considered Murphy's question. James had a flashback of the sight of Kinsley at the Custard Cottage, polishing off her double-scoop cone in record time.

"This is *so* good," she moaned. "I haven't eaten for hours, so forgive me if I stuff myself in a most unladylike manner. Now, whose idea was it?" She glanced up at the ceiling while searching her memory. "We talked about it a bit when we both lived in New York, but then we broke up because I wanted to lead a slower life. After ... the funeral, we came back here and Gary told me that he had quit his job and was ready to live anywhere as long as we could be together. I'd never heard anything so romantic!" She loaded another chip and held it an inch away from her lips. "The whole run-off-to-Vegas-thing was all Gary. I haven't even had a chance to tell my parents yet!"

She held out the bowl of *chili con queso* to James and Murphy. They both declined and watched in fascinated silence as Kinsley devoured the rest of the dip. "Now I'm thirsty!" she laughed giddily. "I'm going for more punch."

As soon as Kinsley moved off, Lucy, Bennett, and Gillian gathered in front of James and Murphy. Gillian's face was shining from the exertion of her unique style of frantic dancing and Bennett's eyes twinkled as a result of several cups of fiesta punch. Lucy, on the other hand, seemed cross. She continuously tugged on her dress at both ends while casting covert glances at Dwight, Colin, and Gary.

"I can't believe she married that punk!" she spat over the strains of a mariachi band.

Gillian pushed a cloud of orange hair off her forehead. "Maybe he told her everything and they entered into their union with open hearts and open minds."

"Damned unlikely," Bennett muttered.

"What about our other suspects?" Murphy inquired.

Lucy shrugged. "Dwight's barely spoken to anyone since he's been here and believe me, more than one of Lindy's co-workers has tried to bring him out of his shell. He just stands against the wall and glares at Colin."

"I don't think he's crazy about having girls flirt with him only *after* they've been shot down by Colin," Bennett commented.

"Pah!" Lindy spluttered, pushing her way between Bennett and Gillian. "Dwight's just a wet blanket. Colin's tried to talk to Dwight a bunch of times, but he keeps getting the brush-off. Believe me, I've been watching those two."

"Yeah, you kind of disappeared for a bit. Were you hiding behind a curtain or somethin'?" Bennett teased.

Surprisingly, Lindy blushed. "Maybe. Come on, it's time for the piñata."

Lindy abruptly turned off the stereo to a chorus of boisterous complaints. Ignoring these, she announced Lucy's triumph and declared that, as the guest of honor, Lucy got to take the first swing at Dora. She then blindfolded Lucy with a festive chartreuse scarf, put a yardstick in her hands, and spun her around three times.

"Now, I took all the pictures off the wall, but try not to knock out anyone's teeth. I don't think my insurance covers party hazards." Lindy backed away. "Vámonos!" she exclaimed. "Hit it, Lucy!"

Lucy took a great swing at the air and clipped the piñata on the foot, but the pink, purple, and yellow papier-mâché creation was tougher than it looked. She took another swing, which landed square on the piñata figure's rump, but it didn't break. The crowd began giggling en masse as guest after guest failed to cause even the tiniest of cracks to appear on the piñata.

It was at this point that James decided to take a visual stock of the three suspects. As he glanced around, he was shocked to see that Kinsley lay draped across Lindy's sofa, her head in Gary's lap as he watched images of Times Square flash on the muted television. Kinsley's eyes were closed and it looked as though she had fallen asleep. Gary absently stroked a strand of her blonde hair and seemed utterly content. A small smile uplifted the corners of his mouth as he noticed his wedding band catch a glint of light from the disco ball twirling from the ceiling of Lindy's living room.

Colin was next in line to take a whack at the piñata, but Dwight was nowhere to be seen. In fact, McClellan appeared to be absent as well. James did a quick walkthrough of the downstairs and then stepped out into the freezing night by way of Lindy's kitchen door. He carried a full bag of trash with him and made a big show of stuffing it into a dented metal can on the side of the house as he scanned the street. There was Dwight, hands stuffed into the pockets of his coat, walking briskly toward his car.

Seconds later, he was gone. But just as James was about to return to the warmth of the house, he noticed another car pull out and head in the same direction as Dwight's Volvo wagon. He watched until the taillights disappeared around a curve in the road and then froze in fear as a figure detached itself from the shadow of an ancient maple in the front yard of the house next door. The man, for James was certain that no woman possessed the looming and powerful presence of this specter, stepped into the circle of light created by Lindy's lamppost, and James exhaled in relief. It was only McClellan.

Back inside, shouts of triumph followed by exclamations and the clinking of hard objects striking the wood floor indicated that someone had finally released the contents of the piñata. In the living room, the sound for the TV had been restored and Dick Clark was tapping on his expensive watch and gesturing at the ball behind him.

"In just a few minutes, folks, that ball, weighing over one thousand pounds and made entirely out of Waterford crystal, is going to drop." He plastered an expectant grin on his ageless face. "Better get close to the person you'd like to kiss, as we'll be starting the countdown following these messages."

Dick Clark was replaced by a car commercial showing an attractive yet rather smug-looking woman expertly fielding one hairpin turn after another.

"I don't think there's been an original car commercial in years," James heard Lucy comment from behind him. "Did you see what Lindy put in the piñata? It was stuffed with candy and little bottles of tequila! They'll be talking about this party at Blue Ridge High for years!"

James mumbled something unintelligible, dismayed to see that Murphy was pouring champagne into two plastic flutes. She glanced up as she poured and smiled as their eyes met. Feeling a tightening in his gut, James searched about for an excuse that would prevent him from being sandwiched between his ex-girlfriend and his current girlfriend at the stroke of midnight.

"Please," he uttered under his breath in a panic. No luck. Dick Clark's porcelain veneers were once again glowing on the television screen.

"Hope you've got your champagne handy, because we're just thirty seconds away from a new year!" he chirped.

At that moment, as Murphy was crossing from the kitchen into the living room and Lucy was yanking her dress into place and preparing to plant a romantic kiss on James's lips, Gary made an attempt to wake his slumbering bride.

"Kinsley," he said, lowly at first, but loud enough for James to hear. He repeated her name twice more, and then tried to push her to a sitting position. She immediately slumped back onto the couch, falling facedown into the cushions. "Kinsley!" Gary's voice held a note of alarm as he rolled his new wife over and tapped her cheeks with the palm of his hand.

Gillian, who was standing nearby, leaned toward the couple and asked in concern, "Is she all right?"

"Ten!" Dick Clark announced, and the room began counting in unison.

"Nine!" Lucy yelled as she closed in on James's right flank.

Gary looked up at Gillian with appeal in his eyes. "I can't wake her up!"

Gillian bent over Kinsley's form and frowned.

"Five!" Murphy chimed in on James's left, and she held out a flute for him to take.

James didn't reach for the drink. His eyes were fixed on Gillian. Suddenly, his friend waved at him. "James, I need you!"

"Three!" the partygoers screamed.

Just as Lucy was about to place a proprietary hand on his arm, James pushed forward through the crowd and sank to his knees next to Kinsley. He saw the rise and fall of her chest but was frightened by the slackness of her face. For a second, he was transported back to Luray Caverns and was gazing upon Parker's lifeless form in horror.

"Two!"

Through the tangle of people, James was unable to see Murphy, but Lucy had repositioned herself in order to watch James, and he caught her eye immediately.

"Call an ambulance!" he roared over the other guests, who had just hollered "One!" at the top of their lungs.

And then the room erupted. "HAPPY NEW YEAR!" was shouted over and over again all around the house, paper horns were blown, streamers were ripped from the ceiling, and balloons were batted about as they floated down, released from their crêpe anchors.

A set of impossibly long fingers clamped onto James's shoulder.

"Step aside, please," McClellan ordered in a bass rumble that seemed to permeate through the cacophony of the revelers. He checked Kinsley's pulse, gently lifted an eyelid in order to examine her pupils, and then turned a stony stare upon Gary. "How long has she been like this?"

Gary shrugged. "I dunno. Two hours, maybe. She's had a bunch of that red stuff, and she's been through a lot lately," he added defensively. "Who are you anyway? You a doctor or something?"

"I'm with the State Police," McClellan answered and then scooped Kinsley up into his praying mantis arms. "I'm taking her to the hospital. I can get her there a lot quicker than waiting for the paramedics. Emergency services are always stretched to the limit on New Year's Eve," he informed Gary and then started walking.

"Wait a minute!" Gary protested, but then he paused, as though he wasn't quite sure what his protest was about. "I'm coming with you, then!" he added and then trailed after the sergeant, who cut a swath through the crowd and left a wake of gaping mouths and anxious whispers.

Within seconds of McClellan's departure, two members of the local law enforcement arrived. Lucy's boss, Sheriff Huckabee, and her least favorite co-worker, a redheaded chauvinist named Keith Donovan, entered the house. Huckabee, who bore a close resemblance to a walrus due to his large girth and flaring gray mustache, made a beeline for Lindy.

"Party's over, Ms. Perez."

"What is going on?" Lindy put her hands on her hips as she watched her guests make hasty departures.

"One of your guests is a murderer," Huckabee replied as Donovan rudely hustled Lindy's friends out the door. "But don't worry, we know *exactly* who it is."

EIGHTEEN

BARBECUED CHICKEN BREAST

Sodium
per
Serving:

1060 mg

JAMES SLEPT LATE ON New Year's Day. Amazingly, his father didn't seem hell-bent on waking him up in order to have his breakfast cooked. In fact, it was a phone call from Lucy that finally forced James to rise from the layers of blankets made warm by his slumbering body.

"I'm at the station," Lucy explained, meaning that she was calling from her desk at work. "Huckabee's told me everything about our case so I thought I'd get our phone tree going, starting with you."

Yawning, James rubbed sleep from his eyes. "Okay," he croaked, "but I'm going to fix some coffee while you talk."

"Gee, can you at least *pretend* to sound interested?" Lucy's enthusiasm turned sour.

Downstairs, James was delighted to see that a pot of coffee had been brewed and the glass carafe was still warm to the touch. "Yes!" he declared in relief, and Lucy believed he was responding to her.

"That's better. Now," she inhaled for dramatic effect, which was lost on James. He was too busy fixing his coffee just right and wondering if there were any eggs left in the fridge. "First of all, Kinsley's going to be fine. She was released from Shenandoah General early this morning."

"That's great news," James replied guiltily. In his state of fatigue, he had almost forgotten about the young woman's frightening physical state the night before. "She was like Sleeping Beauty," he remarked. "What was wrong with her, Lucy?"

"She was poisoned!" Lucy whispered with a mixture of horror and delight. "With a very high dose of Wildnil. Does that brand name ring any bells?"

James took a grateful sip of coffee and felt the blood coursing sluggishly through his veins pick up a bit of speed. "That's the potent drug stolen from Colin's office, right?"

"Yep. A whole mess of it was put in one of the bowls of *chili con queso*."

"Wow," he breathed. "But how can she be fine? I thought that stuff was really potent to humans?"

"Apparently it takes a long time to work if it's ingested," Lucy informed him. "At first, it just makes you super sleepy. Dwight should have injected it directly if he wanted Kinsley to die, but who knows what he wanted!"

"So Dwight's definitely the killer, huh." James was more than ready to accept this assumption and put the mystery of Parker's death behind him.

"Dwight was questioned all night and it's not looking good for him. There was an ampoule of Wildnil beneath the driver's seat of his car and a pair of muddy boots in the trunk that are an exact match to a set of tracks left outside of Colin's office. McClellan and his team are searching Dwight's house today."

"Has he confessed to anything?" James wondered.

"No. Just the opposite. He claims that someone has set him up and swears that he's never been to Colin's office in his life and has no reason whatsoever to hurt Kinsley."

That gave James pause. "That does raise a point. Why *would* he wish her harm?"

"I don't know." Lucy sounded impatient.

"And Parker? Does McClellan think Dwight killed her?"

"He's playing his cards close, but think about it. Dwight could have easily slipped out of the office and transformed into Mr. Sneed." Lucy was growing bored with James's questions and was obviously anxious to spread the tale. "The state cops will need to find some evidence in his house to link him to that crime. Right now, he's only being held for attempted murder."

"Only?" James spluttered. "I don't get this. If nothing else, Hutchins seemed like a sensible person. How could he be so stupid as to leave his boots in the car?"

"People aren't always rational when it comes to murder, James," Lucy responded with a touch of condescension. "I'll call you later if I hear anything else. Start the phone tree, will you?"

In no particular rush to inform the rest of the supper club members about Dwight's arrest, James ate some low-fat oatmeal with a low-salt butter substitute. He drank a second cup of coffee and then called Lindy.

"I'm still trying to put my poor house back together!" Lindy grumbled. "Teachers are the *worst* party guests. I've seen them trash other people's houses, so I don't know why I expected better behavior from them, but I did!"

James interrupted her litany of complaints, ranging from the amount of punch spilled on various pieces of furniture to the fact that garbage was deposited in both her houseplants and umbrella stand, to tell her that Kinsley was hospitalized but physically unscathed.

"I know all about it, James! She was poisoned!" she shrieked. "And at *my* party! When the Blue Ridge parents get wind of that little tidbit I'll be out on my ear. First, Parker's killed on my field trip and then her sister's poisoned at my house. I'm officially cursed!"

"No one's going to blame you," James soothed his friend. "It sounds like Dwight is our bad guy. How did you know about the poison already?"

"As soon as the ER doc told the police that he suspected Kinsley had consumed something toxic, the cops took samples of all of the leftovers. I wasn't allowed to clean anything up until this morning. I was told the *chili con queso* was spiked because its salty taste masked the taste of the Wildnil."

"And a vet would know all about Wildnil. Looks like Dwight is going to jail for a long time." James drained his coffee cup and began to feel like a human being again. "I know this is off the subject, but did you have any luck with Chavez last night?"

"Well, I was hoping for a New Year's kiss, but now I realize that he'd never make a move on me in front of the other teachers. He *did* stay with me until the bitter end." She issued a frustrated sigh. "I swear he was going to say something important, too. He took my hand and gazed at me with those beautiful, coffee-colored eyes, and then that Donovan jerk interrupted us. Chavez went home and I may never know what he was going to say!"

"Hmm," James murmured sympathetically. "We'll just have to find another way to get you two alone. And soon."

"What about you, James?" Lindy asked sharply. "From where I was standing, there was more than one female looking to get a little love from *you* last night. Have you ever had two women after you at once?"

"No," James gulped. "And just for the record, I don't like it. I have problems enough handling one woman at a time."

Cheered, Lindy laughed and promised to phone Bennett before she resumed her cleanup.

After an extremely long and luxuriantly hot shower, James bundled up in a heavy wool sweater, jeans, and lined boots before fixing a mug of black coffee for his father and heading out to the shed. He did a double take when he noticed Milla's minivan in the driveway and heard the sounds of a relaxed conversation emanating from the shed.

"Pop?" James knocked and then slowly opened the door. He didn't know what he expected to find, but Milla and his father were both engaged in perfectly innocuous activities. Jackson was painting and Milla was organizing his paints and brushes by arranging them in cutlery boxes according to size and color. Jackson's radio was set to a soft jazz station, and a plate of partially eaten ham biscuits sat next to a bowl containing the remnants of a fruit salad.

"Happy New Year, James!" Milla gave James a hug and a kiss on the cheek. "Can you believe this marvelous work? Your daddy is a genius!"

Looking around, James had to agree. Stacked all around the small space were paintings of hands. Hands sewing, hammering, twisting electrical wires, bagging groceries, changing oil, stirring soup. Each set was as different as a pair of eyes. The skin tones, minute lines, small hairs, freckles, scars, age spots, and other unique markings were as varied as the occupations illustrated.

"Whose hands are those?" James asked. He stepped closer to his father as Jackson added a stroke of green to the palm of a hand holding the foot of an infant while guiding it into a pad of ink.

"Doc Spratt," Jackson answered without taking his eyes from his work. "He insisted on doing your footprints himself."

James stared at the tiny foot, cradled with gentle firmness in the nest of the doctor's skilled hand. The action was tender and proud, and James could almost sense the excitement that his parents must have felt. How his father was able to capture all of these feelings by painting two hands and one foot was beyond him, but Jackson had found a way.

"Amazing, Pop." James gestured around the room. "Are all of these hands you've seen before?"

"'Course!" Jackson snorted. "I just need to see someone's hands once and for no good reason at all, I can recollect them like that." He snapped his fingers. "I haven't been around about town in a while, but folks don't change too much from one year to the next." He hesitated. "Not in the hands, anyway."

Milla collected the plates of food. "I'm going to load the dishwasher, and then we're going shopping, Jackson Henry. I'm no artist, but there are things a person needs when they sit in one spot all day and we're going out to get them!"

James waited for his father to argue, but he simply grunted, stood, and began to clean off his brushes.

After the pair drove off in Milla's minivan, James undertook the chore of taking down the Christmas decorations, boxing them, and hauling them to the storage space his family referred to as the attic. Calling the rickety pull-down ladder and drafty area above the bedrooms an attic was a stretch, and James had debated over whether or not to bother with the family advent wreath, the boxes containing all of the ornaments James had made in school, or the treetop angel hand-sewn by his mother. It was the thought of Milla coming over to an unadorned house that motivated James into setting up a tree and stringing lights around the lamppost outside. Now, however, he grumbled vociferously over having to return them by way of the steep and narrow ladder.

"At least I'm getting some exercise," he said after standing up and bumping his head on an angled roof rafter. By the time the house was restored to its pre-holiday order, James noticed that Milla had brought over a floral arrangement consisting of carnations and greenery and had set it out on the kitchen table. She had also purchased a new dishtowel in a cheerful plaid. These little touches—ones that the Henry men didn't know how to add—were already making their small house more pleasant.

"Milla is a miracle!" James told Murphy later that day as they met at Dolly's Diner for dinner. "She took Pop to an art supply store *and* to a furniture store to pick out a new chair."

"That's great news. See? It's a whole new year." Murphy smiled and sipped her tea. "Who knows what can change for the better?"

James reached across the table and squeezed her hand. "Mine is starting off pretty well so far, thanks to you."

Pleased, Murphy looked around the diner. "I thought I might see Lottie here. It seems as though she's finally agreed to go out on a date with Scott. I was kind of surprised because her ex-boyfriend is your typical beefy-jock type, so I thought Scott didn't stand a chance." She shrugged. "But apparently he made something for her, and she was just swept away by his creativity. I thought she mentioned coming here, but they probably hang out later than old folks like you and me."

As the two moved on to the subject of Dwight and his antisocial behavior at the party, Kinsley and Gary walked into the diner. Murphy jumped up and waved the couple over to join them.

"You're looking pretty good for someone who was poisoned!" Murphy teased Kinsley.

"Thank God someone can kid around with me." Kinsley rolled her eyes and elbowed Gary. "Mother Hen over here is barely giving me room to breathe."

Gary frowned. "Can I help feeling protective? Someone tried to kill my wife!" He opened his menu but didn't read it. "At least they got the bastard."

Kinsley's smile faded. "I went to see him this morning."

"What?" James, Murphy, and Gary all shouted in unison. Startled, Kinsley's elbow knocked into Murphy's teacup. It tipped over and a river of hot liquid streamed onto Gary's lap.

"Jesus!" he yelled, leaping to his feet. "Watch it!"

"Oh, honey!" Kinsley tried to dab at the stains with her napkin. "I'm sorry. It was an accident."

Gary looked down at his wet crotch and the stain spreading on his jacket. "This is suede," he grumbled as he inspected his jacket. He then stomped off to the restroom. Kinsley followed him with her eyes, which appeared weary and tinged with a sadness that seemed unfitting to a new bride.

"Why did you visit Dwight Hutchins?" Murphy asked quickly, before Gary could return.

Kinsley was still troubled over the tea incident. Reluctantly, she faced Murphy. "I just wanted to know why he tried to hurt me. What had I ever done to him?" She traced circles on the table with the dregs of tea. "Besides, I wanted to look him in the eye and ask him if he killed my sister." She dropped her gaze and concentrated hard on not crying.

James handed her his napkin just in case. "And did he talk to you?"

Kinsley nodded. "He claims he's been framed. He repeated this over and over again. He swore he didn't break into Colin's office, that he didn't poison me, and that he would never harm a hair on my sister's head." She shook her head. "By the time I left, I was torn between hating him for lying to me and wondering how long he'd been in love with Parker."

Murphy had quickly transformed into reporter mode. "Did he accuse a specific person of committing these crimes?"

"No," Kinsley replied and then forced a smile as Dolly approached.

"You poor, darlin' baby girl!" Dolly exclaimed and cupped Kinsley's lovely face in her wide hand. "I am *so* glad to see you up and around. You pick anything you want and Cliff'll make it for you, special." She appraised Kinsley closely. "Seems to me like you could use some red meat. How about some spaghetti with meatballs as big as your fist?"

"Sounds perfect." Kinsley nodded gratefully at Dolly, and the threesome small-talked for a few minutes about the weather and the latest celebrity gossip. In the middle of a discussion about the latest box-office hit, Kinsley's expression turned anxious as Gary reappeared at the table. "Are you okay?" she asked her husband solicitously.

"I'm not going to sit here in wet pants, that's for sure." With one hand on his hip, he held out the other for her to take. "Let's go."

Kinsley paused. "But I already ordered dinner and, Gary, I'm really hungry. I didn't get a chance to eat lunch today."

"She's always hungry," he said to James and Murphy. Though his tone was light, no laughter reached his eyes.

"We'll drop her off at home afterwards," James offered, silently bristling on Kinsley's behalf. "She can't miss out on Dolly's meatballs. They're famous."

"Or you could go home, get changed, and then come back and join us?" Murphy suggested in a sugary voice.

Gary waved off her invitation. "I'll just grab Mickey D's on the way home." He then gave Kinsley a disapproving look. "Though I'm pretty damned curious about why you went to see the maniac who tried to kill you—especially when you told *me* you were going to get your nails done."

Kinsley grabbed Gary's arm. "I didn't plan on visiting… him. I went to the nail salon, but they were closed. I totally forgot about today being a holiday." Her eyes welled. "I just sat there, in the parking lot, wondering *why, why?* There's only one person that could answer that question for me, so I went to see Dwight Hutchins. Suddenly, there I was at the county jail, sitting at a table across from him."

Dolly arrived with a platter the size of a Yule log and inserted herself between Gary and his wife. "You eatin' today, Mr. Lowe?" she asked the shorter man without her customary excess of exuberance. James was certain that Dolly must have stationed herself so that she could overhear most of the conversation. He was also certain that she wouldn't be too pleased about how the newcomer was treating Kinsley.

Faced with Dolly's fierce maternal stare, Gary quickly backed away. "You can explain everything to *me* later," he grumbled and walked off.

"I'm sorry, guys." A single tear ran down Kinsley's smooth cheek. "I guess he's just stressed. He used to act like that at Solmes. It's one of the reasons we broke up." She twirled spaghetti around and around on her fork. "I could never understand why he got so upset when the market did something unpredictable. It wasn't like it was *his* money that was lost."

"Actually, it may very well have been his money," Murphy said quietly and quickly sought James's eyes. "I think it's time to tell her the truth."

James agreed, though his heart ached for the woman sitting beside him. Murphy told Kinsley what she knew about Gary being fired as succinctly and straightforwardly as possible. She then fell silent as Kinsley busied herself with her spaghetti.

"You didn't know about the front running," James stated softly.

Kinsley speared a meatball with her fork, peered at it as if it were an enemy, and then sliced it in two with her knife before shoving it in her mouth. She wordlessly answered James by shaking her head so that her hair glimmered beneath the lights.

"Sitting in that room today, Dwight told me that he and Gary were roommates their freshman year at Princeton. You could have knocked me over like a bowling pin when he said that." She took a deep breath. "He believes that Gary is behind the burglary and ... and putting the Wildnil in my dip." She drank half a glass of water in three gulps. "Apparently, Gary was always playing mean jokes on people in their college dorm and continued the pranks after they both joined the same fraternity. Since they were fraternity brothers, Dwight saw Gary at house functions, but Dwight lived in the dorms while Gary moved into the frat house."

"Dwight doesn't strike me as the type to join a fraternity," James remarked.

Gesturing with her fork, Kinsley said, "Me either. And Dwight said he got burned out on all the partying by the end of their freshman year. So he stopped hanging out at the fraternity and he hardly saw Gary after that. Then, Gary suddenly appears in the Shenandoah Valley. Allegedly, Dwight hadn't seen him for *years* until last night."

James and Murphy picked at their barbecued chicken breasts as they struggled to figure out if Dwight was simply creating a smokescreen or if Gary was somehow connected to all three crimes.

"I'm really confused," Kinsley muttered and put down her fork. "I got so angry at Dwight when he said those things. I screamed at him. I called him a liar and a bastard and ... a lot worse than that. I think the cops were shocked that that kind of language could come out of my mouth."

Murphy signaled to Dolly. "How did he take you not accepting his story?" she asked Kinsley.

"He just sat there. Resigned." She sighed. "But he was adamant about not hurting Parker. It was the one thing that got him fired up even after I yelled at him. He told me that he loved her but she was too wrapped up in beautiful Colin to see him as anything other than a guy who was good with their patients."

When Dolly appeared to check on their progress, Murphy pushed away her dinner plate and ordered three slices of chocolate cake and coffees all around.

"The bit about Parker rang true to me," Kinsley answered and then smirked, "but it's pretty clear that I couldn't tell if someone was lying unless their damned nose started growing!"

"I know you've been through a lot, Kinsley." Murphy placed a hand on the distressed woman's forearm. "We're here to help you in any way, and if you want my advice, I would tell you to find out *exactly* what kind of person the man you married is."

Kinsley's eyes widened as Dolly placed three cake slices on their table. Each one could have served four people.

"Dolly!" James blurted. "These pieces are a trifle big!"

Dolly shrugged and her massive bosom moved up and down along with her shoulders. "Seems like you folks could use a dose of sugar tonight." She gave her wide hip a slap. "Always makes me feel better when I'm workin' out some kind of problem."

"You're a wise woman," Murphy said, smiling at the proprietor who slowly ambled off, humming loudly as she paused to refill coffee cups throughout the diner.

Kinsley swiped a pinkie across the top of her cake and then sucked the icing from her finger. She squared her shoulders and picked up a fresh fork. "The first thing I'm going to do is call a woman who mentored me when I started at Solmes. She'll tell me all about the front running."

"And after that?" Murphy persisted.

Kinsley looked crestfallen, but anger surged through her voice like a wave breaking on the shore as she said, "You mean, am I going to find out whether my new husband—the man that I've fallen in love with all over again—stole drugs from a local vet, tried to poison me, murdered my sister, and then pinned all the crimes on an old roommate?"

Murphy looked abashed. "I'm sorry. I wasn't—"

"*Of course* I want to know the truth about him! But how?" Kinsley gazed at James and Murphy with appeal in her eyes.

"Don't worry," Murphy answered with assurance. "I've got an idea."

NINETEEN

DRIED APPLE SLICES

Sodium
per
Serving:

30 mg

"ARE YOU SURE THIS is a good idea?" James asked
Murphy for the third time. "I really think the police should be hiding in Kinsley's pantry instead
of us."

Murphy chewed on a pretzel twist. "Lucy's
here. She's practically a deputy."

"And she's the one who came up with our hiding spots?"

"Yes. Except that I insisted on being in here with you instead of
her, so she and Bennett are in the coat closet. Lindy and Gillian are
in an upstairs bedroom with their cell phones charged and ready.
They're the 9-1-1 team. If things seem to be getting ugly, those
two will call for help." Murphy offered James a pretzel. "These are
honey mustard. Delicious. Oh, but you'd better stick to these dried
apple slices instead. Pretzels are way too salty for you."

James frowned as he bit into a rubbery apple slice. "This is ridiculous! We're standing in Kinsley's pantry, eating her food, and waiting for her to start a scene with Gary so that we can be witnesses to a confession?"

"You got it," Murphy said happily. "We are going to nail the louse, and I'm going to have the best front page story of my entire career. Shoot, I might even write a book about this. Lucy will get offers from a dozen different law enforcement agencies—hopefully very far away from Quincy's Gap—and your other friends will be town heroes. We've got nothing to lose."

"When did Kinsley agree to all of this?"

Murphy shrugged. "On the phone last night, right after she talked to her friend from Solmes and found out that Gary had been fired for front running. First, I had to settle Kinsley down, and then we figured out how we could ambush her new husband to see if he's involved with Dwight."

James was befuddled. "So you think Gary and Dwight are partners in crime?"

"Of course. They must have been planning this for months. With Parker gone, Dwight gets the practice, and now that they've been legally wed, Kinsley's death would mean that Gary would get a least a portion of Kinsley's millions. Gary probably promised to pay Dwight off in exchange for the part he's played." She chomped on another pretzel. "What's a few years in jail compared to a lifetime of wealth?" she asked rhetorically.

Suddenly, they heard the sound of the garage door being opened. Murphy snapped off the pantry light and eased the door closed. "I've got tape recorders stashed in four rooms," she whispered in excitement. "So even if we miss parts of the newlyweds' conversation, we'll have something to hold over Gary's head later on."

"I hope you ladies know what you're doing," James murmured. "If Gary *is* guilty, then there's no telling how he's going to act."

Murphy shushed him as Kinsley entered the kitchen from the garage, noisily flinging her car keys and purse onto the counter.

"I'm glad you were willing to rent *Wall Street*," Kinsley said cheerfully. "I haven't watched it in ages, and I thought it would be fun to see what we're missing."

"High stress, five-dollar coffees, long hours, and rude customers," Gary replied. "We've got it much better now. Did you get a chance to look at those Florida Keys brochures, baby?" His voice practically purred as he spoke. "We could spend the whole winter on the beach drinking cocktails."

"Oh, Gary!" Kinsley laughed. "You know I promised to go back to Blue Ridge High next week. I'm really psyched about teaching. We can go somewhere for Spring Break."

"But it's cold *now*, babe." Gary continued to plead his case. "How about Mexico? We could go and come back real quick and you'd only miss a week or two of school. Think about the margaritas."

"I think I'd like to take a break from Mexican food for a while. I *was* just poisoned, you know," she reminded him. "Here, take your sesame chicken before it congeals any further. Boy, do I wish there were more restaurants in this town." Kinsley sniffed. "Even this dim sum is only so-so. Remember that incredible Chinese place across from Solmes? What was that called?"

"Lu Lu's Lo Mein Palace," Gary responded with his mouth full. "How could you ever forget that name?"

"I don't know," Kinsley answered and then stopped to chew. "But I've been thinking about our life there a lot lately. I even called Elaine Salinsky to catch up on all the gossip. Do you remember her?"

There was a lengthy pause before Gary finally spoke. "Kinda," he said, and then asked lightly, "What did she have to say? Did she mention me?"

"Why don't you tell me why she might have?" Kinsley's tone was firm. "And think carefully about how you answer this, because a lot rides on what you say."

Gary laughed nervously. "What is this? You Judge Judy or something? I quit, babe, and Solmes got pretty bitter about it. The big cheeses knew they were losing their best trader, so they did their damned best to blackball me. Made up some shit about front running. It's a good thing I gave up that life." He snorted. "No one would hire me now."

There was no reply from Kinsley. James could almost hear Murphy silently screaming, *Don't fall for that lame explanation!*

Kinsley rattled a few more bags, which James assumed contained more take-out, and the smells of soy sauce, fried rice, and crispy fried won tons seeped into the pantry. As his stomach gurgled in expectation, James ruefully thought that he'd probably never be able to eat Chinese food again, unless they found some way to cook it without sodium. And then it wouldn't taste like Chinese food, he imagined.

"Elaine said you were living high on the hog at the time you … left Solmes." James noted that Kinsley decided not to pin Gary down about whether he was fired or chose to leave on his own accord.

The sound of a pair of cheap, wooden chopsticks being snapped apart echoed in the kitchen. "Pieces of crap! Look at all these splinters!" Gary complained. "Well, I wasn't using these kinds of chopsticks, that's for sure. I made enough to buy a pair of those nice glass ones."

Kinsley pursued her line of questioning. "Elaine said you moved to a pretty swank place on the Upper West Side. Did you get some kind of special bonus from Solmes that I wasn't privy to?"

"Listen to you," Gary chuckled. "'*Privy to*,' la te da!" he mocked her, his voice carrying more and more suppressed anger as he growled, "Old Elaine's been saying lots of stuff about me. You two had a real nice girl's chat, didn't ya?"

"I just don't want any secrets between us, Gary," Kinsley answered honestly. "Can you tell me that you haven't kept anything from me?"

"No, I haven't." Gary slapped his chopsticks on the counter. "Now, can we watch the movie?"

Kinsley waited a bit and then said, "Sure. I'm sorry, hon. I guess I'm just feeling lonely in this isolated valley without Parker. When we were together, it seemed like a beautiful place, but now..."

"And what am I, chopped liver?" Gary spluttered, and then he quickly cheered up. "Hey! Let's move back to New York! I'd love that!" He clapped his hands together in glee. "Just think of the food, the bars, the shows. Let's do it!"

"Um, I was thinking more along the lines of Kansas," Kinsley responded timidly. "I miss my family, now more than ever."

"Sorry, babe," Gary answered without much sympathy. "I know you're hurtin', but I can't do Kansas. We'll head to a big city, maybe L.A., get a cool place, something really modern and hip, maybe with a sweet pool, and then kick back and enjoy life."

When Kinsley next spoke, her voice was more muffled and James realized that she must have moved into the living room while Gary was busy picturing a life of leisure.

Kinsley had rented a small house in one of the town's older sections. Just two blocks off Main Street, its current owners, Missy and Bobby Greenwood, had modernized the cottage. The Greenwoods had added on a garage and updated the kitchen so that the three-bedroom home could serve as the perfect place to raise a family. However, the young couple served in the military and had been sent to Germany for a year's term. As a result, the Greenwoods' first child would be born on foreign soil and Kinsley would take loving care of their charming house until she decided where to take up a more permanent residence.

"Gary, I want to live more simply!" Kinsley declared from the living room. "I want to give to a community—to be a part of a town. I want people to know me when I go out for groceries or rent a movie, and I don't want to be anchored down by constantly thinking about money. In fact, I've already talked to the local ASPCA about donating all of Parker's money to their charity so they can build a beautiful new facility."

"What!" Gary roared. "Why didn't you talk to me first? Have you signed any papers?"

James heard Kinsley turn on the television instead of replying. "Just so you know, I may give them mine as well," he heard her taunt, and then Gary said something too low to be heard from inside the pantry.

"I can do whatever I want!" Kinsley shouted back. "I'm moving home to Kansas, and I'm giving away every penny except what I'll need to buy a small house with." Her voice escalated with every word. "Why don't *you* take all that money *you* earned *front running* and invest it?"

"I already did and I lost it all. Satisfied now, you bitch!" Gary hollered in return, and then a silence descended upon the house, interrupted only by the sound of an exercise show on the television. Judging from the tempo of the music, James assumed that the show's participants were engaged in a vigorous aerobic workout.

"You lied to me," Kinsley hissed. "You didn't quit your job to *comfort* me! You got fired and came here to offer your shoulder for me to cry on so that you could sucker me into marrying you!" She stomped across the hardwood floors. "Well, I'm calling our family lawyer. I'm sure he can arrange for an annulment," she snapped her fingers, "just like that!"

Gary's footsteps followed her to where she stood. "Don't you dare!"

"Or what, you little leech?" she said with a sharp edge to her voice. "You'll kill me?"

The air became charged with rage.

"I wouldn't test me on that one, babe," Gary stated evenly. "You're my wife and if *anything* should happen to you, then I get every dollar that you're so hell-bent on pissing away."

James felt himself go rigid. The antagonism between the couple was speeding to a crescendo that was likely to end in violence. With both hands clenched around the stem of a baseball bat, James felt wound like a spring. At the slightest hint of alarm from Kinsley, he planned to jump to her aid, but sitting there in the dark, it was hard to judge whether he could act in time. He shifted his weight to make certain that his limbs hadn't fallen asleep after crouching in the narrow pantry.

"Don't do anything," Murphy whispered. "She's going for the jugular now."

Apparently, Murphy was right. "I'm not afraid of you," Kinsley mocked her husband, which seemed to James like a dangerous tactic to take. "You're a deceitful, greedy louse," she continued, "but you don't have the guts to kill anyone."

Gary snorted, a sound he seemed fond of making. "I don't need to do the dirty work. I've got someone else to do that for me."

James heard the sound of metal scraping on metal.

"What are you talking about, Gary?" Kinsley's wrath filled the house. "Are you referring to my sister's murder? Are you trying to tell me you're some kind of puppeteer and that you had her killed?"

There was no reply.

Kinsley's footsteps moved with slow deliberation.

"Put that down, Kinsley. You're being ridiculous."

"You and that loser, Dwight, you're in this whole scheme together. He gets Parker's practice and you get my money. Is that it? Well, game's over!" she raged. "Get out of my house!"

He snorted again. "I'm not going anywhere. We're going to forget this whole conversation, and we're going to go on a little trip. See? I've already rented a car and a nice suite of rooms down in the Keys. Our bags are packed, too." He chuckled. "This isn't an optional trip, *sweetheart*. You're coming with me. Now put that poker down."

James almost stopped breathing. *What was Kinsley planning to do with that fireplace poker?*

"Get out of my bag!" Gary shouted as James heard the sound of a zipper being opened.

"What are these vials?" Kinsley sounded dumbfounded. "Wild-nil!" She stomped back to Gary. "What do you plan to do with these? Poison my cocktail while I'm sunning on the beach?" She crossed the room again. "I'm getting rid of you for good."

"Put that phone down!" Gary roared, and when it was obvious that Kinsley wasn't listening, his steps began to pick up speed as he neared his wife.

"Help me!" Kinsley screamed, and James burst out of the pantry with Murphy right on his heels.

A few seconds later, Kinsley stood with her back flattened against the living room wall, the phone clutched against her chest as though it would protect her. Lucy stood in front of her, but something was odd about her posture. She seemed to be sagging sideways, as though she were slowly losing her balance, and she wore a surprised expression on her face.

Gary was on the floor, struggling like a wild animal as Bennett attempted to pry the poker from his hands. James was shocked to see that the point of the tool was glistening with blood.

"Lucy!" James saw the wound in her thigh and stared in transfixed horror as blood flowed from the hole.

Torn between aiding Bennett and supporting Lucy as she crumpled toward the floor, James ran to Lucy. He cradled her head as he eased her to the floor and then turned, looking for a piece of cloth he could use to staunch the flow of blood. He dashed into the kitchen and grabbed a dishtowel, and as he applied pressure to Lucy's wound, he saw Murphy rip the poker from Gary's hands.

"Gillian! Lindy!" Murphy yelled. "Call for help!"

There was no answer from upstairs.

"There's no dial tone," Kinsley breathed. She held out the phone for everyone to see. Her face was white as flour and she stood immobile, staring at her husband as though he were a complete stranger.

On the floor, Gary began to laugh. "You idiots! You can't do anything to me! You've got no proof! Nothing!"

Murphy raised the poker. "Shut up. Now put your hands in the air."

"No," said a low and deadly voice from the other side of the room. A masked man stepped out of the shadow at the base of the staircase and raised a gun. "*You* put your hands in the air. All of you."

Gary scrambled away from Bennett's clutches and stood just behind the man clothed all in black. "It's about time you got here. How did you know this group of morons was coming after us?"

"Only you, Gary. And that's fine with me. Someone's got to deal with your dead body." And then man raised his arm.

Gary's eyes flew open in fear. "What—?"

The man fired two shots into Gary's torso.

One of the women screamed as Gary's body slid down the wall, leaving a path of bright blood on the stark white behind him.

Without another word, the man turned his gun on the rest of the group and backed toward the door. He reached his arm behind his hip and twisted the knob. Slipping outside like a ghost, he disappeared into the night.

Inside Kinsley's living room, no one moved.

"My cell phone," Lucy finally croaked from the floor while trying to reach inside her coat.

"I'll get it. Don't try to move." Murphy gently retrieved the phone from an interior pocket of Lucy's jacket. Her voice trembled violently as she spoke to the 9-1-1 operator.

James met Bennett's eyes and the mail carrier snapped to life, springing up the stairs leading to the bedrooms two at a time. Kinsley was cowering on the floor, hugging her knees and hiding her face in her arms.

Before James could even rise to his feet, Bennett called his name from the top of the stairs. "James! They've both been knocked out cold!" he shouted. "Come on, man."

Stirred into action by the fear of what horrors could have been inflicted upon his friends, James hustled up the stairs to find Lindy and Gillian splayed upon the bedroom carpet. Their breathing was even and there was no sign of trauma to their heads.

"Maybe he injected them with something," James whispered.

"This is some mess, some mess," Bennett muttered, kneeling over Gillian.

The sound of sirens approaching caused them both to sigh in relief.

Bennett moved to the window and looked out. "Lucky that we're right in town. The cavalry was just around the corner."

As James hastened down the stairs and opened the front door, his heart froze in shock at the sight of Sergeant McClellan standing on the stoop. His long hands gripped the nape of the masked man's black shirt.

"Could you give me a hand?" McClellan asked. He and James dragged the inert figure inside.

As soon as they released him onto the floor, McClellan rolled the motionless man onto his back. Outside, several sheriff's cars and an EMT van pulled to a screeching stop in front of the house. Blue, red, and white lights burst into the living room, striping the walls, ceilings, and floors with blinding color.

Despite the noise and the flashing lights, James could focus on nothing else but the man beneath him. Even as the paramedics pushed him aside to reach Lucy and Gary, his eyes were fixed on the masked face. Even as he heard footsteps thunder up the stairs, he couldn't blink. Even as Murphy called his name over and over again, he heard nothing. His attention was zeroed in on McClellan's sticklike fingers as they reached forward and, in what seemed like agonizingly slow motion, rolled the mask, inch by excruciating inch, up over the gunman's face.

Staring at the handsome features—the square jaw, the narrow nose, and the flawless skin peppered by stubble, James tried to comprehend the image his eyes had relayed to his brain. His mind rebelled, struggling against the logic of what he saw.

The man in the mask was Colin Crabtree.

TWENTY

PEPPERMINT PATTY
HERO CAKE

Sodium
per
Serving:

466 mg

THE SUPPER CLUB MEMBERS were gathered around Lucy's hospital bed, waiting in polite silence as she spoke on the phone to the sheriff of Madison County.

"Thank you for the offer, sir. I will certainly consider it." She replaced the phone on the nightstand and then grimaced as she straightened her injured leg.

"How are you?" Gillian asked, patting Lucy's hand in quick, agitated taps.

"I'm fine. Really." She smiled at her friends. "Getting stabbed by a fireplace poker was great for my career! Both the Madison and Augusta departments want me to come aboard as a deputy sheriff as soon as I'm well enough."

Bennett frowned. "What's wrong with working for Shenandoah County?"

"Nothing." Lucy shrugged. "But they haven't offered me a position. I suppose Donovan's been whispering mean nothings in Huckabee's ear again. You know, how I'm a loose cannon, don't follow procedure, regularly endanger the lives of citizens, blah, blah, blah."

Lindy sat down in one of the two chairs in front of a filmy window that faced the parking lot. Behind her head, fat snowflakes swirled through the air, lazily falling upon the black pavement until it appeared to be sprinkled with chalk dust.

"Does that mean you'd move to another town?" Lindy clasped her hands together as though she feared the answer.

"Maybe," Lucy answered softly and then turned her blue gaze upon James.

He wanted to tell her not to go, but he knew that he had no right to influence her decisions just because he didn't want her to vanish from his life. "We'd never be the same without you," he told her, meaning that the supper club wouldn't feel right without her presence. But he also realized that he wanted her in his life. The thought of Lucy being completely gone from Quincy's Gap instantly filled him with anxiety and sorrow.

"There's our heroine!" cried a voice from the threshold. There was Milla, carrying a baking tray that bore a large sheet cake covered in white frosting. "This is my peppermint patty cake," she declared, setting the cake down on the swivel tray next to Lucy's bed. "The cake is chocolate, the icing is peppermint butter cream, and the word 'hero' is spelled out with tiny crumbles of chilled peppermint patties. I know it's the masculine form of the word, but I just didn't have room to write out 'heroine,' my dear." Milla leaned over and cupped Lucy's cheek in her hand. "You are something else, young lady." Tearing up, she reached into her purse and blew her nose into a tissue. "Let's cut this cake, and you all can explain to a simple old woman what in this world happened yesterday."

Lindy volunteered to do the talking while the rest of the supper club concentrated on the rich chocolate cake layered with mint-flavored icing so buttery, creamy, and sugar-laden that James could feel his teeth shrieking in protest. He was pleased to see that Lucy had set aside her dietary restrictions for the moment and was eating the largest slice of them all with fervor.

"This frosting," Lucy moaned after Lindy had finished talking and everyone had eaten his or her slices of cake. "Milla, you know my biggest weakness now."

"It's your kryptonite, huh?" Milla laughed. "Don't worry dear, I'll keep your secret. But boy, oh boy, there were a whole *mess* of secrets in that class of mine!" She shook her head in disbelief. "So you're telling me that Colin Crabtree and Kinsley's new husband killed that sweet Parker and were planning on … getting rid of Kinsley, too?"

"That's what we've heard from the State Police," Bennett answered. "The two of them almost got away with it, too. Lucky for everyone, McClellan's been shadowing Colin for weeks. Seems he never trusted the guy."

"Then who poisoned Kinsley at your party, Lindy?" Milla wanted to know. "And using *my* very own *chili con queso* recipe, too?"

"Gary," Lindy said. "But he didn't want to kill her then. He just wanted her to get sick so that he could set up Dwight to take the fall and he, Gary, could rescue Kinsley and earn her trust. We think he was going to kill her in Florida. He had both a rental car and a hotel room booked in the Keys, and had also rented a private sailboat. Looks like he was going to dope her up with Wildnil and toss her overboard."

"That horrible little troll!" Milla waved her cake knife in the air. "After what that girl's been through, I hope he rots away in jail until he's nothing but skin and bones."

Lucy pointed at the ceiling. "Gary's a floor above me. He's in the ICU. McClellan said the only reason the guy's still breathing is that Colin shot him with a .22 and missed his major organs." She smirked. "I'd say he's lucky, but I've heard mumbles from my nurses that he may never walk again. I guess one of the bullets damaged his spinal cord."

Gillian sighed and fluffed her hair, which had acquired canta-loupe-hued highlights in the last twenty-four hours. "Money is *so* corruptive. It tainted Colin and Gary, and *robbed* Parker of her very life. The Buddha knows it will take years of love and healing for Kinsley to trust again. Poor soul!"

"The word around school is that her parents are here and are going to stay with her until she's ready to move back to Kansas," Lindy said. "So at least she's not alone."

"I hate to say it, but finding out that Gary is a scoundrel doesn't seem like a big surprise," Milla scoffed.

"Gary did have a black aura, but I was *terribly* distraught to see Colin's handsome face beneath that ski mask!" Gillian wailed. "I thought he was one of the *good* ones. I mean, he took care of sick animals!"

"But he wasn't very good at that job, remember?" James added, pleased that he could remind Gillian of the man's imperfections once again.

"Colin was Mr. Sneed all along." Lucy poured herself a glass of water from the pitcher on her nightstand. "He just picked up the clothes from a thrift store and the hat caught his eye because it looked like the kind of thing an old man would wear. He never even noticed the fishing lure! The wig and beard came from some online costume shop, so we never would have been able to solve the crime by visiting local stores." She paused and stared at her water glass. "I told you guys that strangulation was a personal crime. The crazy thing is, Colin knew all along that Parker had gone as a chaperone in Kinsley's place." She sipped her water. "That man committed a premeditated murder so that Gary could step in and comfort Kinsley. It was a seriously huge gamble, but neither of them cared."

"It's all *too* awful. And what about the quiet vet ... Dwight?" Milla sounded worried. "He was innocent all along?"

James nodded. "Kinsley's hired one of the state's top criminal lawyers to help get him out of jail right away. Murphy's been trying to interview him for the last two days, but Kinsley's been taking up all the allotted visiting time." He smiled. "Rumor has it that they are making plans to build a million-dollar animal rescue facility in Parker's name."

"What a wonderful tribute!" Gillian clapped with glee. "And *so* many animals will benefit. Just think of some pitiable puppy or kitten trying to survive outside on a day like today. It breaks my heart ..." She choked up.

Bennett handed her a tissue from the box on Lucy's nightstand. "We're celebrating the end of this nutty affair, woman. Don't get all blubbery on us now."

"There's still something I don't get." Milla rose and began wiping off the cake knife with a napkin until it gleamed beneath the overhead lights. "How are Colin and Gary connected? A vet and a stockbroker from different states? I don't get it."

"They've been planning this for a long time," Lucy explained. "And they've been friends for a long time, too. Boyhood friends."

"Their families *summered* together," Lindy mimicked a haughty, aristocratic tone. "In Bar Harbor, Maine. The boys were enrolled in an eight-week theater camp every year. They learned how to act *all* the classics and apparently decided that if Shakespeare's characters could commit murder on a regular basis, then they could kill off a few folks as well."

"Ah!" Milla slapped herself in the head. "I should have guessed the Maine connection by the lobster references Gary made during my class."

"Gary and Colin kept in close touch after graduating from college. Apparently, they were both frustrated about not becoming wealthy right away. Gary especially," Lucy continued. "So they decided to find an heiress to seduce, marry, and knock off. Unfortunately, the other girls they flirted with didn't take the bait. It wasn't until the Willis sisters came along that their scheme had any hope of working."

Milla licked a dab of icing from the end of her fork. "How do you know all this?"

"McClellan called this morning," Lucy said. "Both of our felons are doing their best to rat out the other. So much for lifelong friendships!" She snorted and then turned sober. "Though I think I've got some amazing friends right here in this room. We did this as a team. Murphy too. I thought she'd be here today. Has anyone seen her?"

James picked at some crumbs on his plate. "She's writing articles as fast as her fingers can generate them. I guess a lot of big city papers are going to run her pieces."

"Good for her," Lucy mumbled and then sank back against the pillows, suddenly looking exhausted.

"We've worn you out!" Gillian cried and then began pushing Bennett out the door. "Time to go, everyone."

"Oh my, she's right," Milla agreed. She gathered up plates, forks, and napkins and pulled on her coat. Kissing Lucy on the forehead, she asked, "When will you be released, dear?"

"Tomorrow."

Milla was concerned. "I don't suppose you can drive home. Do you have a ride?"

"I'll come get her," Lindy quickly volunteered. "I'm sure I can get out of school a bit early."

A cough from the doorway alerted them to the presence of new visitors. It was Sheriff Huckabee and Principal Chavez. Both men stepped aside as Bennett and Gillian made their exit.

"Ms. Perez?" Chavez gestured to Lindy. "May I have a word with you in private, please?"

Lindy gulped, said goodbye to Lucy, and left the room. Milla scurried out after them, leaving James to stand awkwardly by as Huckabee entered.

"So I hear you've been gettin' job offers from other departments?" The fleshy sheriff tugged on the ends of his mustache.

"Yessir," Lucy replied as James turned to leave.

"Well, I got one more for you. How about it, Lucy? You wanna be a deputy right here in Shenandoah?"

Lucy appeared undecided. She glanced at James, a look of appeal on her face. Huckabee followed her eyes and examined James curiously.

"You her career advisor or somethin'?" A hint of disapproval laced his question.

James shook his head, and then, spying a memo pad next to the phone, scrawled out a single sentence. He then folded the paper and slipped it into Lucy's hand.

"Get some rest," he told her and smiled on his way out the door. As he waited for the elevator, he noticed Lindy and Chavez huddled together on two chairs in the waiting room. Chavez was holding Lindy's hand and gazing into her eyes as though she were the only person in the world, though dozens of people sat all around them. James could tell that whatever Chavez was saying was filling his friend with joy.

As he watched, the twosome suddenly flung their arms around each other and exchanged a passionate kiss. The waiting room fell completely silent, and when the couple finally noticed and separated in embarrassment, the onlookers whistled and applauded the display of affection.

James grinned at the look of rapture on Lindy's face and pushed the button for the elevator. At the same moment, Lucy unfolded the note he had written. Her mouth curved upward in a small smile and her eyes twinkled.

"Sheriff," she said proudly, "I accept your offer. I'd like nothing more than to be a deputy of the Shenandoah County Sheriff's Department."

Huckabee shook her hand with excessive firmness and then ordered her to get some rest. After he left, Lucy stared and stared at the single phrase written upon the note until she eventually grew too weary to look at it anymore and fell into a contented sleep.

When the nurse arrived thirty minutes later to check Lucy's vitals, she gently removed the piece of paper from her patient's limp hand.

Reading the one sentence, the nurse shrugged and placed the scrap on the nightstand. The words *We wouldn't be the Flab Five without you, so don't go* meant nothing to her, but judging from the peaceful smile on her patient's wan face, it was something quite precious to Lucy Hanover.

"Good work, boy." Doc Spratt slapped James heartily on the back. "You're down to a normal range again. One thirty-five over eighty-five."

James let out a relieved sigh. "Well, that's good to hear. Still, I feel like there's nothing I can eat anymore, doc. No fat, no salt, no sugar, no carbs. What's the point? I can't live on salad, water, and grilled chicken!"

The old doctor chuckled. "I know how you feel, son. Have what you want, in moderation, and then, every now and again, say to yourself 'what the hell' and go whole hog. Eat a donut, get the popcorn with the cup of butter, have those mashed taters drownin' in gravy…"

He patted James on the arm, made some notes in a file, and then snapped it closed. "Live your life, James Henry. Make it a full one, for the sake of those that didn't get the chance." He met James's eyes and held them for a minute and then pretended to pull an orange lollipop from behind his ear. "Now where did that come from, I wonder?"

After settling his bill, James stepped outside the medical office building and into a fresh inch of snow. It was blindingly white and pure beneath a muted blue sky. James could feel the blood pulsing through his veins and the crisp air tingling his lungs. He inhaled deeply, his arms wide open as though he might embrace the Blue Ridge Mountains emerging from the snowy hillsides like giant ocean waves. He glanced at the orange lollipop and then, with a smile on his face, headed in the direction of the building housing *The Shenandoah Star*, his boots crunching through the crust of snow.

It was getting late, but he saw lights shining from the windows above newspaper offices. He quickened his pace, seeking the warmth of Murphy's welcoming home. Ringing the doorbell, he hid the lollipop behind his back and thought about Doc Spratt's advice. *Live your life, James Henry. Make it a full one, for the sake of those that didn't get the chance.*

When Murphy answered, James handed her the lollipop and then took her in his arms.

"It's cold out there," he whispered. "Let's light a fire."

ACKNOWLEDGEMENTS

Many thanks to Holly, Anne, and Mary for their reading and commentary—you gals are the best. Thanks also to Mary for bringing me enchiladas after Sophie was born. You gave me that idea to write about Spanish and Mexican food. My gratitude to the fab Midnight Ink team: Barbara Moore, Karl Anderson, and the skilled artists including Ellen Dahl and Linda Ayriss who created this wonderful cover. For their expertise in the world of finance, I'd like to thank my brothers, Mead and John, and Dad for supplying me with information on front running. Thanks as well to Dr. Ted Stanley for tips on carfentanil citrate. And to my friends at the Short Pump Panera (John, Dave, Brad, Ellen, Robert, Theresa, et al.) for coffee and good company.

And last but never least to my darlings—Tim, Owen, and Sophie—for pulling me away from the computer to enjoy real life every now and then.

Read on for an excerpt from the next
Supper Club Mystery by J. B. Stanley

Stiffs & Swine

Coming soon from Midnight Ink

ONE

TUNA CASSEROLE

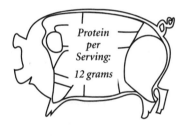

JAMES HENRY, HEAD LIBRARIAN of the Shenandoah County Library system, counted out five quarters. He hoped to use the vacuum at the self-service car wash to rid his aged white Bronco of the sand that had accumulated on the floor mats during his vacation at Virginia Beach. There had been a thunderstorm on the last afternoon of his vacation, and the sand that had been dampened and clumped into the mat's grids had the consistency of a bowl of grits.

As he grumbled over the exorbitant cost of five minutes' worth of vacuuming time, James removed the snakelike hose from the tin base, slid the quarters into the slot, and expectantly waited for the vacuum to roar into life. When it remained silent, he jammed his index finger on the return change button and was given nothing in exchange for his efforts. He assaulted the button, pushing vigorously, but the machine refused him so much as a single quarter.

Now, irritated and sweaty, he draped the vacuum hose in a sloppy coil back on its steel hook and approached the dollar bill changer. His wallet, which was stuffed with slips of paper bearing the names of books he wanted to read, only contained a ten and two singles. The first single had a fleabite on its top left-hand corner that was approximately three millimeters in size, and the machine spit it out like a child rejecting a forkful of Brussels sprouts.

The second single must have passed through the hands of an origami artist. It appeared to have been folded horizontally and vertically, balled into a monetary knot, and stained by coin dust and dirty fingers before James received it in change from a gas station outside of Norfolk. In addition to the worn paper, the bill had been decorated with a woman's name written in bubbly letters, a drawing of cartoon lips, and a series of *x*'s and *o*'s. The bill changer began refusing the dollar the second James placed its edge inside the machine. He tried again. The machine ejected the bill so rapidly that it fluttered to the ground before James could catch it.

"Look here, you!" He pointed a threatening finger at the machine and made one last attempt to straighten out the dollar's kinks against the lip of the bill changer. Taking a deep breath, he whispered, "Just take it. Take the damn dollar." He pushed the bill in. The machine pushed it out. In. Out. In. Out.

"Damn it!" James hit the bill changer with the palm of his hand and then stuffed the dollar back inside his wallet.

"You don't look very relaxed for a man fresh back from a week at the beach," an amused voice said from the interior of a sheriff's department cruiser. "Am I going to have to run you in for property damage?"

James smiled, delighted to see the lovely face of his friend, Lucy Hanover. As usual, her beautiful skin radiated good health, and her large, cornflower-blue eyes sparkled with good humor. Her caramel hair was pulled into a tight French twist, and the sophisticated hairstyle allowed James to gape over how thin Lucy's face had become since the beginning of the summer.

"Have you lost more weight?" he asked her. "Your face ..."

She nodded. "I'm doing a protein diet right now. It's really helped me get toned, and I'm not hungry on it. Maybe the rest of the supper club should give it a try." She examined herself in the rearview mirror. "I think gorging on all that Mexican food over the winter may not have been the best idea for a dieting group. Between the enchiladas and the donuts at the station all spring, this summer has been all about being disciplined."

"Those enchiladas tasted good going down," James said as he eyed her uniform, which consisted of beige pants and a chocolate-brown shirt bearing the embroidered shield just below the shoulder. He took a step closer to the brown cruiser, noting how bright the yellow star painted on the driver's door appeared against the dark background, and peered into the window at the gun belt strapped around Lucy's waist.

"Wow!" He looked her over, unaware that his blatant observation of her trimmer figure could be perceived as too forward or even downright rude. Luckily for James, Lucy was too flattered by his attention to be offended.

"It's been awhile since we've all been together," she said, clearly pleased to be the source of James's admiration. She turned off the car engine and relaxed in her seat. "I'm excited about getting back to our regular dinner meetings tomorrow night."

"Me too," James replied. "I can't believe how busy we've all been. I guess we all needed a change of scenery. Every one of us has been out of town—just on different weekends."

"Speaking of gettin' out of Dodge, how *was* the beach?" Lucy's tone was purely conversational, but the brief blaze that entered her eyes warned James that a full interrogation was imminent. When he hesitated, she quickly added, "Did Murphy go with you?"

Here it was. The moment James had dreaded for over five months. He was finally going to have to tell Lucy that Murphy Alistair, editor and reporter of *The Shenandoah Star Ledger*, was officially his girl-friend. The supper club members knew that they had been dating, but James had never made it clear that they were serious enough a couple to take a vacation together.

In truth, James had had a wonderful spring with Murphy. They went to the movies, local plays, music shows, and a slew of events all over the Valley so that Murphy could glean material for her articles. When they weren't hiding away in a mountain inn or browsing antique shops or farmers' markets, they were at work. They rarely spoke on the phone during the day, but after James left the library, he often went straight to Murphy's. In her neat and taste-ful apartment, they shared delicious meals and then made love with the windows open. Soft music swirled through her bedroom, and the stars perched so low in the summer sky that James felt as though they were in danger of being blown away by the fan rotating on the sill.

The only odd thing about their time together was that Murphy preferred that James not spend the entire night with her. She was working on a book, she had told him enigmatically, and did her best writing late at night. When he asked what it was about, she told him it was a work of fiction and that she'd tell him all about it once it was finished. James knew that many people had aspirations to write a book but found that their dreams never materialized into reality, so he didn't take Murphy's claim about being a novelist too seriously. Still, he respected her desire to give it a shot, and so he snuck back home before midnight, feeling much younger than his years as he crept up the squeaky stairs to his bedroom.

All in all, James and Murphy had shared five blissful months together. And to James, the best part was that they never, ever argued.

That is, until Murphy arrived at the beach to spend the Fourth of July weekend with him.

James had been alone for the first four days of his vacation week. Because of the multitude of responsibilities required to operate a daily newspaper, Murphy could only take a few days off work. And though James happily anticipated Murphy's appearance on Friday, he was utterly content at the beach without company. He slept late, took leisurely strolls, and let the days slip by as he read book after book and drank giant cups of iced coffee.

Though he hadn't been aware of it until he left Quincy's Gap behind, James had desperately felt in need of some down time. After all, he and his supper club friends had become embroiled in yet another murder case over the winter, and his relationship with Lucy Hanover had not taken the romantic turn he had once hoped it would. Instead, Lucy fell head over heels for a hunky aspiring sheriff's deputy and dropped James like a stone. And even though Lucy later regretted her decision to chase after the handsome deputy, James rejected her appeals to give their relationship another try. It was too late anyway, as James was already involved with Murphy.

In addition to hunting down a murderer and coping with romantic upheaval, James's home had undergone a major kitchen and bathroom makeover. The house and yard had been a mess, and Jackson Henry, James's father, had hired an assistant. Together, the pair of them had banged and clattered well before six each morning. Exhausted, James was almost grateful that Jackson had reverted to his hermitlike lifestyle in order to produce new paintings to be sold from a famed D.C. gallery. His temperamental parent locked himself in his shed for hours every day, only surfacing for meals or to receive visits from Milla, the owner of Fix 'n Freeze, a company revolving around cooking classes and small-scale catering.

Milla had become such a regular fixture in the Henry home that James often wondered if she would close her business in New Market and conduct her classes from the Henry's cozy kitchen instead. Not that James was complaining, but after an entire spring of Milla's fantastic cooking, he had packed on at least ten of the twenty-plus pounds he had lost the year before.

Still, Murphy didn't seem to mind the expansion of doughy flesh that had appeared around James's middle, and he was grateful that she didn't complain about his preference to make love with the lights off. Recently, however, it seemed to be the only thing she didn't complain about. During their three days together at the beach, Murphy was bossy, sulky, and she displayed an irrational jealousy every time a pretty girl walked by them on the beach.

"Are you done staring at that girl?" Murphy had barked when an attractive young woman wearing a pink bikini and matching pink headband sauntered past them during the first afternoon of Murphy's arrival.

"I was just looking at her tattoo," James had responded honestly. "She just seemed too preppy to have the lyrics of one of those gangster rap songs tattooed across her shoulder blade."

Murphy had scowled. "You checked her out long enough to see whether the tattoo artist had spelled everything correctly, that's for sure!"

"Isn't people-watching part of the beach experience?" James had said, trying to placate his girlfriend. "You know, making comments on people's suits, their sunburns, tattoos, cute kids?"

Ignoring him, Murphy had strode down to the water and, garnering plenty of stares for her own trim body and sun-streaked hair, dove into the Atlantic and began to swim away from the shore with such confident strokes that it seemed as though she never planned to return.

After their tiff at the beach, Murphy had nagged James for allowing his hotel room to become untidy and demanded that he reduce the level of air conditioning. Once he had straightened the room and set the temperature gauge to her satisfaction, she insisted on sitting on the balcony and planning every second of their next two days.

"Can't we just relax and do things as we feel like it?" James didn't like to follow a schedule when he was on vacation. "If we run around and check off everything you've got listed here, we'll be exhausted!"

"Well, I want to visit the lighthouse *and* rent jet skis." Murphy tossed some brochures onto the table. "And I haven't been to the battleship Wisconsin in years. I'm going to write a couple of travel articles on the Norfolk area while I'm here. I've been so busy editing my manu—" She halted abruptly and then pointed at him. "You're a guy, you should like military history."

James had bristled. He liked all kinds of history, but would rather read about it on the beach than traipse around a battleship beneath a blazing August sun alongside hundreds of other perspiring tourists. Eventually, Murphy wore him down and he agreed to spend Saturday and Sunday as she saw fit, but he didn't enjoy himself, and there had been nothing romantic about their time together.

"Guess we're not quite ready to buy a house with a picket fence and have an army of kids," Murphy had joked at the end of their weekend, but James saw no humor in their situation. They had bickered and snapped at one another too many times in such a short interval, and James spent the entire drive home wondering whether he and Murphy were as compatible as he had once believed. She had suddenly become jealous, controlling, and insecure, but he had no idea why.

When he had asked her about her atypical behavior, Murphy had brushed him off and claimed he was exaggerating the situation. However, since they had returned to Quincy's Gap, her demeanor had remained crotchety at best. James was worried that she was keeping something from him, but Murphy insisted that he was overreacting and being paranoid. Still, they had not spent the night together since their botched holiday weekend, and that said a lot to James about Murphy's desire for space all of a sudden.

"Yoo-hoo!" Lucy waved her hand at James, forcing him back to the present moment. "Planet Earth callin'. You ready to land your rocket and answer my question?"

James started. "Yes," he answered, more tersely than he intended. "Murphy came for the last few days. It's just that things didn't turn out as I had hoped they would."

A glimmer appeared in Lucy's blue eyes. "That's too bad," she said without a trace of sincerity, and then her expression grew cloudy. "Guess things rarely end up how we hope they will."

The pair fell silent and then Lucy suddenly seemed to remember something. Digging through a pile of papers, empty plastic soda bottles, and other assorted trash, she pulled out an envelope. After examining the return address, she brushed some crumbs from the business-sized envelope and held it out for James to see. "Have you gotten a letter from the Hudsonville Chamber of Commerce?"

"I haven't gone through all of my mail yet. Why, should I be expecting one?"

"Yep, but since you haven't read it, I wanna watch your face while you do! Here." She passed the letter to him. "Apparently we're celebrities now. Well, at least in Hudsonville anyhow."

"Hudsonville?" James asked. "Where is that?"

"Way south off of I-81. Close to the North Carolina border. I hear it hosts the region's biggest barbecue festival." Lucy smiled mischievously. "But don't let me spoil the surprise. Read on."

James briefly examined that town seal, which showed a drawing of an anxious-looking Native American handing a suckling pig to a complacent pilgrim. Pine trees grew in abundance on a hillside behind the two figures and the text *Incorporated 1885* was written in block letters above the tallest tree. The letter read:

Dear Ms. Hanover,

First of all, congratulations on becoming a deputy for the Shenandoah County Sheriff's Department. I am confident that the citizens of Quincy's Gap and its environs will benefit from your past experience in apprehending criminals.

The officers here at the Hudsonville Chamber of Commerce have followed the endeavors of you and your friends in our local newspaper, *The Hudsonville Herald.* We are very impressed by the fact that your group ensured the capture of several extremely dangerous felons. For the most part, media has granted the credit for each of these arrests exclusively to members of the law enforcement. We have friends in Quincy's Gap, however, and know the whole story, as do most of the fine citizens of our county. *The Herald* has run a very popular series on your supper club.

In short, you and your friends are celebrities here in Hudsonville, and we would be honored if your group would consider spending the week with us at our forty-seventh annual Hudsonville Hog Festival as guest judges. We would like you to judge the Queen Sow Contest as well as award the cash prize and trophy to the winner of the Blueberry Pie-Eating Contest.

Of course, the town of Hudsonville will gladly pay for your lodgings at our town's nationally rated bed and breakfast, and our local sponsors will provide you with plenty of free meals and merchandise during your stay.

The festival begins in two weeks and, while we apologize for the short notice, we truly hope that you will join us for this fun, family-oriented, and finger-licking-good festival.

If you have any questions, feel free to call me anytime.

A Mr. R. C. Richter signed the letter. Several titles, including President of the Hudsonville Chamber of Commerce, as well as four different telephone numbers were listed below his name.

"Is this for real?" James folded the letter and slid it back into the envelope.

Lucy nodded. "Sure is. The word is, their *original* celebrity judge cancelled at the last minute, so they're scramblin' to find a replacement."

"They must be desperate if all they can come up with is the Flab Five!" James laughed and then stopped smiling. "You know, we're going to need a different name, considering how incredibly *not* flabby you are."

Lucy shrugged, ignoring James's last comment. "Come on, James. We're celebrities, too. I think Murphy's coverage of our activities has made it into more than just *The Star* and *The Hudsonville Herald*. We're big news in these parts. The deputies on our bowling team tease me about us bein' household names all the time."

James blinked in surprise. "Are you on the team? I though *Deputy* Keith Donovan was adamant about keeping it an all-male team." James grimaced as he spoke Keith's name. He and Donovan hadn't gotten along since high school.

"I'm not *on* the team." Lucy frowned. "I just go to the games. That jerk Donovan hands out all the duty assignments, and he's given me desk jobs whenever he can, while he and Glenn handle all the larceny and A&B cases. The most exciting thing I've done all summer was transfer someone from jail to the courthouse!"

"A&B?" James inquired, hoping to keep Lucy from sulking.

"Assault and battery." Lucy's radio crackled. A dispatcher announced a stream of unintelligible code, and Lucy sat up in her seat and reached for the keys, her eyes twinkling. "Gotta go, James. We've got a case of possession of a firearm by a convicted felon. See you at Gillian's tomorrow night."

Photo by Bruce Nelson

ABOUT THE AUTHOR

J. B. Stanley has a BA in English from Franklin & Marshall College, an MA in English Literature from West Chester University, and an MLIS from North Carolina Central University. She taught sixth grade language arts in Cary, North Carolina, for the majority of her eight-year teaching career. Raised an antique lover by her grandparents and parents, Stanley also worked part-time in an auction gallery. An eBay junkie and food lover, Stanley now lives in Richmond, Virginia, with her husband, two young children, and three cats. Visit her website at www.jbstanley.com.

30,469

WWW.MIDNIGHTINKBOOKS.COM

From the gritty streets of New York City to sacred tombs in the Middle East, it's always midnight somewhere. Join us online at any hour for fresh new voices in mystery fiction, book club questions, author information, mystery resources, and more.

Midnight Ink promises a wild ride filled with cunning villains, conflicted heroes, hilarious hazards, mind-bending puzzles, and enough twists and turns to keep readers on the edge of their seats.

MIDNIGHT INK ORDERING INFORMATION

Order by Phone:
- Call toll-free within the U.S. and Canada at
  1-888-NITEINK (1-888-648-3465)
- We accept VISA, MasterCard, and American Express

Order by Mail:
Send the full price of your order (MN residents add 6.5% sales tax) in U.S. funds, plus postage & handling to:

> Midnight Ink
> 2143 Wooddale Drive, H259
> Woodbury, MN 55125-2989

Postage & Handling:

Standard (U.S., Mexico, & Canada). If your order is:
> $24.99 and under, add $3.00
> $25.00 and over, FREE STANDARD SHIPPING

AK, HI, PR: $15.00 for one book plus $1.00 for each additional book.

International Orders (airmail only):
> $16.00 for one book plus $3.00 for each additional book

Orders are processed within 2 business days. Please allow for normal shipping time. Postage and handling rates subject to change.